best of intentions

LK FARLOW

DEDICATION

Dedication: To my Phoobs. I know sometimes I'm a little (okay, fine, a lot) crazy, but I always have the best of intentions when it comes to you.

"YOU READY?" I ask my best friend, smirking at my reflection as I straighten my bow tie in the mirror.

Yeah, that's right. A bow tie, and a vest…the things we do for the people we love. But today's the day he marries Natalie—my little sister. And this vest is far more comfortable than my Kevlar, so I suppose it's worth it. Not to mention, Tatum, my adorable as fuck almost four-year-old niece, begged us to wear them. And if there's one thing on this earth I can't resist, it's her pouty lip. Kid's got power.

Alden doesn't even hesitate. "Yeah, man. I'm ready. More than ready."

I run a hand through my hair and drop down into the chair next to him. Some days it weirds me out that he's not only marrying my little sister but is also my niece's father, a fact only brought to light within these last few months. But as I sit here with him, all relaxed and calm, it strikes me just how much he means it. He's completely ready to spend the rest of his life with Natalie.

Then again, it doesn't really surprise me. I've known Alden most of my life, and the dude's always put one hundred percent into everything he's passionate about, and my little sister is definitely at the top of that list. Even if it is a bit weird for me, I'm thrilled for them.

Love like that doesn't exist for everyone, that's for damn sure. And truthfully, I couldn't think of two more deserving people. They fought hard for their happy ending—they put in the work and fucking earned it.

Once upon a time, I figured I'd find me a nice girl and settle down—you know, way on down the line. Then she happened. Or, hell, maybe I happened. Either way, I saw the light. Moral of the story, I'm not long-term material. So, nah, there's no wedded bliss in my future. Only lots of great sex— the no-strings kind—and that's just fine by me. I still get the intimacy that all humans crave without all the cards and flowers and oh my God, you missed our two-week anniversary bullshit.

It's a total win…at least, that's what I tell myself.

I'm sure I sound a bit jaded, and hell, maybe I am, but it's with good reason and fully in the better interest of the other party. But that doesn't mean I'm not happy for them—truly. You'd be hard pressed to find a couple more perfect than those two. They're that couple; moonbeams and rainbows and little cartoon hearts shoot out of their eyes every time they look at each other. If I was anyone else, it'd probably make me sick.

Another bonus of the day is seeing Jenny, Natalie's fine-as-fuck friend, all gussied up. Actually, scratch that. I hope that Nat picked a burlap sack for her to wear, because being close to her while she's dressed to kill all night might actually kill me.

Jenny's loud, opinionated, and brash—a total spitfire. Until I come around, that is. In my presence, she gets all clammed up and nervous. It's cute, really. Fuck. Did I just call the girl cute? What am I, twelve?

Alden and I are both seemingly lost to our own thoughts, and a comfortable silence stretches out, blanketing the room.

Then Carlos—Alden's second in command at the café he and Natalie run together—pops into the room. "It's almost time. You ready?"

Alden smirks. "That seems to be a pretty popular question today. But, yeah, I'm ready. More than. It honestly feels like I've been waiting an eternity."

Carlos claps him on the back. "Glad to hear it. Mrs. Reynolds said five minutes till it's time. Which means we need a celebratory shot." He crosses the room to where the bar cart is stashed in the corner and pours us each a shot of spiced rum. Alden and I stand and join him. He passes us each a small glass before raising his own in the air. We follow, lifting ours as well. "To finding the person who shows you how to be happy, and being smart enough to keep them."

We clink glasses and down the shots, the warmth of the rum leaves a trail, settling in my gut, almost like a premonition. But before I can overthink it, Alden bursts out laughing. "Dude. Did you just make a fucking Trolls reference?"

"Maybe." Carlos shrugs. "It seemed appropriate."

"Tatum would approve for sure," Alden replies, a wide grin splitting his cheeks. "Now, c'mon, it's time to go claim my wife."

I sling an arm around his neck and pull him close. "Chill out, caveman."

He laughs and shoves away from me. "Just wait, tough guy. One day, some girl is gonna lay you out flat on your ass." I waggle my brows and Alden shakes his head. "Not like that. I mean, the way Natalie did me."

I roll my eyes and head toward the door. "Not gonna happen, bro."

Except when I open the door, I'm met with the vision of Jenny in her bridesmaid dress. And it's not a sack. Not by a long shot. I stagger back as I take her in. She's a goddamn vision. The offending piece of fabric only covers her right shoulder, leaving the left deliciously bare. The chiffon material drapes and crisscrosses over her chest, hugging her breasts together in a way that makes me imagine my hands there instead, before floating down in swish, ending right above her knees. And the color, my God, don't even get me started. It's about a shade darker than her skin and slightly rosy, leaving me to wonder if her nipples are a similar hue.

I shamelessly rake my eyes over her, groaning when her fuck-me heels come into view. She turns at the sound of it and instantly a pretty blush stains her cheeks. I bet it would travel down her neck and across her chest if she could read my thoughts right about now.

"Oh!" she gasps, doing a slow perusal of me in my suit. If the glint in her eye is anything to go by, she likes what she sees. Bet she'd like what's beneath it even more.

I shoot her a cocky wink. "Oh, yourself. You ready to walk down the aisle with me?" The impact of my words doesn't hit until Jenny sways in her sky-high heels. Fuck. I pretty much implied it was us getting married. I scrub a hand over my face while Alden and Carlos snicker at my fumble.

"Sure," she whispers, stepping closer to me.

"I'm gonna run and make sure we're good to go," Carlos says before turning to Jenny. "Have you seen Tatum?"

"She's in the bridal suite with Natalie and the grand-mothers."

"Good, good. Alden, head on out to the altar." I'm not really sure how Carlos became the event coordinator, but dude's taking his job seriously—and he's doing a damn good job. "When the music starts, Tatum will walk first; wait until she reaches the midway point and then y'all will follow arm-in-arm. Got it?"

I give him a mock salute. "Got it."

He rolls his eyes before setting off for the chapel, leaving Jenny and me decidedly alone.

Against my better judgment, I drag the pads of my index and middle fingers over Jenny's bare shoulder and down her arm, causing her to suck in a sharp breath. "You look real good, Jenny."

She nibbles on the corner of her juicy, bottom lip, and I'm struck with the desire to do the same. "You do too," she whispers, her voice as breathless as I feel.

What in the hell is happening here? Women—no matter how smoking hot—do not make me breathless. Especially long-term girls like Jenny Jones. She practically has engagement rings in her eyes as she bats her long, inky lashes at me.

I take a pointed step back, desperate for space. Space to clear my head—to get out from under whatever kind of good-girl-voodoo spell she has me under. Swear to God, it's always the good ones. They're all doe-eyed and sweet words until you get them in bed. Then they're all scratching nails and filthy talk. Which begs the question, is Jenny a little minx in bed or is she as vanilla as the frosting on Natalie and Alden's wedding cake? Shit. No amount of space can help when these types of thoughts keep sneaking in.

And really, when did I start seeing Jenny as sexually desirable? Sure, she's always been a looker—I mean, I'm not blind. But, she's so far from my type it's not even funny. I like them tall, leggy, and—most importantly—only interested in one night. And everything about Jenny screams 'til death do us part. I guess that makes sense though, because the thought of dipping my wick in the same pot for the rest of my life is basically a death sentence in and of itself.

I'm once again shaken from my thoughts. This time it's Jenny tugging on my arm. It sounds crazy, but I swear I can feel the sear of her touch through my clothing. "What?" I ask, my tone harsher than needed. I'm on edge, and her touching me isn't helping.

She drops her gaze, replying to her feet instead of me. "It's…we missed our cue. We need to go."

Stiffly, I nod once, linking my arm with hers before escorting her down the aisle.

YOU KNOW that feeling you get deep in your belly when your crush pays attention to you for the first time? Well, Nate's arm in mine is like that, only a thousand times more intense. It's as if an entire swarm of bees have taken up residence inside of my body, because I am positively about to buzz right out of my skin.

I know these thoughts are childish and silly, but in my eyes, Nate Reynolds is the perfect man—he's the ideal, the guy I compare every other potential suitor to. Which is beyond absurd, because he hardly knows I exist. I'm literally nothing more than his little sister's best friend, who happens to show up at family events from time to time.

Add in the way he ghosted his fingertips over my shoulder while telling me I looked good, and yeah, I'm a goner.

It's frustrating as hell. Around everyone else, I'm outgoing—outspoken even. But the minute he's within a ten-foot radius, I transform into this mumbling, bumbling version of myself that can hardly compose full sentences. The man's hotness renders me mute—how can I win his affection if I can't even form coherent and thought-provoking sentences?

Truly, the universe is cruel. If the aforementioned issues

weren't enough to prove it, the way he looks in his suit really drives the nail in. With some guys, their clothing wears them, all ill-fitting and baggy. But Nate…Nate wears the bejeezus out of his—every item looks tailor-made for his tall, muscular frame. From jeans to his uniform—mmm, drool—to this damn suit, he looks runway or photoshoot ready. And don't even get me started on the bow tie.

Thankfully, our trip to the altar is a short one. Even still, for five out of those fifteen steps, visions of me dressed in white and him waiting for me raced through my mind. Those thoughts were unwelcome and unwarranted, mind you— let's just chalk them up to my blood sugar being off. I may have a crush, but I am in no way, shape, or form delusional. I don't fancy myself in love with him, or secretly think we're going to get married and make little police officer babies. It's more the equivalent of doodling our names together in a heart in the margin of my notebook—harmless. Innocent even.

Well, mostly innocent. You know, aside from the late-night fantasies when I'm feeling lonely, and visions of him shirtless and sweaty keep me company, along with my B.O.B. There's just something about man sweat. But, still, that's completely natural too. I think. Right? Either way, it's still harmless, because he'll never know, and I'll certainly never act on it. I mean, I'm not even in the friend zone. Nope, I'm in the little sister's friend zone, and that's a hellacious type of limbo very few have ever passed through to the other side.

At the end of the aisle, we go our separate ways, with me taking my place next to where Natalie will stand, and him at Alden's side.

Natalie and Alden's daughter is next in the procession. But in true Tatum fashion, she doesn't walk down the aisle, she dances. She struts her stuff and shakes her little booty as she makes her way toward us, haphazardly tossing flower petals as she goes.

Knowing Tatum as well as I do, I recognize this little jig as her happy dance. She is hands down the cutest kid ever.

At the end of the aisle, she pauses, looking from her dad to the guests, to the remaining petals and back again. Little cutie hesitates so long that the music changes, signaling it's time for the bride.

When Natalie and Mr. Reynolds enter the room, a collective gasp can be heard—Tatum's being the loudest of all. "Mama looks like a princess for reals," she whisper-shouts, causing a chorus of laughter to ring out, lightening the emotional moment.

She's not wrong either. In all my life, I don't think I've ever seen a more beautiful bride. She's glowing and radiates joy. Which, if you ask me, is exactly how a woman should look on the day she says I do.

"Tater Tot, what are you doing?" Natalie whispers when she makes it to the front.

"You just look so pretty, Mama."

Natalie's dad leans down and presses a kiss to his daughter's cheek before taking his seat.

"Thank you, sweet girl. You do, too." Natalie steps forward and crouches down to her daughter's level—a feat in the heels she's in—and wraps her in a big hug. "You wanna finish those petals off so your daddy and I can do this thing?"

Tatum's eyes widen as if she's only now realizing she didn't complete her job. Truthfully, I think we're all just now realizing it. Natalie one hundred percent stole the show when she entered the room.

Instead of replying right away, Tatum takes her time. She glances down to the remaining rose petals and then over her shoulder to Alden before finally landing her gaze back on Nat. "Y'all gonna kiss?" she asks, scrunching up her little button nose.

"Yeah, baby, we're gonna kiss."

Tatum rolls her eyes. "Ugh. Yuck." Alden laughs and

attempts to cover it with a cough, but his little girl isn't buying it. "Fiiiine."

We all burst out laughing—even the stodgy officiant—when she flips her basket over, dumping the remaining petals on the floor.

I keep my gaze focused on the two of them, unwilling to chance a look over toward Nate. Knowing my luck, I'd get so swept up in his yumminess that I'd miss a cue and everyone would catch me drooling—no thanks.

Natalie and Alden's ceremony is something straight out of a fairy tale. They opted to hold their big day on the grounds of The Grand—a local upscale spa and resort that is right on the bay. Their ceremony is inside the Grand Ballroom, a space so naturally beautiful that they didn't even need to decorate. Their vows are the definition of swoon-worthy, and their first official kiss as husband and wife is borderline X-rated—seriously, it almost had me squirming, and it absolutely had Tatum gagging and covering her eyes. It was one hundred percent the perfect wedding.

But now…now it's time for the reception, which is being held in a large open-air tent on the patio. Not to mention, with them owning a café, I know the food will be next-level good, and I absolutely love dancing. Who knows—maybe if I'm extra lucky a certain hot cop will ask me to dance.

No, you know what, it's the twenty-first century, and I'm a modern woman—maybe I'll ask him. Yeah, I think I will. But before that can happen, I'm going to have to find some courage—preferably of the liquid variety.

———

I step into the reception space and find myself immediately in awe. The round tables are draped in sheer white linens and the centerpieces are a simple mix of greenery and assorted candles. Twinkle lights hang from the exposed beams, casting a romantic glow over the entire room. It's the vision of a Pinterest-perfect wedding.

My mission to find an alcoholic beverage is one that will not be derailed, even if it probably isn't the best decision. I'm on my way to the bar when I catch a glimpse of Nate standing with Alden and Carlos, his head thrown back in laughter over something one of the guys must have said. He looks like pure deliciousness; the way his Adam's apple bobs has me clenching my thighs and grabbing a flute of champagne from the first passing waiter. The fact that champagne is my least favorite drink no longer matters—I need something to take the edge off stat.

Down the hatch goes the bubbly, in one fell swoop. The dry, sweet-tasting liquid leaves a bitter aftertaste, but I don't mind. It'll be worth it in the end—I hope. Quickly, I avert my eyes and continue toward the bar, calculating how long it's been since I ate last—bad news, it's been a while.

As I step up to the worn wooden makeshift counter, I scan the room, not looking for Nate, or so I tell myself. Especially when I see him chatting up Giselle, an Amazon of a woman who works with me at the café and looks as though she's fresh out of the pages of a fashion magazine. If that's the kind of girl he's into, then I don't stand a chance.

But...I'll never know for sure if I don't try. And there's something about tonight—there's some kind of magic in the air that whispers try and talk to him...ask him to dance. Then again, that could also be the champagne I chugged on an empty stomach. Either way, I'm listening.

The bartender makes his way to me, and I promptly order two shots of bourbon, skipping over the handcrafted wedding day signature cocktails. Natalie and Alden picked a delicious-sounding and probably potent blackberry whiskey lemonade. From what I've been told, it's tangy and sweet with hints of rosemary, and if I had planned my meals and insulin better today, I bet I would have freaking loved it.

I toss back my shots one after the other, savoring the burn…enjoying the way it warms me from the inside out. The temptation to order another round is strong. The only thing stopping me from doing so is the fact that I want to be relaxed, not white-girl wasted. There's no bigger turn off than being sloppy drunk.

It takes me three excruciatingly long minutes from ordering to finishing my shots. Three minutes in which I waffle back and forth between asking Nate to dance and staying my ass right here at the bar. The fear of rejection is strong, but the fear of what-if is even stronger.

I signal the bartender, this time ordering a sparkling water with a twist of lime, scan the room for Nate, straighten my spine, and set off toward him. He's once again standing with a group of guys, but this time I don't recognize them.

I walk with purpose, my head held high and an air of confidence that I don't really feel—fake it till you make it, right? I approach the group boldly, not stopping until Nate and I are practically toe-to-toe.

He smirks down at me, looking far too handsome for anyone's good—especially mine. I get lost in his warm brown eyes, loving the way his cocky gaze heats me from the inside out, much like the bourbon coursing through me. I snap out of my daze when one of the guys he's with snickers a little at my prolonged silence.

"What's up, J?" Nate asks, concern—probably of the brotherly variety—laces his tone. "Is everything okay?"

I feel my cheeks warm as I nod. "Yeah. Um, yes. I wanted…I was just wondering if you'd, um, like to dance?"

I see his rejection before I hear it. It's in the stiff set of his shoulders and the hard line of his mouth. I know it's coming, and it guts me. I avert my eyes, focusing on my drink as if it's the most interesting thing in the room.

"Ahh," he starts, but I cut him off.

My eyes brim with unshed tears, but I refuse to show Nate

how much power he has over me—how much him turning me down affects me. Really, I can't believe I was idiotic enough to think he'd ever say yes. "It's fine. N-no worries. I… yeah. No big deal." I shrug, trying for nonchalance. The pitying looks—not only from him but also his friends—tell me I've failed miserably.

"I don't dance, Jenny. It's nothing personal."

"Right," I whisper before turning to flee the scene. As soon as my back is to him, the first tear falls. I want nothing more than to seek out a dark corner where I can nurse my wounded pride in solitude.

I'm steps away from my final destination when I feel a warm, callused hand encircle my wrist. Hope blooms in my chest. Maybe he changed his mind…

"Wait," a gravelly voice says, and my hope fizzles—it's not him after all.

"YOU ARE ONE DUMB MOTHERFUCKER," my longtime friend and partner, Duke, murmurs as Jenny turns and all but hauls ass away from me.

I scrub a hand over my face. "Tell me something I don't know."

"I can think of a lot of shit you don't know, but here's what I'm gonna tell you. You may not be smart enough to say yes when a ten asks you to dance, but, brother, I'm no fool." And just like that, Duke sets off after Jenny.

As I watch him go after her, I can't help thinking that maybe I've made a huge mistake. I watch, unable to look away, as he grabs ahold of her delicate wrist. Something about him touching her has me bristling in a way I'm not sure I understand. Over the years, Duke and I have had plenty of arguments, but until right here and now, I've never once had the desire to hit him. Hell, I've never had the urge to hit anyone over a woman.

"You really gonna let him get your girl?" Xavier, another guy on the force, asks, sounding smarmy as hell.

"Not my girl," I grumble under my breath.

"You sure, lady killer?" he asks, goading me, much to the delight of the other guys in our group.

"Positive," I grit out, doing my best to ignore the stupid-ass nickname that the entire force seems to have adopted for me—well, everyone except Duke. He knows better.

"So, it won't upset you if he sweeps her off her feet on the dance floor and right into his hotel room?"

Involuntarily, my fists clench at my sides. "Asshole's not taking her anywhere."

X levels me with a stare. "Brother, you can't have it both ways. You aren't interested, no sweat. But believe me, some other man—probably many—will be. You can either go after her or not. But you can't act like a moody teenage girl when someone else shows her attention."

Logically, I know he's right. But I'm too annoyed to be logical. Too fired up over the thought of Duke's hands skimming over her mouthwatering curves, when it should've been me. Only, I was too stubborn to say yes.

I grind my molars as he leans down and whispers into her ear. A freight train hurtling toward me couldn't drag me away as I watch him butter her up. A myriad of emotions fills me as her face goes from guarded to relaxed to smiling. I'm practically shaking with some feeling I'm not quite willing to name when he manages to earn that sweet laugh of hers.

I've never in my life felt territorial over a woman, and yet I'm a damn raging bull when he takes her drink and deposits it on the nearest table before leading her to the dance floor. All bets are off when the jackass catches my eye, smirks, and winks at me before settling his hands on the swell of her hips. As of this moment, he's no longer one of my closest friends; he's just become the matador taunting me with my very own red flag—Jenny.

The song they're dancing to is slow, and while there is a respectable amount of space between the two of them, they're still too damn close. Legit, this is like a train wreck—I don't want to watch them together, and yet, I can't look away.

"You look like you're about to go apeshit," Xavier murmurs, sounding all too pleased.

"Yeah," one of the other guys pipes up. "Like your head's gonna explode or something. Who knew our lady killer could get so territorial?" I look over my shoulder to glare at him just in time to see him mime an explosion with his hands.

"What the fuck ever," I mutter, stalking away from them and straight toward the bar. This is a whiskey situation if there's ever been one. At the counter, I order Jameson neat, downing it in one gulp. It burns on the way down, momentarily distracting me from Duke and Jenny.

My reprieve is short-lived when a husky, feminine laugh sounds out above all the others. Deep down, I know it's hers —I've heard it on countless occasions and memorized it a million times over. It's her real laugh, the same one she gives when she and Natalie are goofing off or when she's playing with Tatum.

A quick glance out onto the dance floor, and sure enough, there she is, with her head tossed back, lips parted, and cheeks flushed. Fuck. Instantly, images of her with the same euphoric expression on her face, while she rides me, flit through my mind.

I'm not sure what's going on, but it's like some arbitrary switch I didn't even know about has been flipped, and suddenly she's not Natalie's friend Jenny or Alden's employee Jenny…no, she's fuck-hot Jenny that I want between my sheets.

Duke notices me tracking them and lifts his brow at me as if to say well, what're you gonna do about it? Smug bastard that he is, he knows exactly what he's doing.

My anger fades as it all clicks into place—he's not making a play for Jenny, he's ensuring that I do. Shaking my head, I make my way toward them, ready to do whatever it takes to get her out of his arms and into mine.

Duke notices me cutting through the crowd toward them

and expertly twirls Jenny so that her back is to me. I don't slow my approach until I'm directly behind her. "May I cut in?"

She whips around to face me. "Thought you didn't dance," she states simply.

"Usually, I don't."

"Don't make any exceptions on my account," Jenny scoffs and moves to return her attention to Duke.

Without thinking, I gently grip her chin and keep her gaze on mine. "I'm not making an exception. I'm righting a wrong. I wanted to say yes when you asked, but stupidly, I declined. So. Now, I'm asking you. Jenny Jones, would you please allow me the honor of this next dance?"

A pretty pink blush creeps up her neck, staining her cheeks. It's a damn good look on her. She turns to Duke, as if seeking his approval—smart man that he is, he simply nods and steps back, allowing me to take his place.

The timing couldn't be more perfect. Just as she steps into my arms, the song changes from upbeat to slow and moody. I wrap an arm around her waist, settling my hand possessively on her hip, pulling her small body into mine. Her hands instinctually fly to my chest, and, I swear, it's as if her touch sears right through my shirt.

She blinks up at me, body stiffer than an ironing board, all doe-eyed and innocent looking. I smirk down at her as I bring my free hand to trail over the skin of her exposed shoulder. She gasps at the contact and melts into me. I swear to God, I love it. With the tips of my fingers, I drag them down her arm to her elbow. I wrap my hand around her and pull her impossibly closer. Her head nestles against my chest as we sway to the music.

I keep her on the dance floor for at least four songs, unwilling to let her go. Thank God they were all slow, because I don't think I'm ready to really feel her move. Even now, with us merely rocking back and forth, her body feels so damn good pressed up against mine—and don't even get me started on the way she occasionally presses her nails into my chest.

On song five, my luck runs out. The bass thumps low as she spins and presses her back into my front. Jenny may struggle to talk around me, but her body is saying all the things her words don't. She swivels her hips as the tempo climbs, and the semi I've been sporting is in real danger of rivaling the damn tent the reception is being held in.

Seemingly unaware of my mental—and physical—struggle, Jenny keeps right on grinding her ass into me. Deciding to go with it, I palm her hips and move with her. My rhythm isn't quite as good as hers, but we're in sync enough for me to know we would be on-fucking-fire if we were doing this dance between the sheets instead. Right, because that's what I need to be thinking about right now.

The melody crescendos and Jenny reaches back with one arm, wrapping it around my neck, her fingers grazing the skin of my nape. Fuuuuuck—who knew that was such a turn on? She glances up at me, and it takes every bit of self-control I possess not to kiss her—not to claim her glossy, pouty, delectable looking lips as my own.

But, I don't—I'm all too well aware that if I give in, if I allow myself to taste her here and now, I won't stop until she's writhing beneath me, begging me for more. And therein lies the problem—I don't do more. I'm a one-night guy, and she's a forever girl. If only my dick would get in line with my logic.

Being the little temptress that she is, Jenny keeps her eyes on mine as she slowly licks her lips. I can feel my body losing the war to my mind. A taste. One small, teensy taste. Come on, what will it hurt?

I instinctively sway closer, brushing her nose with mine. She lets out a startled breath at the contact—the tiniest of gasps—yet it's enough to have my mind running wild, imagining her making the same noise as I slide into her. Have mercy, how is it possible this sexy woman is the same awkward girl my sister is best friends with?

Just like that, thoughts of Natalie break the spell, and the fog she has me in dissipates. I'm telling you, it's that good-girl voodoo. Stuff's not only real, it's strong. Just as she rises onto her tippy-toes, I take a step back, placing a healthy amount of distance between us. The action causes Jenny to stumble forward, landing her right back into my arms. Only, instead of looking grateful for being caught, she looks unmistakably hurt. Dammit.

"Jenny, I—"

She shakes her head and offers me a smile. I watch as a mask settles over her pretty features, blocking off her feelings from my prying eyes. I don't like it one bit. "I wanted a drink anyway," she says, spinning on her heel and beelining toward the bar.

Whether I'm unwilling or unable to let her walk away from me on bad terms, I'm not sure. All I know is I can't do it. "Great. Then I'll go with you. It seems our dancing has me pretty damn thirsty too." Among other things, such as aroused and confused—but mostly aroused.

Jenny tosses a glare my way over her shoulder. "Oh, did I say thirsty? I meant hungry." She shrugs sweetly.

"I could eat; I'm still a growing boy, after all." I pat my flat abs and shoot her a wink. She huffs and rolls her eyes, which I figured she would. Being doubly rejected by the same guy in one night has to sting a little. But what she doesn't get is I'm not shooting her down out of lack of interest, because fuck yes, I am interested. Honestly, it's more out of respect for her —and her friendship with my sister.

I'm all too aware that she's interested. It's evident in the way she acts around me, especially tonight. It's in the way her eyes track me when we're in the same room and she thinks I'm not looking. It's the way her body leans toward mine like a magnet, drawn helplessly to me. I could easily bed her—hell, it'd probably be the best night of her life. It's the morning after that would be a whole slew of issues. I would undoubtedly hurt her when I bid her farewell with the dawn, thus making all future events where we're together awkward as hell.

Sure, this is all hypothetical. And I sound like a conceited, pompous ass even to my own ears. But, in my mind, it's justified. The last thing I ever want to do is hurt a girl as pure as Jenny Jones. The women I sleep with know the score—they don't expect a second date, much less my phone number. And Jenny—fuck, she deserves more than being some jackass's one-night stand.

"Well, you go right ahead and get you some food. I'll just run to the ladies' room." She smiles victoriously, obviously assuming she's bested me. And that's fine. I'll let her think she has. For now.

"Okay then. We can catch up more later," I say, placating her.

She hurries away from me, the only acknowledgment she even heard my words is the half-hearted wave she gives without turning back to face me.

Oh, Jenny, you're not getting rid of me that easily, I think to myself before counting down from five in my head. The second I hit one, I take off behind her.

A head start's only fair.

AS SOON AS I enter the main building and know I'm out of Nate's sight my shoulders slump. It's really not fair for him to have such a powerful effect on me. Then again, maybe I'm the issue. I mean, how many times—in one night—will it take for me to realize he's just not that into me? How many times will I embarrass myself around him?

I dart down the hall and into the restroom and plant my hands palm down onto the countertop. My lower lip trembles as I take in my flushed cheeks and glassy eyes. No. I will not cry. Not over him—or any man, for that matter.

If Nate Reynolds doesn't want me, well, fine. It's no one's loss but his. There are certainly plenty of other fish in the sea. Even if they aren't six plus feet of brooding hot cop. It's not like he's got the market cornered. I just need to…redirect… my interests, so to speak.

I take a deep cleansing breath, inhaling my resolve and exhaling my schoolgirl crush on Nate. I can do this. I straighten my posture, give my cheeks a pinch for a little color, and readjust the thigh holster holding my pump before turning to head back to the reception. Who knows, maybe I'll find someone else to dance with.

With a quick shove, I fling open the bathroom door, only

to come face-to-face with the devil himself. Sighing, I try to step around him, but he moves with me. Kind of hard to redirect when the thing you're trying to avoid is literally blocking your path.

"Decided to take up stalking in your free time?" I snap, impressed at the strength of my tone. For once, I'm not tripping over my words. Go me!

Nate simply smirks at me, looking so damn fine. Which just aggravates me even more. Only he could make stalking sexy.

"You do know it's illegal, right?"

"You're right," he says in a stupid, mollifying tone that makes me want to throat-punch him. "Stalking is illegal. But, that's hardly what's happening here, Jenny."

The way his lips wrapped around my name, his voice all low and raspy, has heat unfurling low in my belly. Jackass. "Oh, so you didn't follow me inside?"

"Maybe I did, maybe I didn't. For now, let's chalk it up to a happy accident."

I stare at him blankly. Why on earth would running into him be a happy anything? Maybe a few hours ago, I would have agreed. But now, happy would be avoiding him like the plague.

"C'mon, let's grab something to eat."

"I'm not hungry," I say right as my traitorous stomach rumbles.

"Sure you're not. But, I am." He looks down at me, dragging his eyes over every inch of me. "Starving, actually."

Hope—stupid, silly, ridiculous hope—blossoms in my chest. Jesus, could I be more pitiful? He's like my very own Pied Piper. I frown at the comparison, because that makes me a rat helplessly following him and his magical—no, Jenny! Do not think about his pipe.

Before I have a chance to respond, Nate links his arm with mine and sets off, presumably back out to the reception tent, damn near dragging me. It's on the tip of my tongue to yank my arm free from his, chew him out, and just retreat back to the safety and comfort of my hotel room.

But the senseless, pathetic part of me lets him lead, because as much as I hate to admit it, I'm a little excited to see where he may be taking me. Judging by the fact that he's already whisked us past the double doors leading out to where the tent is set up, it's not to eat.

"I thought we were—" I start to speak up, but my words dry up when he guides me through a small side door and into the balmy night air. Looking around, I see we're in a secluded pergola at the edge of where the grass meets the sand. We're close enough to the patio that the sounds of music and laughter from the reception mingle with the soft crashing of the waves.

"You thought what?" he asks, never once breaking his stride.

"I-I thought we were gonna get something to eat." If I'm being truthful, I need to eat. I've spent most of the day running around like crazy, trying to make sure Natalie was as relaxed as possible. But I don't speak up, mostly because I'm too intrigued by where we could be going and a little because I simply don't want to eat with him, as childish as that sounds.

"We will. I just want to do this first."

I pull my head back in confusion. "Do what?"

He abruptly releases my arm and turns to me. "This," he murmurs before cupping my cheek and laying his lips against mine. He sucks lightly on my lower lip, drawing it into his mouth, eliciting a soft moan from me.

His kiss is far sweeter than I imagined it would be—he's so strong and virile, I figured his kiss would match. In all of my fantasies, his lips were dominating and searing, completely commanding mine.

Don't get me wrong, there's nothing wrong with how he's

kissing me—like I'm some delicate, precious jewel—it just doesn't reconcile with who he is. This kiss is nice, and Nate Reynolds…well, he isn't.

Not really.

Sure, he's a good person and has a kind heart. Would do damn near anything for anyone. But he's also powerful and sexy and intimidating—a real man's man. Honestly, I would have never guessed he was capable of such gentleness or restraint.

He presses two more small, open-mouthed kisses to my mouth before flicking at the seam of my lips with his tongue, begging for entry. In a daze, I open to him, falling easily into the gentle dance our tongues are engaged in.

His pace never speeds, and his hands never stray, which is a little disappointing. Unless…this is a pity kiss. A way for him to ease his conscience for being a dick to me twice in one night. The thought is ice water to my libido, and I pull away. "What in the hell was that?" I demand, internally vowing not to let my emotions get the best of me.

Nate has the decency to look embarrassed. "Jenny—" he starts, but I'm not having it.

"No! No, sir. Don't you Jenny me, with your bedroom eyes and sexy voice. You are giving me freaking whiplash. You're moodier than a damn teenaged girl. I'm not some badge bunny you can play games with. I'm not here for a good time at your convenience. You either want me or you don't, and it's beyond obvious you don't—your actions have shown that over and over again."

By the time I'm finished, my chest is heaving. We stand in silence, chests heaving as we stare at one another. Finally, Nate exhales a long breath and scrubs a hand over his face. "Fuck, Jenny. I'm…it's not that I don't want you. Trust me, you're a walking wet dream—any guy would want you."

"What's the issue, then?" I ask, stepping back from him. "Is leading girls on your kink or something?"

He huffs out an amused laugh, and it takes my all not to slap the stupid, sexy smile off of his stupid, sexy face. "You're something else, you know that?"

My scowl deepens, which only seems to please him more.

"No, leading girls on is not my kink. And, it wasn't my intention to lead you on." He holds up his hands in surrender, knowing my patience is a thin thread ready to snap. "I realize I've been sending you mixed signals all night. But here's the thing: I absolutely want you. I just know that nothing good would come from us being together."

I blink at him, shocked by his honesty. When I don't say anything, he takes it as his cue to continue.

"You're so beautiful, Jenny." His previously amused tone shifts, his voice deepening. "And while I'd love nothing more than to take you back to my room and worship you from head to toe, I won't. You're light and good and pure, and you deserve a man who will worship you for more than one night. I'm not the guy for you."

"You're not the guy for me," I echo back, my voice hoarse.

A million different emotions flit across his face before he leans down and presses his lips to mine once more. This kiss is chaste, friendly almost, and he certainly doesn't linger. "But, damn, I wish I was."

Figuring it's well past time to go our separate ways, I turn to head back to the party. "Where're you going?" Nate asks, stopping me.

I jerk my head in the direction of the reception tent, wondering why he even cares.

He glances at me, biting his lip—why is that so sexy?—before dropping his gaze to my shoes. "Mind if I join you?"

I'm expecting my knee-jerk reaction to be anger, or at the least indignation. As quickly as the image of me yelling and screaming and demanding to know how dare he comes, it passes in the blink of an eye, and all I'm left feeling is mild indifference.

Sure, knowing nothing will ever happen between us stings, but there's also a kind of mercy in that knowledge. The what-if has been eliminated, hopefully paving the way for a friendship between the two of us—after all, panty-dropping grin aside, Nate's personality is what draws me in the most, and I'd rather count him as a friend than nothing at all.

"Go right ahead," I say to him with a smile, allowing him to take the lead. Boundaries defined or not, the minute he steps in front of me, my eyes fall to his delectable ass—I mean, I'm only human.

NATE

Half an hour and one drink later, Jenny's taste still lingers, as does the way her body fit so perfectly against me. And don't even get me started on the soft moans that passed from her lips to mine. Jesus, Lord in heaven, help me, because my sanity is dangling by a thread.

Currently, we're posted up at one of the many round tables surrounding the makeshift dance floor, as the bride and groom dance their first dance as a married couple. My gaze darts around the room, not really wanting to focus on the way my little sister is staring into my best friend's eyes. Jenny, on the other hand, looks positively entranced. Her gaze is misty as she watches Natalie and Alden glide across the floor to some sappy song about forever and always.

"They're so good together," she whispers, turning to me. "Don't you think so?"

I grunt out my agreement, and she laughs.

"Does talking about romance with me really get you that…" She trails off, leaving me hanging.

"That what?" I prompt.

She taps her bottom lip thoughtfully, and all I can do is

imagine my dick tapping against it instead. Get it the fuck together, man.

"Well, when I started talking to you, you got this look on your face. Almost like you had an atomic wedgie. So, it's either talking to me that caused the face, or it's talking about love and feelings with me. I'm really hoping it's the latter."

I can't help but laugh. "An atomic wedgie? What are you, eleven?"

She shrugs her delicate shoulders. "Hey, it's the most accurate description I could think of. You actually looked physically pained by my question."

The thing is, it isn't her question that got me. Nah. It's the fact that she's able to sit here next to me and carry on as if we both don't officially know just how much chemistry we have together. It's almost like...now that she finally got a taste of me, her metaphorical reset button was pressed. She's suddenly cool, calm, and collected—as if my presence no longer affects her. Which is just fucking perfect, seeing as her proximity alone has me wanting to drag her off to the nearest flat surface so I can hear those soft, breathy moans of hers again.

I don't even realize I'm staring at her until she nudges me with her elbow. "Take a picture, playboy; it'll last longer." Her easy, carefree tone grates my nerves—which I fully realize is shitty of me, and yet I can't stop it.

Spending time with her tonight has been the greatest form of torture. Maybe if I wasn't such a fuck-up, I could be the man for her, but I refuse to ruin her. Jenny is far too bright to be brought down by my brand of bullshit. And that's exactly what would happen if I took a chance on her—or hell, any woman for more than a night.

Nate the lady killer, that's what the guys at the station like to call me. I always force a smile and laugh right along with them...if only they fucking knew just how close to home that hit.

I startle when Jenny's small, warm hand comes down on mine. "Are you okay?"

I bristle at her question. "Why wouldn't I be?"

Her eyes widen at my defensive tone. "Whoa there, big guy. Take a breath."

She pulls her hand away, and immediately I mourn the loss. Jesus, get it together, Nate, you're acting like a psycho.

"Honestly," she continues, her voice soft. "I wasn't trying to imply anything. You just looked tense. I...I was actually gonna ask if you wanted to get out of here."

A smirk pulls at my lips as I glance around the tent. Guests are still roaming about, dancing and eating. Hell, they haven't even cut the cake and little Miss Jenny is suggesting we skip out. Maybe my good girl isn't such a good girl after all...

"You think anyone would miss us?" I ask, fully aware that we have yet to do ninety percent of any of the traditional wedding bullshit—you know, like cut the cake or whatever that shit is when the bride throws her bouquet at all the female guests. Though, gotta be real, I won't miss watching my best friend remove my little sister's garter.

This time she's the one smirking at me. "Absolutely, but they'll make it."

I know I should tell her no—I should send her on her way to fulfill whatever maid of honor duties she may still have, and I should find someone else—anyone else—to warm my bed for the night.

But, I don't.

Because deep down, I know that hooking up with someone else won't chase away the newfound desire I'm drowning in for my little sister's best friend. Not to mention, the thought of her doing the same—of her spending tonight with someone other than me—is enough to have me standing from the table we're at, grabbing her hand, and yanking her up to follow me.

"Lead the way, GG."

She quirks a brow at me. "You…you do know that my name starts with a J, right?"

I can't help but laugh. "Yeah, Jenny, I know." I give her hand another tug, and we're on our way, fleeing the action of both of our best friends' wedding.

———

Hand-in-hand, we make our way out of the event space and into the lobby, pausing at the elevator bank. "My room or yours?" I ask, and she cracks up. "What? Why is that funny?"

"Because," she sputters, damn near doubled over in laughter, giving me a glimpse of her glorious cleavage. "That totally sounded like a line."

She straightens, and I drag my eyes back up to hers. "Yeah, yeah. Whatever." I punch the up arrow and reiterate the question once we step inside the car. "Like I said, my room or yours?"

Her tongue swipes across her bottom lip as she mulls it over. "Mine. I want to get out of this dress."

Immediately, I'm hit with a million dirty images. Like me helping her out of that dress, slowly tugging the zipper down while pressing a hot kiss to the space where her neck and shoulder meet. I can damn near see the fabric pooling at her feet, leaving her completely bare to me—minus her fuck-me heels.

Jesus, what an idea.

Trying to regain my composure, I inhale through my nose and grip the elevator railing with enough force to turn my knuckles white.

When I don't immediately reply, she skims her index finger over the top of my hand that's gripping the rail. Instantly I release the breath I was holding. "Yeah, GG. That's fine. What floor?"

She searches my eyes for a long moment before whispering, "Three."

I punch the button, and we settle into an awkward silence as we ascend. When the doors open, I step back and allow her to pass me and lead the way. Less than a minute later, we're standing in front of her room.

"Gotta get my key, hang tight."

When she reaches the fingers of her right hand into the front of her dress, I swear, I almost knock her hand out of the way and offer my assistance with the retrieval. She wipes the card on the hem of her dress and passes it over the sensor in the handle. It flashes green, and I turn the knob, holding the door open for her.

I'm not sure what I was expecting the inside of her room to look like—I guess I figured there would be clothes strewn all over, you know, stereotypical girl shit. But what meets me couldn't be further from it—her room is neat and tidy, with her duffel bag stashed under the desk and her toiletry bag on top of it.

She heads straight for her bag, crouching low to rummage through it. She stands and turns to face me. "I'm just gonna get changed really fast. Make yourself comfortable, okay?"

I give her a brisk nod as she walks into the bathroom. It's really all I can manage, because there's no way in hell I can be comfortable knowing she's just about naked with only a door separating us.

Pacing the length of the room, I'm on my third pass when I hear the door open. "Hey, uh, Nate?" Jenny calls timidly.

"Yeah?" I call back, willfully keeping my back toward her.

"I...I need some help unzipping my dress."

Involuntarily, my spine stiffens, and I barely hold back my groan. I pivot around to face her. "Sure. C'mere." I crook my finger at her and internally recite the department's code of conduct, the National Anthem, the last names of all the officers on the night shift—fucking anything to keep my mind from replaying my earlier fantasy about this very thing.

She glides over to me, nibbling on her bottom lip before turning to offer me her back. My eyes practically eat her up before I step in a little closer, breathing her in. She smells like pure temptation and every desire I've ever had come to life. I exhale roughly against where her neck and shoulder meet—the very same place I imagined kissing less than an hour ago. Her skin pebbles into gooseflesh, and she teeters in her heels. I grasp her shoulders to steady her, and we both freeze at the contact. It's hardly intimate, yet it feels like the most intense foreplay of my life.

The way Jenny trembles beneath my innocent touch tells me she feels the same. God help us both.

I keep my right hand planted firmly on her shoulder while gently dragging my left along the edge of her dress, over her bare skin until I meet the closure. It's got some microscopic hook above the zipper, but I have it popped open in no time. We both tense when I grip the small metal pull. Lifetimes pass as I slide it down, my knuckles dragging over her smooth skin. I stop breathing when I realize she's not wearing any kind of bra. Lust pools in my gut when I make it to the end of the track, only to see her panties are nothing more than a lacy wisp of fabric.

"Fuck, Jenny," I rasp out, fighting like hell not to spin her around and close the gap between us.

She releases a shuddering breath and steps away from me. Good girl, Jenny. Distance is good. "I'm gonna go finish changing now." Her voice is nothing more than a rasp, and all I can do is nod—nod and remind myself of all the ways I'm no good for her—for any woman—for more than one night.

FOR THE SECOND TIME TONIGHT, I'm hiding from Nate Reynolds in a bathroom. Only this time it's to keep me from tackling him to the bed and exploring every inch of his sculpted body. Not that my unskilled hands would know a thing about how to touch him, but I'm a fast learner—I bet I could make it work. Plus, how hard could it really be?

Great. Now I'm thinking about him being hard.

I finish stripping off my dress, wishing I had time for a cold shower—Lord knows my libido needs to chill out and stay in her own lane. Instead, I settle on splashing my neck and chest with icy water from the sink. The feel of the coolness against my heated skin is like little pinpricks, but it does the trick.

Once I feel like I'm no longer at risk of making a fool of myself, I turn off the faucet and dry off with an overly fluffy hotel towel. I regret the pajamas I brought with me the minute I slide them on. I didn't think twice about the small, flouncy cotton shorts and matching tank that exposes a sliver of skin just above the waistline of the bottoms when I packed them. I mean, why would I? No one ever sees me in my jammies but me—and now Nate will, too.

Giving myself a once-over in the full-length mirror, I

cringe. My entire body is basically on display for him. And more importantly, so is my pump. Ugh.

I wish I wasn't so self-conscious about people seeing it, but I learned quickly in my teenage years that assholes abound, and most struggle to accept anyone who is different than they are. So what if my pancreas doesn't work…so what if I need insulin to stay alive? I'm still freaking human—but to immature high schoolers, I might as well have been an alien from outer space. Unfortunately, after a few cringe-worthy adolescent experiences, I'm still body-conscious years later.

I make quick work of pricking my finger and checking my blood sugar levels—shockingly, it's within my target range, what with the lack of food and my few drinks. However, if I want to keep the equilibrium, a bedtime snack needs to happen. After a mental tally of what snacks I packed, I settle on the pack of peanut butter crackers I know are in my purse and calculate the bolus.

One last glance in the mirror, and I secure my device to the inside of my panties, tucking my tubing into them as well for good measure—Lord knows there's nowhere else to hide them in these pjs. God, please don't let him notice it, and please don't let him think I'm trying to seduce him.

Finally, I step out of the bathroom, only to stop short when I see that Nate is lounging on the far side of the bed—my bed. Why is he in my bed when there is a perfectly good chair?

He glances up at me and smirks, raking his hungry gaze over my body. "You gonna join me, GG?"

There's that nickname again.

"S-sure," I mumble out, stepping fully into the room. I walk over to the bed and climb into it. The sound of Nate groaning—all deep and husky—alerts me to the fact that I'm inadvertently giving him a straight shot down the front of my top.

Quickly I move to an upright position, clutching the neckline of my shirt to my chest. Hand on the Bible, I've never been more thankful that I inserted my infusion set into my bottom and not my belly. "Sorry. Uh—"

Nate pulls the covers back and gestures for me to slide under. "Nothing to be sorry about. Hell, if you want, you can do it again, and give me a minute or two to commit it to memory."

Strangely, his pervy wisecrack instantly lightens the mood, and we both laugh. "Wanna watch TV?" I ask, grabbing the remote from the side table.

"Sure."

Right as I press the power button, my stomach rumbles. Dammit, I forgot my crackers. As expected, Nate is quick to comment. "You hungry? I can call for room service."

His thoughtfulness has those stupid bees buzzing again. "Actually, I have peanut butter crackers in my purse."

He moves to a fully seated position. "Hold up. Lemme get this straight. You'd rather have a kiddie snack than a thick, juicy burger and fries?"

"Guilty, and I bet they'd taste even better if you got up and grabbed them for me." I shrug and offer him a sweet smile when he scoffs and rolls his eyes.

Nate hauls himself up off the bed and saunters over to my purse, pausing before reaching into it. "Not gonna lie, I feel a little weird digging around in here."

Snorting out a laugh, I ask him, "Why?"

"I don't know. I guess it's just one of those things that gets drilled into guys—not to snoop through a lady's purse."

"Riiiight," I draw out the word. "But you're not snooping. You're retrieving something I specifically asked for."

"True." He plunges his hand the rest of the way in and roots around for a second. "Jesus, GG, what all do you have in here?" he asks, his eyes wide.

"What do you mean?"

"You have an entire vending machine in here."

Now it's me who's scoffing. "Do not."

"Do so." And to prove his point, he starts pulling out my various snacks and lining them up on the dresser. Two things of crackers, a pack of gummies, a Kind bar, a beef jerky stick, and a baggie of Goldfish.

Sheepishly, I look down at my lap, studying the remote like it's the most fascinating thing I've ever seen in my entire life.

"Hey, no shame in your game. And, since you have a buffet in here already, there's no need to call down for food." He tosses my crackers with perfect aim, landing them directly next to me on the bed.

I tear into the packaging and stuff one into my mouth, mumbling a 'thank you' around the peanut buttery goodness. I devour two more and glance up to Nate, wondering what's taking him so long. The sight I'm met with has me choking so hard I may as well have a mouthful of dust.

He's standing there before me with his dress shirt long gone and his belt undone, the buckle all but pointing to his junk like a flashing neon arrow. "Uh…" I trail off, at a total loss for words.

Nate shrugs like he hasn't a care in the world. "You changed into your pjs, so now I am, too." He returns to unfastening his pants and shucks them off, leaving him in nothing more than a pair of skin-tight black compression briefs. Sweet merciful Jesus, I think I'm dying. But, oh, what a way to go.

His ever-present smirk turns to a full-blown grin when he notices the greedy way my eyes are roving over him—almost the same way a kid takes in the presents beneath the tree on Christmas morning.

He clucks his tongue at me. "Unlike you, I'm completely willing to stand here long enough for you to commit this to memory—I'm a giver like that. Hell, you can even snap a pic on your phone if you want."

I bring my hands up to cover my heated cheeks. "My God, you are shameless."

I feel the bed dip as Nate rejoins me. "Nah, GG, I just work hard for these goods and know it'd be a disservice to keep them all to myself."

I bark out a laugh; once again, he's managed to lighten the mood. "Do you even hear yourself when you talk?"

Instead of answering, he slides under the covers with me and rips open the pack of fruit snacks. "Fuck, these are good. The same kind Nat buys Tatum."

"I know. She got me hooked on them, too."

We both zero in on the remote laying in my lap at the same time, but he snags it before I can even think to move—damn police officer reflexes. After a few seconds of channel surfing, he settles on an old Cops rerun—how fitting.

We chat throughout the show, talking about everything and nothing all at once. Finally, about four episodes in, I roll to my side to face him and ask, "What made you become a cop?"

My breath catches when he follows suit, bringing us nose-to-nose, so our breath mingles. He is one hundred percent close enough to kiss. Unfortunately, there will be no more kisses though. Because…friend zone.

"Honestly?" he asks, and I nod. "It started when I was a kid, from watching shows like this and Rescue 911. Then as I got older, I guess the seed was planted, and I just kept watering it. Now, I like knowing that I am helping make my community—the only place I've ever really called home—safer. I like knowing that what I do, day in and day out, makes a difference. Don't get me wrong—some days it sucks, and it's hard, and it hurts. Some days, I just want to sit and drink and cry after a shitty shift. But every day I put on my badge, I feel a sense of pride and…just this belonging…like I am exactly where I need to be."

His response sucks the air from my lungs, leaving me

utterly breathless and completely speechless. Turns out Nate Reynolds's goodness doesn't only apply to his looks—it extends down to his very soul.

At my lack of reply, his cheeks go ruddy. "Yeah, that was pretty—"

"Amazing!" I cut him off, not wanting to hear him downplay what is very clearly something he's passionate about. "Seriously, Nate. That blew me away."

He pushes himself up to a semi-upright position, shoots me a cocky as hell wink, and pretends to brush his shoulder off. "It's all good; I tend to have that effect on people."

"Oh, Jesus, you're too much."

Running his teeth over his lower lip, he grins. "You don't even know, GG."

"Is everything an innuendo with you?" I ask, snuggling down deeper into the fluffy duvet.

"Nah. Only like…ninety percent of things. But, enough about that. Is working at Bayside your life dream?"

"Uh, that would be a no. Don't get me wrong, there's nothing wrong with being a server, but it definitely isn't what I want to be when I grow up."

"What do you want to be?"

I hesitate, wondering if he really cares. "I love the food and beverage industry. I love the creativity, the camaraderie— and at times, the competitiveness. What I really want is to work my way up to maybe owning my own place one day."

Nate nods thoughtfully. "I dig it. I can totally see you being the boss."

As the night wears on, we talk about everything and nothing. We talk about our favorite childhood memories and my obsession with red Starbursts. We float from topic to topic until finally, with my head nestled—platonically—on his chest, sleep draws me under.

I BLINK MY EYES AWAKE, noticing several things all at once. One: I'm not in my room. Two: there's someone in bed with me. Three: I've got her wrapped in my arms like I never want to let go, and she's got her ass pressed into me like we're glued together.

The question is, whose room am I in? My bedmate shifts in her sleep, causing her to slide across my shoulder and tickle my nose. I inhale and her scent fills my lungs. Jenny. I'm in bed with Jenny. Last night rushes back to me—our kiss, sneaking out of the reception, talking until we both fell asleep.

She stirs again, pushing her tight little ass farther into my groin, and Jesus Christ that feels good. All that's separating us is my boxers and her little sleep shorts—in other words, practically nothing. My hips involuntarily press forward, and Jenny lets out a sleepy little moan.

I have one arm under her head and the other wrapped around her waist. The urge to slip my hand beneath her shirt is something fierce, but I don't. I keep my palm firmly pressed to her belly and remain unmoving.

Which makes one of us.

The little minx keeps shifting and rubbing against my

dick, like she's trying to start a friction fire. I'm about a minute from coming in my briefs.

When her hand finds mine and brings it to her breast, I know I have to put a stop to this—even if it is fifty wet dreams coming true at once.

"Jenny, wake up," I murmur into her ear. Fuck if it helps, though. Nah, she just rolls her hips and lets out the sexiest sigh I've ever heard. "Seriously, you gotta get up."

I try and move my hand away from her body, but she curls her fingers, causing me to palm her perfect, perky tit. Oh, damn, this is so wrong. The hard bud of her nipple presses into my hand through her tank top, and my mouth waters imagining it in my mouth instead.

"Jenny, you have to stop," I say, my voice rough and gritty with desire.

She moves her hand from mine, and I think I'm finally getting through to her. I go to slide my arm out from under her, thinking we probably both need some space, but she stops me dead when she reaches back and palms my erection, sliding her hand from root to tip.

"Fuck, GG, fuck that feels good, but—"

She partially rolls, twisting at her hips so she can look at me—and hell if she isn't awake and alert. "I know what I want, Nate." Her voice is nothing but pure lust.

"I'm not—"

She cuts me off again. "The guy for me, I know." Her words fall off, and she moves to a seated position, nibbling on her lower lip. My body immediately misses hers.

I follow and move to an upright position as well. I open my mouth to speak, but she beats me to it.

"Look, I know you don't do relationships—or even monogamy—and that's fine. I know what I'm asking for. I want you. I want to be with you. Even if it's only for one night."

"A-are you sure?" I stutter out, like an inexperienced fifteen-year-old.

She doesn't respond right away, but thanks to the light filtering in through the crack in the bathroom door, I can see her. I can see her as she slips the straps from her tank top down her shoulders and pushes her shirt to just beneath her breasts. I can see her dusty pink nipples, and fuck if they aren't a perfect match for the dress she wore earlier.

"I'd rather have one night than a lifetime wondering. I'm a big girl, Nate—we can do this and still be friends when the sun rises."

She sounds so confident and so sure. Fuuuuuck. Who am I to deny her? I dive in and capture her lips with my own, kissing, nipping, sucking, and teasing. Jenny gives as good as she gets, and before I know it, I have her on her back, and I'm settled between her thighs.

I thrust my hips forward, and she moans into my mouth. "God, GG, the way you sound—I can't wait to hear it when you—"

She bites at my lips. "What are you waiting for?"

Jenny's right—what am I waiting for? I roll off of her and back to my side of the bed. "Gonna grab protection," I murmur, so she doesn't think I'm leaving. "Why don't you go ahead and lose everything keeping me from seeing and feeling that beautiful body of yours?"

"Okay, Nate," she whispers, sounding damn near ready to float away.

I stalk to where I left my pants and fish my wallet out of the back pocket, retrieving the condom I keep in the billfold. When I turn back to the bed, I see my good girl followed my instructions perfectly. Her nightclothes and panties are laying in a heap next to her—so fucking hot.

I lick my lips as I toss the little foil packet toward her. She clutches it to her chest as I push my briefs down, stepping out of them as I move toward her. Her eyes eat me up as I lower myself down onto the bed.

Back under the sheets, I position myself back between her already spread thighs and press a hot kiss to her temple. This time when I roll my hips into hers, I'm met with nothing but damp, hot skin. "You're already so ready for me," I murmur into her ear.

Unexpectedly, she laughs. "Jesus, Nate, it's like I can hear your smirk." Reaching up, she draws me down to her mouth and kisses me like her life depends on it. We touch and rub and grind until we're both so worked up it's unbearable.

I take the condom from her and sheath myself. "Are you sure?" I ask one last time, hardly able to believe I'm about to sink into my little sister's best friend.

She pushes her hips up toward me, wrapping her legs around my waist. "One thousand percent."

And that's all I need to hear. I push inside her, and I swear to God, it's unreal how tight she is. We move together like we share the same brain, our bodies completely in harmony with one another. It's the most delicious, erotic push—pull of my entire life. She fits me like a glove and meets me thrust for thrust.

Jenny pushes her hands through my hair before winding her arms around my neck, pulling me down to her. I lick and suck and bite at her neck as she whimpers out my name.

"You feel so good," I grit out, palming the right side of her ass as she clenches around me. "So, so good."

She falls over the edge before she can form a reply, and damn it all if I'm not a millisecond behind her.

Our harsh breathing is the only sound as we both recover from what was, hands down, the best sex I've ever had. Holy. Shit. I think I just had an out of body experience, because sex has never—and I mean, never—felt like that. It's like her body was made for mine, which is fucking insane.

A million other equally absurd thoughts assault my

brain—thoughts that should have me hauling ass back to my room—but instead I nuzzle deeper into her neck, peppering the smooth skin there with soft, open-mouthed kisses.

She shifts under me, trailing her nails over my back, a dreamy sigh spilling from her lips. "Jesus, Nate."

I'm about to echo her sentiments when a beeping-buzzing noise fills the room. Jenny goes stiff as a board at the sound, and my eyes shoot to her phone on the bedside table, but it never lights up. What the…?

My confusion doubles when Jenny places both hands on my chest and pushes me off of her. Here I am, reveling in the afterglow of some damn good sex, and she's all but ready to shove me out the door. Which is ironic, seeing as I'd usually have been dressed and on my way—I'm definitely not typically into the post-coital cuddle.

I'm about to ask her what's up when—beep-beep-buzzzzz —it happens again. I know it's not her phone, and it's not mine either, so what in the hell is it?

She stands from the bed, taking the sheet with her so that it is wrapped tightly around her body, leaving me alone in the bed, naked and cold. Again, I repeat, what the…

Wordlessly, she stalks toward the bathroom. I know I should give her privacy—that a gentleman would give her privacy—but, I'm no gentleman, so I follow along.

Just as she goes to shut the door, I'm there blocking it from fully closing. Beep-beep-buzzzzz. There it is again, and it sounds as if it is coming from…her?

"Jenny, what's going on?"

She shakes her head and pushes on the door. Nah, not happening. Gently, I push back, creating an opening wide enough for me to step through.

Jenny sighs, but it's not of the soft sexy variety from five minutes ago. No, this sigh is full of exasperation. Yeah, well, welcome to the club, sweetheart.

"Whatever. Stay then," she grumbles, sounding thoroughly annoyed.

I plant myself on the ledge of the tub. "Planned on it."

Confused as hell, I look on as she pulls a small black device from beneath the sheet she's using to conceal her body. She taps a button, and the screen lights up. "Shit," she whispers.

"What is that?" I ask her, but she ignores me. That shit's not gonna fly. "Jenny, what are you doing?"

Guess she's pretending I'm not here as she grabs a little bag from the counter and unzips it, grabbing another smaller bag from inside of it.

All without speaking, she flips open a little canister that almost looks like it would hold film and slides out a little strip. When she pops it into the end of a slim meter and pricks her finger, I realize she's checking her blood sugar. I try and connect the dots as she grabs an alcohol swab from the larger bag and tears it open, rubbing it over the tip of her bloodied fingertip.

Is Jenny diabetic? She doesn't look diabetic...I immediately shake off that thought, realizing it's one hundred percent as stupid as it sounds. People with diabetes—like all diseases—come in all shapes and sizes. The question is, why has she never mentioned it, and what in the hell is that little black pager-looking thing she keeps checking?

Jenny's not-phone buzzes again and she pushes a few buttons on it before clipping it to the front of the bed sheet. She quickly cleans up her supplies and washes her hands before heading back out into the room—still ignoring me.

She goes straight to her purse, where she roots around for a minute. A frown mars her pretty face when she comes up empty-handed. Suddenly, it clicks into my head what she's looking for. "Your snacks are on the dresser."

She straightens and whips around to glare at me. "Thanks." Even pissed off, she's polite. My good girl doesn't have a mean bone in her body. She opts for a pack of gummies and carries them to the bed, where she proceeds to eat them, one by one.

"You wanna tell me what's up?" I ask, really studying her. I mean, clearly, she's diabetic; but is that all it is? Her skin is flushed, and she's sweating—and something tells me it's not from our sex, as earth-shattering as it was. Add to that, her breathing is shallow and the almost queasy look she's sporting…yeah, my Spidey senses are tingling.

She shakes her head. Defiant little thing. "GG, I can't help you if I don't know what's wrong."

"It's…uh…nothing. I'm fine."

I pin her with a pointed look. Why is she being so stubborn and secretive? "Obviously you're not. Talk to me."

"I-I…I'm diabetic. Sometimes around this time of night, my sugar gets low. I also skipped dinner tonight and had a few drinks. Not to mention, our—" She lets out a little fake cough. "—Strenuous activity. It definitely didn't help."

Diabetes is something I know all of jackshit about. Not even gonna lie, even though it's totally baseless, it's an illness I've always associated with older people—definitely not with someone her age who looks the way she does.

"And low sugar, that's bad, right?"

"Nice detective skills," she sasses, and damn if I don't want to kiss her smart mouth.

Wait—she said her sugar dropped because she didn't eat and because of us fucking. Oh, shit. This is my fault.

"Jenny—" I clamp my mouth shut, unsure of what to say. "How can I help?"

She gives me a funny look. "I'm fine. Once my sugar levels out, I'll feel better. I honestly just want to go back to sleep."

My eyes widen. "Sleep? Is that safe?"

"I'm diabetic, Nate. Not concussed."

"Riiiight." I drag out the word, trying not to sound as

dumb as I feel. All of my diabetes knowledge is secondhand from being on scene when EMTs get called out. "Is there anything else you need?"

She stands from the bed and unclips her not-phone, laying it on the mattress before shrugging out of the sheet. I know it's wrong, but with the light from the bathroom completely illuminating the room now, I can't help but ogle her. She's fucking perfection with her high, perky tits, flat, toned belly, and softly curved hips.

"Yeah, you can put your clothes back on." She turns, giving me her back as she redresses. It's then I notice the little tube leading from her not-phone to a little port-type thing on the left side of her upper-butt area.

"What is that thing?" I ask as I slip my briefs back up my legs.

"It's an insulin pump." Well, hell, that makes sense, doesn't it? Now I really feel like an idiot. She turns back to me once she's dressed. "It's a little device that delivers insulin to my body to help me control my blood sugar."

"Yeah, got it." I spear a hand through my hair. "But, how does it know your sugar?"

She lifts her shirt and point to a small, seashell-shaped disk on her stomach. How did I not notice that when our bodies were damn near fused together? "This thing, my CMG—continuous glucose monitor—sends my sugar levels to my pump."

I nod, impressed with all of these devices. "That's actually pretty fucking cool."

She rolls her eyes. "Yeah, really cool."

She plops back down onto the bed and pulls the covers—minus the sheet—up to her shoulders. I round the bed to my side and do the same, earning me an odd look. "What are you doing?" she asks, disbelief lacing her tone.

"Same as you, I'd imagine."

"Humor me."

I give her a small grin. "Going back to sleep."

She snorts. "Didn't take you for a sleepover kind of guy."

Reaching out, I drag her closer to me, tucking her into my side. "Usually I'm not. But tonight I am."

"Whatever," she mumbles, sleep already claiming her. Unfortunately, it evades me.

Every time I close my eyes, vision of Jenny dance behind them. Visions of us actually dating. Visions of me wooing her and us falling in love.

I press my face into the space between her neck and shoulder and breathe her in, as the future we could have continues playing out like a movie in my mind. I can see her so clearly, dressed in white, with my ring on her hand. And then, a few years down the line, I see her belly round and swollen with our first child.

I drag my fingers over the soft skin of her shoulder, loving the way she fits so perfectly against me. And when she reaches out and places her hand on my chest, I'm hit by the rightness of her—of us. I can so clearly envision the future we could have. I can see us growing old together. Content and happy together.

Sleep finally starts to call to me, and my visions blur into dreams. But just as fast, they turn to nightmares, and I'm bombarded with visions of me fucking it all up.

I'm hit with images of me heading out to the bar after shift with some of my buddies, and instead of going home, I leave with someone who isn't her.

No. I wouldn't. I open my eyes, blinking rapidly to clear my mind before trying to sleep again, but it's no use now. The seed has been planted, and every time I close my eyes, I see something worse than the time before.

I imagine Jenny pacing the floor, wearing a trail in the rug, waiting for me to come home, as she wonders where I am.

In vivid detail, I watch as my carelessness slowly drives her crazy, just like it did with…

I unwrap my arms from around her and sit up, jamming my hands over my ears, hoping it's enough to block out the memories.

No, no, no. Jenny deserves more. I won't make the same mistakes again. I won't hurt her. I repeat the mantra to myself over and over again as she slumbers peacefully, completely unaware of my internal battle. But at the end of it, she does deserve better.

And I know if I tried talking to her, if I tried explaining my past and my fears and hesitation, she would either try and soothe me, and be far more understanding than I deserve, or she would run screaming and never look at me the same way again.

Honestly, I'm not sure which would be worse. No, that's a lie. Her convincing me to stay and try would be worse, because I undoubtedly know how that scenario would end.

As much as it sucks—as much as I want to stay—I know what I have to do. Even though she's everything I've ever wanted but never let myself hope for, I know I'll ruin her, and I refuse to ruin her. So, I do the only thing I can. I tuck her hair behind her ear and press a soft kiss to her temple before sliding out of the bed, into my clothes, and out the door.

It was nice while it lasted, Jenny Jones, but like I said, I'm not the guy for you.

THE MATTRESS DIPS BESIDE ME, and my eyes flutter softly as I linger in that space between sleep and awake. The back of a hand brushes my hair away from my face, and I lean into the touch. "Feels so good, Nate," I mumble as I roll to snuggle deeper into him. Last night was nothing but pure magic, and I'm not ready for it to end.

"Nate?" a decidedly female voice shrieks, bringing me into full consciousness. "Jennifer Anne Jones, you better start talking!"

My eyes pop open at what I now recognize as Natalie's voice. Why is the wrong damn Reynolds in my bed?

"Jenny, I'm gonna need you to start talking now—oh my God, is that a hickey on your neck?"

My hand flies to my neck, and memories of Nate licking and biting and sucking at the sensitive skin there invade my mind.

Nonplussed by my lack of reply, Natalie hammers on. "A hickey from my brother? Oh, Jenny, no! Is that why y'all both disappeared last night before we even cut the cake?"

Groaning, I drag the duvet up to cover my face. "Can we not talk about this?" I beg.

"Ha!" Natalie exclaims, pulling the fluffy blanket off of me. "Fat chance. Let's look at the facts: one, y'all both mysteriously vanished at the same time last night; two, you have a hickey the size of a freaking softball; and three, you called me by my brother's name, which leads me to believe he spent the night with you in…oh my God, gross!"

Natalie flies off of the bed like it's covered in spiders and snakes and every other creepy-crawly known to man. "I was sitting. On the bed. You most likely fucked my brother in." She gags a few times as she paces back and forth at the foot of the bed. "You did sleep with him, right?" she asks, pausing to look at me.

The fact that it's Natalie here and not Nate is an unwelcome reality. It's not like I expected our one-night stand to lead to wedding bells, but, Jesus, I at least figured he would stick around until morning. He seemed so content, so into me…until he saw my pump. Guess the joke's on me—again. Like always.

The realization sinks heavy in my gut. I blink my eyes closed to keep the tears at bay and nod to Natalie, confirming what she already knew.

She shudders. "Bleh. TMI."

"You asked," I remind her, my voice scratchy.

"And I regret it." She drops down into the overstuffed chair in the corner. "Speaking of regrets, do you—"

"Regret last night?" I cut her off. "I don't think so. Honestly, I'm all kinds of topsy-turvy. Do I feel a little empowered for actually going after what I wanted? Yes. Does it sting a little that I woke up to him gone? Also, yes. But, at the same time, he didn't make me any promises, and I knew the score, so these hurt feelings of mine are on me, not him."

"Well…" She trails off, searching for the right words. God bless her, this must be an awkward situation for her, quasi-comforting her best friend after a one-nighter with her older brother. Yeah, definitely not ideal. "I really don't know what to say. I kind of want to high-five you, because you know, yay sex! But, at the same time, it was with my brother, which is gross. And he's probably the biggest commitment-phobe I've ever met, and even though I love him and think the world of him, you're not the kind of girl who does casual."

I take the time to digest her words, really chewing on them before replying. "You're right. I don't do casual. But, like I said, the opportunity to go after something I wanted presented itself, and I took it. Nate made it clear he couldn't offer me more than one night, and I went for it anyway." I shrug, feigning nonchalance. "I promise I won't let things get weird between us. I'm a big girl."

Natalie searches my face, as if looking for cracks in the armor I'm wearing. After a few loaded moments, she nods, seemingly pleased. "Okay, well, good. I'm gonna head back to my room to get ready. I'll see you in an hour for brunch?"

"Sounds good. See you then…Mrs. Warner." At the sound of her new name, she blushes and smiles a megawatt smile. Marriage suits her well.

After Natalie leaves, I linger in bed for a bit, letting the memories of last night wash over me. While Nate may only be my second sexual partner, something tells me we connected on a level that's deeper than physical. Unlike the boy I lost my virginity to, Nate owned my body so thoroughly that my inexperience flew out the window. Beneath his touch, my body reacted on pure instinct. Then again, maybe I'm the only one who felt the connection. After all, he dipped out in the middle of the night, making what should have been empowering feel a little dirty.

I force myself out of the bed and into the bathroom where I crank on the shower. As the water heats, I quickly check my blood sugar level before suspending my insulin delivery and disconnecting my pump.

As much as I love my pump—you know, because it helps keep me alive—I also hate it. Sure, Nate acted cool when he saw it, but I can't help but wonder if it's why he crept out before the sun could rise.

Memories of my first, Brian, creep in, unwelcome and unwanted. He was so repulsed by my diabetes. He always asked me to prick my finger and mess with my pump in private—as if he was embarrassed by it. I hated the way it made me feel, as if I was less than him because my pancreas didn't work. But, at the time, I was blinded by his good looks, charm, and charisma. It was almost unfathomable that someone like him would even be interested in me, so I did as he asked.

The final straw was when we finally went all the way. To say I didn't get the fairy tale romance all girls dream of would be a major understatement. At first, when my shirt came off, Brian's eyes feasted over me...until his gaze hit where my infusion set was inserted into my stomach. He actually gagged when he saw it and asked if I could put my shirt back on.

And like the pathetic little girl I was, I did as he asked. Brian then proceeded to take my virginity without any fore-play, with the lights off, and my clothes still on, my panties simply pushed to the side. Apart from a hand on my shoulder for leverage, he didn't touch me, and once he was done, he disposed of the condom, tucked himself back into his jeans, and told me he didn't see us working out in the long run.

Even though Nate is nothing like Brian, even though he treated me with respect and showed me how good sex could truly be, my brain can't help but draw parallels. Seemingly, both of them found me lacking after seeing my dirty little secret. My eyes water and those pesky tears threaten to return, but at least in the shower, I can pretend they're nothing more than water droplets, here to wash away my questionable decisions.

After I shower, I reconnect my pump and resume my insulin before blowing out my hair and styling it in loose waves. I keep my makeup light and fresh looking—I'd love to skip it entirely, but the bags under my eyes from my late night make it impossible.

Dressed casually in a flowy white-and-navy striped romper that ties at my neck—thankfully concealing the marks Nate left behind—with a watermelon-colored cardigan and a pair of wedge sandals, I make my way down to the Grand Hall, where brunch will be served.

Those stupid bees riot in my belly at the thought of coming face-to-face with Nate this morning. But I squash those fuckers down; there's no way in hell I'm letting what happened between us affect me. At least, not outwardly.

The entire elevator ride down, I keep reminding myself that I knew the score. That the only reason he left was to avoid the morning after awkwardness. That it has nothing to do with my…deficiencies.

I lose my breath when I step into the Grand Hall. The space is so incredibly beautiful, from the natural wood-beamed ceiling to the plush settees and velvet chairs gathered around the mismatched tables, which are adorned with floral arrangements that are stunning and understated all at once. And don't even get me started on the floor-to-ceiling windows along the back wall that showcase the picture-perfect waterfront views. This place is a rustic dream come to life.

One of my most favorite things is pinning gorgeous restaurant and bar interiors to my Future Goals Board from the comfort of my couch, and this space is definitely pin-worthy. And judging from the scents wafting through the space, the food is going to be drool-worthy.

A hostess steps out from around the corner and greets me warmly. I let her know I'm here for the Warner Brunch, and she quickly guides me back to where the newlyweds are already seated.

As I lower myself into the seat across from Natalie, I can feel Alden's stare. Obviously, she told him. Which isn't really shocking—they had enough secrets at the beginning of their journey to last a lifetime.

I delay eye contact for a few minutes, taking the time to scoot my chair in and place my napkin in my lap. Finally, Alden clears his throat, and I glance up at him sheepishly.

"So…" he starts, a mischievous glint in his eyes. "You and Nate, huh?"

I look to Natalie for help, but the traitor just smirks at me.

"Yup. It happened, and now it's done. A one-time thing."

Alden steeples his fingers beneath his chin. "Really? You sure?"

My eyes roll on their own accord. "Positive."

"Hmm," he murmurs. "If you say so."

"I do." Subject change please. Talking about my sex life with my boss is crazy awkward, especially when all parties involved freaking know each other. No thanks.

"Where's Tatum?" I ask before pouring myself a glass of ice water from the pitcher on the table.

"She's with Alden's parents. Should be down any second."

I nod. "Are y'all excited for the honeymoon?"

"Yes! So much. But, at the same time, we'll miss Tatum like crazy," Natalie replies, her voice a strange mixture of elation and anguish.

Alden immediately begins whispering in his wife's ear, trying to soothe her. The moment is intimate, and I look away, opting to study the menu to offer them a bit of privacy.

As I read over the choices, family and friends begin filing in and filling the chairs around us. Conversation flows, as does coffee, bottomless mimosas, and Bloody Marys.

After about fifteen minutes, a team of smartly dressed

servers descend upon the table. "If everyone is here, we'll begin taking orders," one of them announces.

Natalie catches my eye, and I can tell we're both thinking the exact same thing: everyone but Nate is here, and I can't help but feel that his absence is entirely my fault.

JENNY

It's been a month and a half since Natalie and Alden's wedding. A whopping forty-two days since I last saw Nate. Coincidence? I think not. I'm honestly not sure whether I'm insulted or impressed by his efforts to avoid me.

Every single time Natalie has invited me over, Nate has been absent. Which, at first, wasn't suspicious at all. I mean, he's a cop and works long hours. But for him to be missing from every cookout and get together they've had—yeah, I'm not buying it.

But today his luck runs out, because I know there's no way on God's green earth he'd miss Tatum's fourth birthday party. Aside from her being the peas to his carrots, she'd never let him live it down, bossy little thing that she is.

Currently, I'm flipping through the clothes hanging on the little industrial wall-mounted rod that I use as a closet, searching for the perfect outfit. I need something that screams *waking up without you totally didn't hurt...not even a little.* Is that a lot to say via clothing? Probably. But I'm damn sure going to try.

The party starts in an hour, and I'm still wrapped in my robe, holding hangers up to my reflection and tossing the maybes down onto my bed. I'm just about ready to start narrowing down my selections when the sound of the doorbell ringing echoes through my cottage. Who in the heck could that be?

A glance through the peephole has me squealing in delight and flinging open the door. Without giving him a single second to prepare, I'm throwing myself into his arms and hugging him tight. "Oh my God! Where have you been?"

"Careful," he whispers in my ear. "You keep this up, and I might get to thinkin' you're excited to see me."

I step back from our embrace, smacking my palm against his chest as I go. "You hush. I am excited to see you. Seriously, where have you been?"

He shrugs. "Around. You know, here...there. You gonna ask me in?"

"What?" I snort. "Are you a vampire now?"

He lunges for me, acting as if he's going to bite my neck. "I vant to suck your blooood," he says, doing his best Dracula impersonation, and we both crack up.

"I've missed this—I've miss you, Jamie."

"Missed you, too, Jenny-cake. Now, invite me in, or I'll storm the castle by force. It's hotter than a football player's jockstrap out here."

Grinning, I push the front door all the way open to lead my favorite—and only—cousin inside. "Welcome to my humble abode," I tell him, sweeping my arm in a wide arc. "It's not much, but it's all mine."

"Not much, my ass," Jamie mumbles as he drinks in my little cottage. Well, I call it a cottage. Really, it's a tiny-house— almost a freaking she-shed—tucked away toward the back of a little patch of woods my grandparents own. The land was bought with the intentions of building a family vacation home down here to escape the cold Smoky Mountain winters.

However, it's been a few years, and construction has yet to start, so my grandparents graciously allowed me to call this little back corner my own. In return, I keep the grass tidy and the flower beds weed free. Really, it's a win-win.

I take in the space through Jamie's eyes, wondering what he thinks of it. It's definitely compact, but it still has an airy feel—largely in part to the two huge sliding glass doors that make up the side wall, and the two skylights. The light, ashy oak floors and cream-colored walls help as well. From the front door, it's a straight shot back to the kitchen, which is decked out with slightly-smaller-than-average stainless-steel appliances—it's not by any means gourmet, like my best friend's kitchen, but it gets the job done.

Along the wall opposite of my sliding doors, I have a little sitting area with a mounted flat screen, a loveseat, a coffee table, and a plush floor cushion that serves as the perfect seat to eat my dinners on.

Beyond that, there's a set of five wider-than-usual steps that double as storage and lead up to the loft area where I sleep. And housed beneath the staircase is a three-piece bathroom that works just perfect for what I need.

"Jenny. This is amazing. When Geema said you were living in a shed, I definitely did not envision something that looked like this. Your pad looks like it could be the feature on small-space-living in Southern Home or some shit."

I blush at his praise. My parents and grandparents are total technophobes, and I have yet to be able to convince them that I'm not living in a hovel. Jamie's been off the grid, so to speak, or I would've had him video chat them just to prove them wrong.

"It's exactly what I need right now."

"Well, I approve and will sing my praises high and low when I get home."

"You're the best, Jamie-pop."

He grins and hip checks me as he sets off up the stairs. "Jenny, why are your clothes everywhere? It's like your wardrobe exploded."

Oh, shit! Tatum's party! "What time is it?" I ask him as I fly up the stairs after him.

"Half past twelve," he replies, cocking his head to the side.

"Crap!"

Jamie quirks a brow at me. "What's your deal?"

"It's my best friend, Natalie, daughter's fourth birthday party, and I'm gonna be late."

"So, get dressed and go. I'll chill here until you get back."

I nibble on my bottom lip. "I…it's not that simple."

"It's a kiddie party, not a fashion show."

I toss myself back onto my bed, directly on top of the clothes I tossed there, and cover my face with my hands. "It really is, though."

Jamie plops down next to me. "Why?"

"Well, there's this guy—"

"Tell Papa J everything!"

Some of the anxiety knotted in my guts melts away as I laugh. "Okay, first of all, never refer to yourself as Papa J ever again. And second…it's Natalie's brother. We hooked up at her wedding in March, and he's been avoiding me ever since."

My cousin pops up off the bed. "Why? Did you go stage five?"

I roll my eyes. "Nope. Even if I wanted to, Nate didn't give me the chance. He was gone before I woke, and I haven't seen him since."

"I see. Well, in that case, you need to look hott—that's with two Ts, by the way." He stands from the bed before offering me a hand. Wordlessly, he begins sifting through the pile on my bed. I'm skeptical when he grabs a pair of black cut-offs and a plain white slouchy tee. "Go change."

I turn my back to him and do as he says, because honestly, everything I know about fashion has been handed down to me by my cousin dearest. Dude's got an eye for what works. I shimmy into the shorts and pull the shirt over my head. It's cute in a casual way, but nothing special. Maybe he's lost his touch?

"I don't know about this, Jamie," I say, spinning back to face him.

"Well, not like that." He moves over to me and quickly draws the hem of the shirt into a loose knot in the front, revealing more of my shape while still being tasteful. "Now, accessorize." A delicate gold chain and arm cuff later, and I see he was absolutely right. I look hott, with two Ts.

As we make our way down the stairs, I ask him, "Are you sure you'll be fine here while I'm out?"

He scoffs. "Well, yes, I would be. But I think I'll tag along."

Knowing that he'll be by my side has a little more of my apprehension leaving me. "You're the best, Jamie-pop."

"Damn straight I am. Let's roll."

I WOULDN'T SAY I've been avoiding Jenny, except the chicken-shit that I am, that's exactly what I've been doing. But today, seeing her is unavoidable. Even worse, I'm filled with equal parts excitement and dread.

These warring feelings have me questioning if I've suddenly become a teenage girl or some shit. However, all of my emotional turmoil over seeing Jenny Jones will just have to wait, because right now, I need to help my niece celebrate.

Gift in hand, I let myself into Natalie and Alden's house as the note on the front door instructs. I head straight through and out the kitchen door to the backyard, where the party seems to already be in full swing.

Their already-amazing backyard has been completely transformed into any kid's dream. There's a bounce house in the back right corner, an oversized bowling setup, chalk to draw on the patio with, bubbles, and more.

My sister spots me immediately and breaks away from Alden to come and greet me. "You're here!" she exclaims, as if I'd be any place else.

"I am. Where's my girl?"

Natalie's eyes glint with something, and while I can't quite name it, I don't like it. "Jenny? She's not here yet."

I grit my teeth together. "Not. Who. I. Meant." Should have seen this shit coming. Ever since our vanishing act at her wedding, my sister and her husband have been giving me relentless shit, trying to get me to admit that I was with Jenny. But, forget that; they don't need to know shit.

Like the little brat she is, Natalie just laughs. "Yeah, I know. Tatum is in the bouncy house with a few friends."

I give her a terse nod and set off in that direction, stopping by the gift table on my way. However, before I can make it across the yard, Alden closes in on me.

"'Sup, brother," Alden calls out, clapping me on the back. "Glad you made it."

I roll my eyes at my best friend, opting to not engage. "Nowhere else I'd rather be."

"Right, right," he murmurs in a smarmy tone that he knows will get under my skin.

"Got something you want to say?" I ask as I scan the back-yard. It is quickly filling with more and more people—most with little rug-rats in tow. But still no Jenny. Not that I'm looking for her.

Alden answers my question with one of his own. "Looking for anyone in particular?"

My eyes fly back to him. "Nope. No one. Just taking it all in."

He nods knowingly. "Ah, and here I thought maybe you were looking for Jen—"

A loud yell pierces the air, cutting him off. "Uncle Nate! You're here!" Saved by Tatum, thank God.

I squat down, bringing me closer to her height. "Of course I am, Tater Tot."

She wraps her arms around my neck and practically tackle-hugs me to the ground. "I'm so-so-so happy you're here! Will you jump with me?"

I look from my niece to the bounce house and back. "I might be a little big for that, but what if we bowl?"

Tatum steps back from me and thinks it over for a second. "Deal." She sticks her little hand out toward me, and I shake it. "Now, c'mon, Uncle Nate. Time's a wasting."

I can't help but smile at her sweet, bossy, quirky nature. This kid really is something else.

We're on our third frame when Jenny arrives. I haven't seen her, or heard her, but I swear, the air changes with her presence. I can physically feel that she's here, and really, it kind of agitates me. What right does she have to have that kind of power over me?

Discreetly, I scan the yard. When my eyes land on her, my agitation morphs into anger. She's dressed casually, yet somehow, she looks like sex personified. And to make matters even worse, she didn't come alone. Who brings a fucking date to a kid's party? And don't even get me started on the D-bag glued to her side, with his pansy-ass glasses and flannel shirt. It's May, and the dude is dressed like a lumberjack.

I try to look away from her and to focus all of my attention on Tatum, but my eyes—and my thoughts—keep drifting to her. She looks so damn beautiful it hurts. I want so badly to pull her aside and ask who the guy is, but that's irrational as hell, seeing as I have no claim to her.

If anything, I should be happy to see she's moved on so easily—after all, I'm the one who repeatedly told her I wasn't the man for her. But, that doesn't mean Hipster McGee is either.

"Uncle Nate!" Tatum yelling draws my attention back to her. "I got a strike! I'm winning!"

"For now," I tell her, doing my best evil villain impersonation.

"Puh-lease," she scoffs with all of the sass of a four-year-old can manage—which is a lot. "Everyone knows girls rule and boys drool."

"Everyone, huh? Everyone like who?"

"Ugh! Tell him, Miss Jenny." My spine goes ramrod straight at her name.

I turn to face her. With my gaze low, I start at her feet and drag my eyes slowly up her sexy, exposed legs. Not caring one bit that her date is right beside her, I pause at the small, barely there sliver of exposed skin at her waist, remembering just how her belly quivered under my touch, before continuing up to meet her eyes.

"Yeah," I rasp out. "Tell me, Jenny."

Her cheeks pink at my charged tone, but her eyes are hard. "It's scientifically proven. There's even a book or two about it, Nate."

I smirk at her. Damn, a lot has changed since that night. In the past, she would have blushed and mumbled something incoherent before excusing herself. I gotta say, though—this new, confident Jenny is hella hot.

"If it's in a book, it must be true," I murmur.

Instead of responding to me, she crouches down and addresses Tatum. With their heads bent toward one another, they talk in hushed whispers too low for me to hear.

I continue ignoring Jenny's boy toy, but with the way he's openly glaring at me, it's getting a little awkward. I mean, what is this dude's issue?

However, I've never been a pansy, so I stick my hand out to him and introduce myself. "Nate Reynolds, and you are?" Hopefully my sizing up the competition—so to speak—comes across as a friendly gesture, even if it's anything but.

"Jameson Reed." He shakes my hand with a strong grip—the kind that says he has something to prove. Well, guess what, buddy? So do I...I'm just not sure what it is yet, because the pretty little thing crouched at my feet seemingly has me tied in knots.

After what feels like forever, Jenny stands. "Tatum, I'd like you to meet my...Jamie."

As if she's only now noticed his presence, Tatum's gaze

snaps over to him. "Oh, um, hi," she squeaks out before giggling down at her feet.

Jamie offers her what appears to be a genuine smile. "I hear today's a special day."

Tatum bounces on the balls of her feet, nodding. "It's my birthday. I'm four."

"Four? Oh, wow. I thought you were at least seven!" Jamie croons, like the suck up he is.

"No, silly. Just four. But, that's still almost growed up. Do you…you have a girlfriend?" She rushes out that last bit, and damn if I'm not waiting with bated breath for his answer.

Except he gives nothing away; he only grins. "Aren't you a little young for all that?"

Tatum rolls her eyes. "My daddy says I am. He says I can't date until I'm thirty. But, if you wanted to be my boyfriend, I bet he'd be okay."

"You're a cutie, kiddo, but we'd better listen to your dad, okay?"

Tatum pouts for a minute but ultimately agrees. This dude is making it hard to hate him with how sweet he's being to my niece. That is, until I see him wrap his pinky finger around Jenny's—a subtle yet familiar gesture.

I'm itching to find an out as an awkward silence settles over our little group. But, when in the company of kids, silence never lasts long. "Mr. Jamie, did you know my uncle Nate is a police officer?"

Jamie regards me coolly. "Is he? That's a good job to have." I can't tell if he's dissing me or not.

"He is! He has a badge and handcuffs and a gun and everything! What do you do?"

"I'm a pilot."

Tatum's eyes double in size. "Like you fly an airplane? A real airplane?"

"Sure do."

"That is so cool!" Tatum squeals. "I've never been on a plane!"

"Wanna know what's even cooler?" Jenny asks, and Tatum nods furiously. "Jamie doesn't just fly the big planes, he also works with a charity organization and helps them. Sometimes he helps flies in supplies to places that don't have easy access, and other times, he helps transport sick people to hospitals that are far, far away."

I'm not sure Tatum even knows what half of that means, but she's looking at Jamie with hero worship in her eyes anyway. "Whoa. Is that why you have those big muscles? From all that helping people?"

At that, both Jamie and Jenny smile. Me, though—I scowl. "Nope, those are from CrossFit."

"Okay, Tater Tot," I interrupt, not wanting to hear anymore of this bullshit. "Let's finish our game so you can go play with your friends."

"Finish? Uncle Nate, just give up. I'm just gonna beat you!"

"You're that sure, huh?" She nods. "Well, I guess you better go and play then!" She wraps my legs in a big hug before moving to hug Jenny next. She hesitates a second, and right when I think she's about to run off, she hugs Jamie, too. The hell?

In the wake of Tatum's departure, the already tense atmosphere turns stifling. For reasons I'm not sure I'm willing to admit, I want to demand for Jenny to tell me who in the hell Jamie is to her.

"Sooo," Jenny drawls, bringing me out of my thoughts. "It was good seeing you again, Nate." And just like that, she walks away.

Jamie extends his hand to me again, but like the petulant child I apparently am, I ignore it. "Right," he murmurs, sounding like he knows something I don't—which just pisses me off more. "I would say it was nice to meet you, but…" He trails off and follows after Jenny.

I keep my eyes trained on him until he reaches her, and when he slips his arm around her narrow waist and shoots me a wink over his shoulder, I have to clench my fists and pinch my eyes shut to remain calm.

Determined to ignore the way Jenny's presence is affecting me, I make my way over to my parents, who are seated under the huge shade umbrella Alden has cranked open. I greet them both with a nod before pulling over a chair for myself.

"Nathaniel Reynolds," my mother scolds in that voice only moms have. "You better give me a better greeting than a shake of your head."

I bite back my smile at her gentle rebuke. I'm damn near thirty years old, and yet, she can still put me in my place like I'm twelve.

I step away from my chair and over to her. "Sorry, Mom." I bend at the waist and wrap my arms around her shoulders, pressing a kiss to her cheek. Before taking a seat, I go ahead and shake my dad's hand as well. "How have y'all been?"

"Good, son, good," Dad answers, bringing his drink to his lips.

I look from him to my mother, knowing she will elaborate. "Busy as can be with little Miss Tatum. I honestly don't know what we're going to do when she starts kindergarten in the fall."

As hard as it was for all of us when Natalie became a mother before she even received her high school diploma, our mom lives for being a Nana.

"I know that'll be a tough transition for y'all," I say absentmindedly, scanning the crowd, not looking for Jenny. The fact that my eyes land on her is nothing more than a coincidence. Or at least that's what I'm telling myself, because after searching her out, I wish like hell I wouldn't have, because watching her laugh at something my best friend said with her head resting on Jamie's chest as he plays with her hair, sparks a fire in my gut that feels a whole lot like jealousy.

Noticing my shift in mood, Mom wastes no time calling me on it. "What's got you looking so sour?"

With a rough shake of my head, I mutter, "Nothing."

"Doesn't look like nothing," she says softly, laying her hand on mine.

My initial instinct is to throw my guard up and snap, and if it were anyone else but my mother, I would. But this woman is an angel on earth, so I dial it back. "Just got a lot on my mind."

"Sometimes talking it through helps."

I flip my hand so that we're palm-to-palm and give hers a quick squeeze. "I appreciate it, but now isn't the time or place."

She follows my line of sight and nods knowingly. "You probably don't even realize this, son, but the entire time we've been talking, you've been glaring at sweet little Jenny. Is she what has you all sour and grumpy?"

Damn intuitive woman.

I start to reply, but my dad steps in. "Melanie, let the boy be." Hell yeah, Dad for the win. "He can come by for dinner one night this week and y'all can gossip then." Never mind—thanks for nothing, Pops.

"Smart thinking." She turns from my dad to me, pinning me with her mom-eyes. "What night are you free?"

"Uhhh." I grab at the back of my neck, rubbing at the tightness there as I mentally go through my schedule. "How's Tuesday night?"

"Absolutely perfect." Fun times.

———

Twenty minutes later, Natalie is rounding everyone up for cake and presents. I'm not even gonna lie, this is my favorite part of kids' parties. Watching my niece's eyes light up as she tears into each brightly wrapped package just does something to me—and also, cake, because, well, cake.

And Tatum's is no disappointment, assuming it tastes even half as good as it looks. I try my hardest not to stare Jenny down as Alden lights the candles on the cake, but it is a futile effort at best. My eyes are drawn to her, seemingly of their own accord.

Normally, I'd have no problem enjoying the scenery, so to speak, but watching her with Jamie—all of their small touches and private laughs—has me ready to Hulk the fuck out.

Once we've sung "Happy Birthday" and Tatum's blown out her candles, Natalie and Alden set to work cutting and distributing slices of cake. I take the plate my sister offers me and make my way over to one of the many folding tables they have set up in the yard.

One bite in, and I realize the cake is even better than it looks, and judging from the lack of chatter, the rest of the partygoers agree. I'm on my third bite when a shadow falls over me. My eyes shoot up to see who's joining me. Of course, it's none other than Jenny, her boy toy in tow.

They take their seats, murmuring to one another in hushed whispers, all but ignoring my presence entirely. I try my best to do the same, but I still find myself straining to listen in on whatever it is they're talking about. This woman has me acting insane…I'm eavesdropping like a child, for Christ's sake.

"Are you having a good time?" she whispers, leaning into him.

"Anytime with you is a good time, Jenny-cake," he replies, and I think I throw up a little in my mouth. Jenny-cake, what the fuck…

She giggles like a schoolgirl. "Ever the charmer." She forks a bite of cake into her mouth, leaving a dot of icing at the corner of her lips. When he reaches over and rubs it away with his thumb, I can't take it a second longer.

"Should you be eating that?" I ask her, my tone hard. Shit, that didn't come out right.

Jenny swallows and lowers her fork. "Excuse me?"

I nod down to the slice of sugary sweetness on her plate. "The cake. Is it something you should be eating?"

She blinks a few times as if stunned by my question. "I'm sorry, but—" she starts, but Jamie covers her hand with his and takes over.

"And why shouldn't she eat it?" Jamie pins me with a fierce glare. "I'm enjoying a slice and so are you—what makes her any different?"

"Maybe the fact that she's dia—" I stop short, knowing I'd be crossing a line if I finished that sentence. Her health and her body are just that—hers, and it's damn sure not my business to spread the knowledge I have of it around to other people.

Even without me spitting the rest of my words out, Jenny gets where I was going. With a tight smile, she breathes in deeply. "While I appreciate your concern, I assure you that I know what I can and cannot eat. This isn't my first rodeo."

Jamie's eyes ping back and forth between us, like he's watching the Williams sisters burn up the tennis court.

"Just looking out for you," I murmur, hoping she hears my sincerity.

But judging from her eye roll, it fell on deaf ears. "Oh, well, lucky me. Whatever would I do without you looking out for me?" Her words have a bite to them, and damn if they don't pinch a little.

I hold up my hands in a sign of surrender. "Look, I'm not trying to fight with you or micromanage you." Somehow, every word out of my mouth seems to be wrong, and I'm only digging the hole I'm in deeper.

Jenny tosses her fork down and pushes her plate away from her. "Are you okay?" Jamie asks, looking at her so tenderly that my jaw clenches.

"Mm. Fine. I've just lost my appetite is all."

An internal war is waging—while I know this isn't the time or place, the urge to call her on the way she's acting is strong. Too strong. "The hell's your problem?" I demand on a harsh exhale.

She gets this sort of crazed look in her eyes, like she's contemplating using the tines of her plastic fork to stab me. This time when Jamie grabs her hand, I'm mildly grateful. "You wanna know what my problem is? Oh, Nate, are you sitting comfortably? Because the list is freaking long."

I gesture for her to elaborate.

"Simply put: you. You're my problem. You're a boy masquerading as a man. I don't know who hurt you, but let me just tell you, hurting others isn't the answer. You think you're God's gift to women and that after one taste, we all become Nate-junkies. Well, newsflash, asshole—as it turns out, one taste of you is plenty. You're nothing but an arrogant, cocky playboy. You weren't kidding when you said you weren't the man for me—you're too into yourself to ever be the right man for anyone. Honestly, at this point, I don't know what I ever saw in you.

"And yeah, Nate, for a long time I did have a crush on you. Stupidly, I had you on some pedestal, but my eyes are wide open now, and I see you for exactly what you are. The fact that you're so incredibly shallow really is the icing on the proverbial cake. Have a nice day, because I'm done."

With that, Jenny shoves her chair back from the table and stalks off toward the house. Jamie shakes his head at me, a snide smirk playing on his lips. "You really are a dumbass, aren't you?" And with those parting remarks, I'm left alone at the table with all of Jenny's words swirling in my gut and guilt swimming in my veins.

AFTER JENNY STORMS off with Jamie hot on her heels, I keep my ass planted in my seat, sulking, even when Tatum begins opening her gifts. The smile on her face as she rips into the colorful packages is almost enough to ease the sting of Jenny's words. To know that she thinks so little of me, especially when I think she's one of the most magnificent women I've ever met... I'm not going to lie, it hurts.

Then again, she doesn't know I feel that way—and she never will. My walls are impenetrable, and they exist far more for her benefit than mine. Knowing that my actions hurt her makes me feel about two inches tall. But I also know that in the long run, I'm saving her from a fate far worse. I know what I'm capable of, and I'd rather a small pain now than utter devastation later. And surely that's where we would end, with me absolutely decimating one of the kindest, most pure women I've ever met.

I can't do it. I won't. Like I keep saying, Jenny Jones deserves better than me. Hell, all women deserve better than me.

"Uncle Nate!" The sound of Tatum hollering my name draws me out of my inner turmoil. I look up to see her running toward me with the American Girl doll I bought her wrapped tightly in her arms. "I love her! She looks just like me!"

Damn straight she does—I paid a pretty penny to customize the thing. "Yeah? You think she's pretty cool?"

"She's the best! I'll love her forever!"

I pull my niece onto my lap. "Do you have a name picked out for her?"

Tatum nods her head. "Heather Lo. 'Cause of my two best friends from the liberry. Nana takes me for story day, and we always sit together."

"That is the best name ever," I assure her. "You know, right after Tatum."

She slings one arm around my neck and presses a kiss to my scruffy cheek. "Thank you, Uncle Nate. You're my most favorite uncle ever in the whole big world!"

I squeeze her to me before releasing her. "I'm your only uncle, Tater Tot, but you're welcome all the same. Happy Birthday!"

I kick back farther into my seat as she runs off to finish opening her gifts. As much as I want to focus my undivided attention on my niece, my eyes seek out Jenny. She's like a fucking lighthouse beacon, drawing my eyes to craggy rocks of the shore, and yet I'm helpless to change my course, even knowing that pure annihilation awaits me.

As the party winds down, my indignation over Jenny's assessment of me battles with my conscience. On one hand, it was my actions that led her to feel the way she does. But, on the other, I hate that I feel even a modicum of guilt, because really, I was only looking out for her. Add in the jealousy twinging just beneath my skin from seeing her with Jamie, and I'm a goddamn mess. I'm torn between snubbing her, groveling, and throwing her over my shoulder like a caveman while declaring "Jenny, mine!"

Jesus, I need a drink.

Thankfully, Alden and Natalie had the foresight to supply

beer for all of the adults at this kiddie shindig. I vacate my seat and set off for the cooler. I dig around in the ice, but only manage to find soft drinks, bottles of water, and juice boxes. Definitely not what I'm after.

"Good stuff's in the kitchen," Alden murmurs as he walks past me, trailing after Tatum as she drags him over to play some game.

"Thanks," I call after him as I turn and head into the house.

Once inside, I pull open the fridge door to find a mecca. Leave it to the foodies to go all out on the beer selection for their four-year-old's party—not that I'm complaining. I snag a bottle of my favorite lager, shut the door, and grab the magnetic bottle opener from the side of the refrigerator. Over the pop-hiss-clink, I hear the back door open again.

Jenny.

Don't ask me how I know it's her without even looking—I just do. I can feel it, as batshit as that sounds. Swear, if anyone ever told me they could feel someone's presence, I would laugh my ass off, and yet, here I am.

I pivot and lean back against the counter to the right of the fridge. We lock eyes in a wordless battle, neither of us willing to back down. The temptation to skim my gaze down her body is strong, but I won't look away—I can't.

Bringing the bottle to my lips, I drink down two swallows. The fact that her eyes momentarily drop to my throat as I swallow doesn't escape my notice, but I let it go. As I pull the bottle away, a little droplet of beer lingers on my lip. Slowly, I swipe the tip of my tongue over it, drawing my lip into my mouth.

Her chest expands as her breathing accelerates, a needy look painting her pretty features, like she's remembering every second of our night together. Turned on is a good look on her.

We remain engaged in our silent clash of wills, both far

too stubborn to back down. Honestly, I'd love nothing more than to go to her and make her talk to me. I don't like the tension that lingers between us, even if I am the cause of it.

"Fuck it," I mumble to myself, breaking the spell.

"What was that?" she asks, cocking her head to the side.

"Can we talk?" I ask, pushing off of the counter.

Her nervous gaze flits around the kitchen as if she's looking for someone to jump out and save her. Speaking of, where is Jamie, her little guard dog?

She gives me a hesitant nod, and I gesture for her to follow me. I guide her into the living room at the front of the house. I take a seat on the couch, patting the spot next to me, shocked and delighted when she actually drops down next to me.

For as compatible as we are in the bedroom, we really couldn't be more different. Whereas I sit with my body angled toward hers, my legs spread wide, elbows resting on my knees, and my beer bottle dangling from my fingertips, she sits with her feet tucked up under her, as if she's trying to take up as little space as possible.

"What do you want to talk about, Nate?" she demands to know, her strong voice filling the space her small body doesn't. Damn, how far she's come from the unsure, nervous girl I met not so long ago. Not gonna lie, her bark is every bit as sexy as her bite. "Or did you just want to stare at me?"

"GG, while you're absolutely something to behold, I actually do have something to say."

Her eyes widen, and she motions for me to get on with it. Sexy, infuriating, impatient woman.

"Look, I think we need to talk about that night."

Her spine straightens. "What exactly do you think we need to talk about?" she asks, her tone ice cold. I go to answer her, but she cuts me off. "You wanna talk about what it felt like for me to wake up to an empty bed?"

"Jenny…I…you knew—" I can't seem to collect my words,

which is BS since I asked her to talk. My lack of intelligible reply doesn't matter though, because it seems my good girl has more to say.

"What I know is that I shared something with you that night that I've shared with very few others." Her chest heaves, and I can't help but wonder what in the hell she's talking about. I know she wasn't a virgin, so what exactly did she fucking share with me? "I let you in, and…and you just left. You were so repulsed by what you saw that you just left." Her big, doe eyes fill with tears and my heart constricts in my chest. I may not have a clue what she's upset over, but whatever it is, I caused it and the look on her face is absolutely gutting me.

Hold. The. Hell. On. "Repulsed? Jenny, what are you talking about?"

She shakes her head, willing herself not to cry. Unable to sit back idly and watch her hurt, I set my beer down onto the table next to the couch and reach for her, drawing her small body into mine. I'm fully expecting her to reject me, so when she melts into me, I pull her closer, so that she's practically sitting on my lap sidesaddle.

"Shh," I whisper into her hair as I run the pads of my fingers over the sliver of exposed skin at the small of her back. "It's okay, GG. I've got you."

With her wrapped in my arms, I keep whispering to her. "You're so beautiful, Jenny. I could never be repulsed by you. Talk to me, tell me what's going on in that pretty little head of yours."

She sniffles a few times and pulls back to look at me. "I knew it was a one-time thing, that's not why I'm upset." She rushes the words out. It's what she follows up with that metaphorically knocks me on my ass. "You saw my pump, and I told you about my diabetes, and then it was like you couldn't wait to escape it."

Oh. Oh, hell. It finally dawns on me what's got her so upset and I feel like a grade-A asshole.

I trace the back of my hand along the side of her face. "Oh, Jenny." My voice is rough, weighted with emotion. "No, that's not it at all."

Her eyes shine, a mixture of hopefulness and uncertainty. She sways a little closer to me, our lips less than an inch apart. "Then what?" she asks, sounding as broken as I feel.

Running my thumb over her bottom lip, I contemplate how to answer her. I need her to know that I'm wholly the issue, but everything that comes to mind sounds like a line or a copout, neither of which will do.

"Jenny," I exhale her name, and she shudders, leaning closer, so that our lips are touching. Yet, neither of us make the move to close the distance. We simply hover, breathing in each other's air.

"There's nothing you could do—nothing you could tell me or show me—that would make me not want you." I speak the words against her mouth, wanting nothing more than to bite down on her trembling bottom lip.

"I...I don't understand." Her words are nothing more than a soft whimper—a plea.

Just as I press my lips to hers, the sound of Jamie calling her name echoes through the house. Jesus. Christ. How could I forget that she's here with someone else? I may be a lot of things—and most of them bad—but I'm not a cheater. That's a hard limit for me.

She pulls back from me and practically flies off of my lap just as he steps into the room. "There you are." His voice holds a slight edge.

"H-here I am," she mumbles back, not looking at either of us.

"Is everything okay?" he asks, stepping closer to her.

"Mmhmm, fine."

He keeps his focus completely on her, as if I'm not even in the room. "You about ready to head home?"

Home. The way he refers to her house as home has me feeling a little greener than I'd like to admit.

"Yeah, Jamie-pop. Just…" She glances back to me. "Just give me a second."

He hesitates before giving her a tight nod. "I'll wait by the door."

"Nate," she whispers, but I really don't want to hear whatever she's about to say.

"Save it." I let out a dry laugh. "You wouldn't want to keep your Jamie-pop waiting." I inject as much venom as possible into his stupid nickname, hoping to convey exactly how I feel without actually having to say it.

Judging from the way her shoulders fall, I'd say I made my point. Without another word, she rises from the couch and walks out of the room.

I linger after she exits, polishing off my now-warm beer before heading to the kitchen in search of a glass of water. I end up getting more than I bargained for when I discover Natalie perched atop of the island, looking like she's waiting to grill me.

Ignoring my sister, I grab a glass from the cabinet and fill it with filtered water from the fridge. I'm mid-sip when Natalie starts in on me. "I know you slept with Jenny."

I choke on my drink.

She ignores me and carries on. "Don't bother denying it, Nate. I. Know. What I don't get is why you've spent most of the day practically pissing a circle around her and glaring at her very gay cousin."

As I cough and hack, my sister's words settle. Jamie's her…cousin. Her gay cousin. Oh, shit.

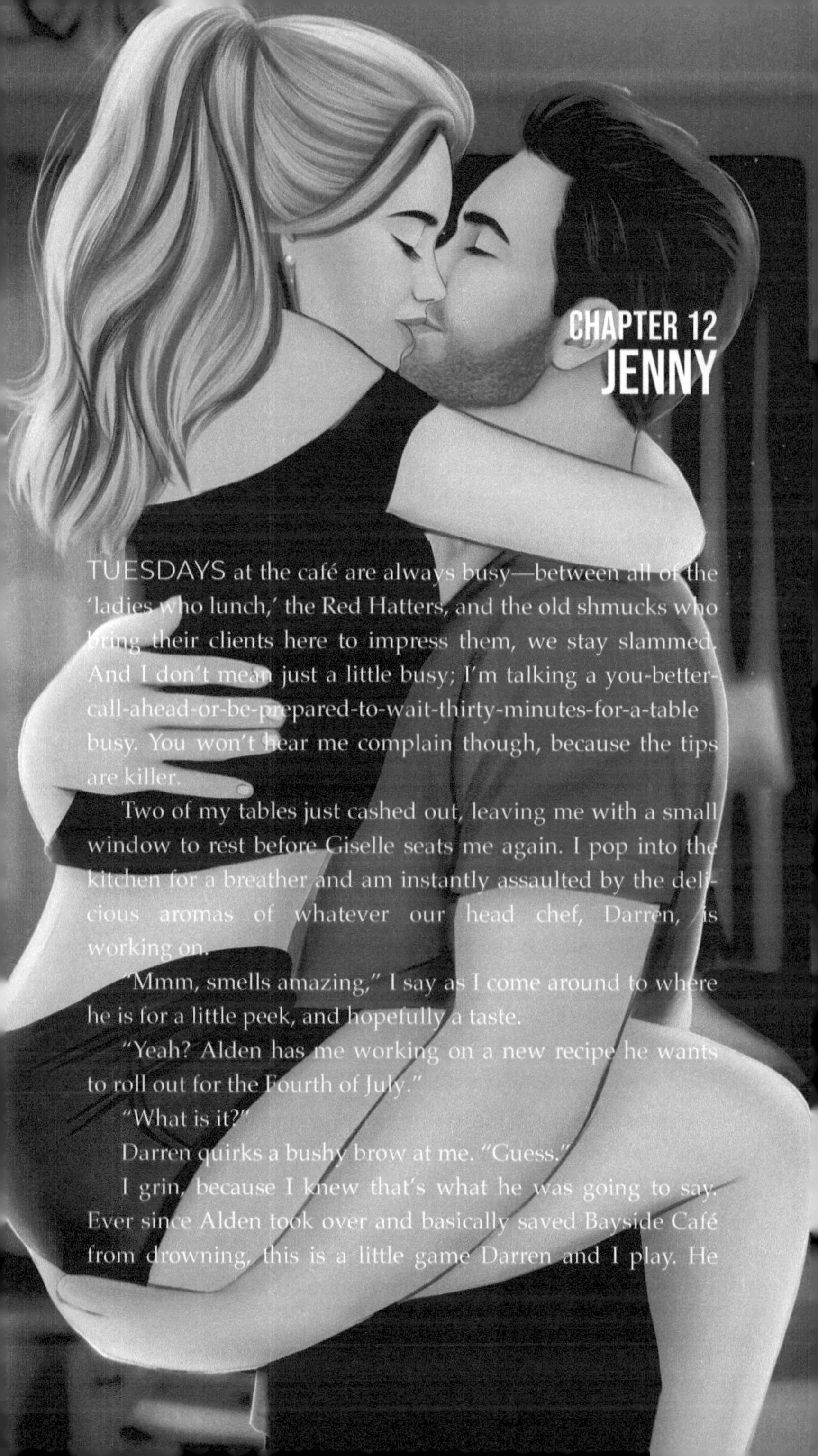

TUESDAYS at the café are always busy—between all of the 'ladies who lunch,' the Red Hatters, and the old shmucks who bring their clients here to impress them, we stay slammed. And I don't mean just a little busy; I'm talking a you-better-call-ahead-or-be-prepared-to-wait-thirty-minutes-for-a-table busy. You won't hear me complain though, because the tips are killer.

Two of my tables just cashed out, leaving me with a small window to rest before Giselle seats me again. I pop into the kitchen for a breather and am instantly assaulted by the delicious aromas of whatever our head chef, Darren, is working on.

"Mmm, smells amazing," I say as I come around to where he is for a little peek, and hopefully a taste.

"Yeah? Alden has me working on a new recipe he wants to roll out for the Fourth of July."

"What is it?"

Darren quirks a bushy brow at me. "Guess."

I grin, because I knew that's what he was going to say. Ever since Alden took over and basically saved Bayside Café from drowning, this is a little game Darren and I play. He cooks—I guess the ingredients based on either smell or blind taste. It's a double-win for me, because I usually get to taste something off the charts amazing and I get to strengthen my palette.

With my eyes closed, I lean over the cooktop and allow my other senses to take over. I can hear the sound of oil sizzling. Inhaling deeply, I smell fragrant garlic mixed with peppers and onions and fresh tomatoes.

"Well, what do you think it is?" Darren asks.

From elsewhere in the kitchen I hear a scoff. "You already know she's gonna guess it, why bother?" Ah, Javier, our sous chef is here, too.

I smirk at his smartass question but pay him no mind. "I know you're making something savory, but I feel like I'm missing something." I tap my finger on my chin. "I'll be honest, I'm not sure what you're making, but if you add in some sweet Italian sausage, it'll be off the chain!"

At the sound of Javier busting out laughing, I open my eyes. Sure enough, Darren is steadily working his special seasoning mix into a bowl of freshly ground pork. "Boom! Nailed it!" I cry out in victory.

Darren grins. "You did good, kid."

"Let me be the first to taste the sausage when it's ready?" I ask, batting my long lashes at him.

"I'll let you be the fifth—after me, Javier, the boss, and Natalie."

"Fair enough." I grab a bottle of water from the small fridge Alden keeps stocked for his staff, chug it down, and head out to check on my tables.

Once I know my customers are all doing fine and dandy, I head over to the hostess stand. "Looks like the rush is just about done," Giselle comments upon seeing me.

"And not a moment too soon. I need a break before dinner service."

"Actually," Alden interrupts from behind us. "You're not

going to be working dinner tonight. Finish your tables, do your side work, and head home."

I shoot him a weird look over my shoulder. "Huh? I'm down to work a double today."

He shrugs. "Plans change. Don't like it, take it up with my wife." Gah—I have to swoon at the way he still refers to Natalie as his wife every chance he gets.

"Why did she tell you to cut me?"

Alden mimes zipping his lips. "I have nothing to do with this. You wanna know, you gotta talk to her. In fact, I was given explicit instructions to have you call her the second you leave here. Don't land me in the doghouse, Jenny Jones."

I roll my eyes. "Sure, sure. But this reeks of a setup!"

Giselle brings her attention back to the reservation book, already bored with us and Alden simply smirks before sending me back out on the floor.

An hour later, I'm in my car and dialing up my best friend. She answers on the first ring. "Hey, what are you up to tonight?"

"Hmm, why don't you tell me, seeing as you canceled the second half of my shift."

Natalie lets out a nervous-sounding laugh. "Well, Mom wanted me to invite you for dinner."

"Why?"

"I don't know, Jenny; she just asked me to."

Yeah, this is definitely some kind of setup. "We've been friends for a few years now, and not once has your mom ever invited me to dinner." I say each word slowly, letting my skepticism come through loud and clear.

Static filters through the line, followed by Natalie's muffled voice. "What? I can't hear you."

More static and then she comes through clear. "Sorry, dropped my phone."

"You're all good. Seriously though, this is weird."

"Look, I don't know why she wants you there, but she specifically asked me to make sure you were. Don't make me disappoint her—Lord knows, I've done enough of that in this lifetime."

"Oh, hell no. You are not playing the teen pregnancy card with me right now, are you?"

"That depends." I can practically hear Natalie's grin. "Is it working?"

I let out a long, overly dramatic groan as I turn onto the winding gravel road that leads to my cottage. "Oh my God, fine." Natalie lets out a loud cheer. "One question though… will Nate be there?"

I throw the gear shifter in park, waiting on her to speak. Why is she hesitating? I don't like this…not one bit.

"Honestly, I don't know. Mom didn't say."

"I'm just gonna assume he won't be, because why on earth would your mom invite me to a family dinner?"

"Exactly. Be there by five-thirty. Do you remember how to get there?"

"I do. Then again, this isn't exactly a GPS kind of town. You've been somewhere once, you know how to get there for life."

"True that. See you later!"

We end the call, and I make my way inside. My feet and back ache, and while I'd love a hot, steaming bubble bath…a shower will have to do.

As I stand under the warm spray, thoughts of Nate invade my mind. Ever since Tatum's party this past weekend, he's been at the forefront of my mind. Even though we talked, nothing between us was resolved. And sweet baby in a manger, the way he held me in his lap and spoke with his lips brushing mine…the mere memory of it has me erupting in goose bumps regardless of the scalding water cascading over my skin.

After my shower, I dress casually in a pair of coral linen pants, a white tank top, and leather flip-flops. I forgo makeup and keep my hair up in the same messy bun I gathered it into before my shower.

With a few minutes to kill, I fire off a text to Natalie.

ME

Hey, what time are we actually eating? Do you by chance know what we are having?

NATALIE

Mom says dinner is at six and that we're having grilled steaks, baked potatoes, and salad. See you soon!

I smile at her reply. That's a perfectly easy meal for me to bolus for. Dinner parties and eating out can be a struggle sometimes, especially when restaurants don't bother providing nutritional information. That's another thing I respect about my best friend's husband: for every single dish on the menu, Alden provides a nutritional breakdown—even if it is a one-time special.

———

Natalie and Nate's childhood home is a traditional colonial style house built from red brick with glossy black shutters, an even glossier red door, and a little copper-roofed portico over the entryway. Put simply, it oozes Southern charm.

Mr. Reynolds keeps the lawn immaculate and the shrubs well-groomed. Honestly, this house looks like something you'd see on HGTV.

As I exit my car, Natalie pulls in next to me. "Hey, hey! Glad you could make it!"

"You say that like I actually had a choice." My words are harsh, but my tone is light and airy.

Natalie just smiles, and together, we head inside.

Everything is exactly the way I remember from my last visit, and let me just say, if MTV did a normal people edition of Cribs, this place would top the list. The furniture and décor are a perfectly balanced mix of generational antiques and modern finds. It's definitely a stark contrast from the log cabin I grew up in. Mind you, I'm not putting my parents' home down—it's just gorgeous in its own right.

The scent of garlic and rosemary greet us the minute we step inside. "Mmm, smells good, Mom," Natalie calls out.

"Mama!" Tatum comes barreling around the corner and tackle-hugs Natalie as if she hasn't seen her in a decade. "I missed you! I painted you a picture today, and we were gonna make cookies, but we needed the butter for the potatoes. But that's okay because Nana let me help make the salad. We chopped up some greens from her garden and now she's gonna show me how to cut up some cucumbers! I got to use a knife! All by myself!"

"Whoa, Tater Tot! Slow down!" Natalie says. "Tell me one thing at a time, okay?"

The three of us set off toward the kitchen as Natalie and Tatum talk among themselves about Tatum's seemingly eventful day. This kid goes from zero-to-sixty faster than a super car. It's no wonder people always joke about bottling kids' energy—they have it in spades.

"Jenny, you made it!" Melanie Reynolds says in greeting, wiping her hands on a floral print dishcloth.

"Am I chopped liver?" Natalie asks, her tone teasing.

Melanie brushes her daughter off. "I see you all the time. Jenny being here is a treat."

Her words cause me to blush a little. "Thank you for

inviting me. If I'd have known sooner, I'd have brought something."

"Your presence is more than enough." Melanie smiles at me in a way that has alarm bells blaring in my head. She has that meddlesome mom look going on, and it has me on high freaking alert.

I grab a seat at the bar and the four of us chatter mindlessly. Well, Tatum chatters, we mostly just listen. I can't say I mind it though. For starters, the kid is amusing. And more importantly, listening to her distracts me from concocting worst-case scenarios about what Mrs. Reynolds has up her sleeves.

However, not even ten minutes later, my worry materializes in the form of Nate Reynolds. "Smells good, Mom!" he hollers from the entryway, his deep, gravelly voice already putting me on edge. When he steps into the kitchen, still dressed in his uniform, I have to force myself not to squirm on my stool. No man has any business looking that damn good.

I mean, have mercy. The way his standard issue shirt pulls tight across his chest, combined with…no, Jenny, do not think about his handcuffs. I squeeze my thighs together and pinch my eyes closed. Good Lord, this man gets to me. After all that's transpired between us, you'd think I'd be immune to him, but nope. Somehow, my stupid attraction only seems to grow. Talk about insult to injury.

"I'm glad you think so," Melanie replies, bending to retrieve a pan from the oven. "I made all of your favorites."

"Uncle Nate! I thought you'd never ever get here!"

Nate doesn't respond to his mother or Tatum. Nope. He's too busy gawking at me. He studies me, probably trying to figure out why I'm here. I can see the moment it dawns on him that we've been set up.

"I see we have a guest joining us tonight."

"We do. I invited Jenny to join us. Your father and I figured it was high time to get to know her a little better."

"You know her plenty," Nate deadpans.

"There's always room to know someone better."

"I agree with Nana." Tatum leaps down from her barstool and twirls in a wide circle. "Plus, Miss Jenny is pretty like a real-life princess. Oooh! Maybe you could be her prince!"

"Now, there's an idea," Melanie mutters to herself. I don't think she meant for us to hear her, but we all did.

Nate and I share a blank look. Luckily, Natalie is on my—our—side. "Alright, you two, that's enough. Tater Tot, why don't you go check on Papa and the steaks?"

A little frown mars Tatum's face. "Papa told me to stay inside. He says grilling is a solo-sport." She stomps her foot. "But there's no I in team! I think he just gets grumpy because I always tell him all the things Daddy does different than him."

We all try and smother our laughter. Tatum is a bossy little thing and at all of four, she definitely knows her way—with adult supervision—around a kitchen or grill. Then again, with two foodie parents, of course she does. Natalie has been cooking with her ever since she was old enough to stand up on her own.

"I'll go," Nate volunteers. I prop my elbows on the bar and rest my head on my hands, discreetly following him with my eyes, ogling his delectable backside until he's out of my line of sight. The second the door shuts behind him, the air settles, and I breathe a little easier.

We chat for a few more minutes before I excuse myself to the restroom. I make quick work of checking my blood sugar and bolusing for my meal. As I'm washing my hands, the door swings open. "Oh, shit, sorr—" Nate's words fall off mid-sentence and I angle my head to look at him. Instead of retreating, he hovers in the threshold for just a moment before stepping into the small space with me, closing the door behind him. "Hello there," he murmurs, turning the lock—like I should have done.

"Uh, hi?" I turn off the faucet and dry my hands, feeling all kinds of cagey in this confined space with him.

"Hi, yourself," he murmurs, stepping closer to me, practically pinning me to the pedestal sink. He stares at me with a hungry gaze that simply doesn't make sense to me. We didn't exactly part on the best of terms last weekend, yet here he is, looking like he wants to devour me whole.

"What are you doing?" My heart thumps a frantic rhythm in my chest. This man is bad for my freaking health.

"Well, I was coming to wash up for dinner." He steps closer, eliminating the gap between us, fitting our bodies together in a way that has me flashing back to that night. "But now, I'm doing this instead."

As soon as he utters those words, I know he's going to kiss me. And even though I shouldn't let him, even though I should turn him away, I meet him halfway, moaning softly when he sucks my lower lip into his mouth.

He nips at it before soothing the sting with his talented tongue. I trail my hands all over the hard planes of his chest and abdomen, relishing in the firmness of his muscles and how they contract and flex under my touch.

With a surety unlike any man I've ever known, he grips my ass and hoists me up onto the edge of the sink, giving us both better access to what we so desperately want. I grind against his hardness, vividly remembering the way he filled me.

When his lips leave mine, I sound my displeasure. But my whimper quickly turns to a moan when he scrapes his teeth over the sensitive skin below my ear before kissing his way down my neck toward my collarbone.

In an act of lust-fueled boldness, I palm him through his pants, and he groans. "Fuck, Jenny. Fuck. Let me make you feel good," he begs against my skin.

I nod, helpless to resist him.

Nate shifts me from the lip of the sink back to standing. My heart stutters in my chest when he drops to his knees in front of me. My eyes glaze over with soul consuming desire when he unties the drawstring to my pants. He slips his thumbs beneath my waistband and starts to pull them down.

"Wait!" I say breathlessly.

"Are you okay?" he asks, with such genuine concern in his voice that it gives me pause.

"I just need to move my pump." I mutter the words in a low tone, my embarrassment warring with my arousal. Thanks to old doubts and lingering insecurities, I'm fully expecting him to pull away—to stand up and leave without a single glance back.

But he doesn't.

"Where is it?" he asks, slowly brushing his thumbs over my hipbones.

"Clipped to the inside of my waistband toward the back left."

With a steady hand, Nate reaches around and unclips my insulin pump and hands it to me. I release a shaky exhale and clip it to my bra, whispering out a soft thank you.

With that issue out of the way, Nate resumes sliding my pants down, bringing my panties with them. He presses a kiss to each hip, sucking slightly on my right hipbone. Jesus, who knew hips were an erogenous zone?

As he moves lower, I thread my fingers through his hair. When his mouth reaches its final destination, he licks and sucks and nibbles like his life depends on my pleasure. He reaches up and hoists my right leg over his shoulder, giving himself more access to me. I'm a bucking, trembling mess on the verge of climaxing. When he adds his skilled fingers to the mix, it's game over, and I damn near black out from the blinding pleasure.

"Jesus, Nate," I sigh. "That was..."

"Yeah," he says, smiling as he wipes his mouth with the back of his hand.

He stands and the awkwardness sets in—for me at least. Where we are and what we did hits me like a tidal wave. What was I thinking? I yank my bottoms back up and spin to face the mirror, bracing my palms against the sink. Honestly, I'm pretty sure it's the only thing keeping me standing at this point. Between my still-quivering legs, my racing heart, and the worry wrapping itself around me like a vise, I'm feeling a little unsteady on my feet.

What if someone heard us? Has anyone noticed we're both missing? How on earth did we go from him avoiding me to him going down on me in the hall bath of his childhood home? What does this mean for us? I thought we were a one-time thing…that the great Nate Reynolds never went back for seconds? Or does this not count since we didn't actually do the deed?

My thoughts are spiraling so quickly that the thought of repaying the favor never even occurs to me. I'm far too busy panicking over the thought of our misdeeds being painted all over our faces all throughout dinner. Dinner with his parents. And Natalie. And Tatum. Maybe I should just fake sick and head home?

Nate wraps his arms around me from behind, speaking low in my ear. "GG, breathe." His tone tells me he's been trying to get through to me for a hot minute.

"It's…I'm fine. Sorry."

He scrubs a hand over his scruffy face. "You have nothing to apologize for. Me on the other hand…" He trails off, worry and regret blanketing his features. "We didn't get to finish talking at the party. I acted like an ass—a jealous ass and I'm sorry. Truly."

I offer him a weak smile. "No worries." I shrug.

"Jenny, I—"

"Seriously, it's all good. Like you said, you're not the guy for me, and that's fine. We're just friends who've fucked, right?"

He rears back at my crassness. I'm aware that I'm acting out of character, but this whole thing with him is too much. He's too much. I could so easily get swept up in him, and Lord knows he's told me time and time again that he'd only hurt me.

"Right," he agrees, but the way he says it coupled with his rigid posture tells me he isn't actually agreeing with me—he's placating me. But I'm too chicken-shit to ask him what he actually thinks.

"So, yeah, thanks…for that." I turn and slip out of the bathroom before either of us can say anything else.

In the hallway, I quickly remove my pump from my bra and calculate my insulin bolus before reclipping it to my pants. I round the corner into the kitchen, almost slamming right into Natalie as she rounds it from the opposite direction. "Gah!" she exclaims, her hand flying to her chest. "You scared the ba-jeezus out of me."

I duck my head in guilt and maybe a little bit in shame. "Sorry."

"Have you seen Nate?"

I will myself not to blush. "N-nope. Haven't seen him."

Her gaze sharpens as she studies me. "Uh-huh. Well, it's time to eat."

"Great!" I say, sounding way too chipper.

She gives me one last quizzical look before linking arms with me. "Nate can find his own way to the table. C'mon."

The Reynolds are the kind of family that waits for everyone to be seated before eating. They say grace before every family meal, and usually that's fine and dandy. But it's been ten minutes since I emerged from the bathroom, and there's still no sign of Nate.

At this point, I don't know if he's still in the bathroom, willing his hard-on away, or I pissed him off and he left. I'm also unsure which option makes me feel worse. To say I could have handled the aftermath of him going down on me a little better is an understatement.

Mr. and Mrs. Reynolds make small talk, trying to distract Tatum from the fact that there's food on the table but not on her plate while Natalie texts furiously, her fingers flying across the screen. If I had to guess, I'd say she's messaging her brother.

Finally, after another five minutes, he joins us at the table. "Uncle Nate! Where was you? I'm so hungry I could eat a horse!"

Nate's lips tip up at his niece's cuteness. "Sorry, Tater Tot, there was something I had to take care of."

I can feel the tips of my ears burn. Surely, he doesn't mean he rubbed one out in his parents' hall bath...right? My eyes flit to him, and he winks. Oh, God, that's exactly what he means.

"Something so important it was worth letting the food get cold?" Luke, Nate and Natalie's dad, grumbles, his brows crinkled in annoyance.

"You could say that. I'm here now though, so let's dig in."

Nate moves to grab a roll, and his mom smacks it out of his hand. "We need to say grace first, Nathaniel. In fact, why don't you lead us?"

"Gladly." He bows his head but keeps his eyes on me. "As we gather for this meal, I want to give thanks for you providing us with another day and for this time together. I especially want to thank you for the lovely Jenny being able to come tonight; she's a beautiful addition to this evening. Please bless everything we'll eat or have eaten tonight to the nourishment of our bodies. Amen."

He smirks at me as he raises his head, daring me to say something—anything. He's freaking baiting me, right here in front of everyone. That asshole. Well, the joke's on him, because in addition to being smart enough to not engage with him, I'm the one who got off while he was left hard…and hard up.

"That was lovely," Melanie compliments, completely oblivious to the tension between her son and me.

Dishes are passed around and plates are made, and even cold, the food is incredible. I listen as Tatum rambles on about how excited she is to start 'big school' in the fall. Poor kid, she has some misconceptions about how kindergarten works, but I think all kids do. I know I did. I legit thought that my dad got to come with me and that he'd eat lunch with me and everything. Talk about a letdown. It's something my parents still tease me about to this day.

Toward the end of the meal, some of the tension I was holding onto finally starts to ease. Aside from his innuendo-laden prayer, Nate has been on his best behavior. I should've known he had more up his sleeve, but hindsight's twenty-twenty, right?

It isn't until he pushes his plate away with food left on it that he strikes again.

"Are you not hungry?" his mom asks worriedly.

He smiles softly at her before dragging his eyes over my way. He shakes his head a little and smirks. "The food was amazing, Mom." He pushes his chair back from the table and pats his stomach. "I'm just stuffed full."

"I don't see how. The only thing you finished is your steak and these potatoes are your favorite."

"I'll take some home and bring it for lunch tomorrow. I know I shouldn't have, but my appetite got the best of me and I had a little snack before dinner." He licks his lips and my thighs clench, remembering the way he licked me. I shake my head at him, signaling for him to knock it off, but he just nods, his eyes glinting, full of unspoken promises.

My cheeks have to be as red as a fire truck right now. I swear, I'm going to kill him.

"Well," his mom hedges. "Okay. I'll send some for Duke as well."

"He'll love that, Mom."

"Did you like the salad?" Tatum asks her uncle.

"I sure did."

Tatum does the four-year-old equivalent of a hair fluff. "Thanks. I helped Nana make it."

Nate smiles at her with such warmth and affection that my heart thaws toward him a little. "Aha. Must be why his tastes extra, extra good."

Tatum beams under his praise. "Better than your snack?"

Nate and I both choke at her question. My Lord, from the mouths of babes.

Nate shoots me another loaded look. "I'm not sure anything could be quite as…tasty as my snack."

Tatum pouts. "What was it? Can I have some?"

Nate rolls his lips inward, trying with all of his might to contain his laughter. Meanwhile, I'm sitting here wishing for the floor to open up and swallow me whole.

He goes to answer her, but I can't take anymore of this conversation and cut him off. "Thank you so much for inviting me tonight, Melanie. Everything was wonderful."

Melanie smiles, but Nate speaks before she can. "What was your favorite part?"

I. Am. Going. To. Kill. Him. In cold freaking blood. Hell, I bet if I explained the circumstances, they'd let me off with an insanity plea, because this man is driving me crazy.

His dad steps in to rescue me. "Son, leave the girl alone." Thankfully, Nate listens.

Aside from a few charged and lingering looks between Nate and me, the remainder of dinner is uneventful. I offer to help Melanie with the dishes, but she adamantly refuses, on the grounds of me being a guest in her home. Nate and Natalie, however, aren't so lucky and are sent to the kitchen to clean up.

Not wanting to outstay my welcome, I use this time to say my goodbyes. First up, the Mr. and Mrs. of the house. "Thank you so much for inviting me over for dinner. It was delicious."

"Would've been better hot," Luke grumbles as he saunters down the hall away from us.

Melanie rolls her eyes at her husband's gruffness. "I'm glad you were able to join us." She reaches out and pats my shoulder. "Maybe we can do it again soon."

My mind flashes to Nate and I doing it again, and I have to stifle a groan. "Uh, sure, that'd be great."

She beams as though I just told her she's won a million dollars.

I step into the kitchen to say goodbye to everyone in there. I hug Tatum, spinning her in a circle as I do. Next up is Natalie—leaning in to wrap her arms around me, she tells me to call her tomorrow and I easily agree.

"See ya," I say to Nate as I turn to head toward the front door.

"What…no hug for me?" he asks, challenging me.

"Yeah, Ms. Jenny, you hugged everyone else. You don't want Uncle Nate to feel left out—Mama says it's not nice to… ex-ca-lude our friends."

I'm torn between wanting to smile at her sweet innocence and high tail it out the door to avoid hugging him.

Nate dries his hands on a dish towel and tosses it down onto the counter. He smirks, crooking his finger at me, beckoning me closer.

With a resigned sigh, I step into his embrace. I'd like to say his touch has magically lost its effect on me, but that'd be a bald-faced lie. The fact that I can't seem to conceal my reaction—goose bumps, shallow breathing, racing heart—to his touch is really just icing on the freaking cake.

He leans down, burying his face in the space between my

neck and ear, his hot breath skating over my exposed skin. "I'm so glad I got to eat you tonight, GG."

I yank out of his hold. "What?"

"I said I'm glad I got to eat with you tonight." He winks, like the cocky little asshole he is.

"I'm sure the pleasure was all yours," I say in an act of boldness fueled by embarrassment.

I pivot on my heel, ready to make a quick escape, but my best friend stops me. "Uh, forget tomorrow morning. Call me tonight."

I NEVER THOUGHT I'd see the day where I appreciated my mother trying to set me up. It's happened a few times over the years, but none of her attempts have ever panned out. Most likely because she's always trying to match me with one of the lady's daughters from her book club—mind you, they don't actually ever read the books. In my mother's words who has time for that when Nancy Jernigan's daughter relapsed on drugs and Janet Kerr's daughter is pregnant with her third kid from a third father? It's probably obvious why the setups haven't panned out, yeah?

But her inviting Jenny to dinner—yeah, she hit the nail on the head with that shit. Definitely the one time I didn't mind her meddling, that's for sure. Her presence was enough to get me going. After the way we left shit at Tatum's party, and the way I let my completely unfounded jealousy get the better of me, left a bitter taste in my mouth.

Hell, I even thought about asking Alden or Natalie for her number, but I figured Jenny wouldn't appreciate that. Not to mention, the endless amount of shit those two would give me for even asking.

Hindsight, I should have used our time together in the bathroom to talk, but seeing her there and knowing we were completely alone—something just came over me. I fucking had to kiss her. One thing obviously led to another, but I don't regret it, even if she did pretty much give me the brushoff after I got her off. Hearing her breathy little moans and tasting her sweetness was one hundred and ten percent worth it—and messing with her all throughout dinner, getting to see that pretty little blush stain her cheeks, was the cherry on top.

Thoughts of Jenny kept me up most of the night. Up and hard as a rock, and let's be real, there's only so many cold showers a guy can take. I'm not even the least bit ashamed to say I got off a few times to the memory of her writhing against me.

Now, here I am, almost twelve hours later, still obsessing over her. And I don't just mean that in a sexual way. Hell, as I scarfed down my usual breakfast of over easy eggs, toast, bacon, and coffee, I found myself wondering how she liked her eggs cooked—I mean, what the fuck?

My usual M.O. is love 'em and leave 'em. I don't do repeats, ever, and they're damn sure out of my mind by sunrise. Yet somehow, a good girl like Jenny Jones has me breaking all of my rules. Rules that exist for a reason.

On my drive over to the station, the radio plays some Top 40 country song that's catchy as hell. As I hum along, I can't help but wonder what kind of music Jenny likes. Does she prefer old school 90s country, like me, or is she more into ear bugs like what's playing now? Get a grip, dude. It doesn't matter what kind of music she likes.

At the station, Duke and I pull up at the same time, as per usual. He and I function like a well-oiled machine. "You look like shit," he calls out in lieu of a greeting.

I sniff the air and crinkle my nose. "Rather look like it than smell like it."

He rolls his eyes and shoulder checks me. "Douche. C'mon, I need some coffee."

We walk in together, hitting up the break room to stash

our lunchboxes and top our thermoses off before heading down for roll call. Thirty minutes later, we're updated on the happenings of Bay Ridge and informed of a few BOLOs.

"That's some shit, right?" Duke asks as we make the trek to the parking lot.

"Huh? What?" I ask, still thinking of a certain green-eyed beauty.

"About Mrs. Norris?" he prompts, waiting for me to catch up.

It's not ringing a bell. "What about her?"

"Brother, were you even listening?"

Truth: I wasn't. Not really. Which kind of pisses me off; I've always been able to compartmentalize—to check my shit at the door, so to speak. In my line of work, I need to be able to give my all—mind and body—when I'm on the clock, even if Bay Ridge is about as safe as Mayberry.

"Jesus, Nate." He holds his hand out to me, palm up. "Keys."

"It's my turn to drive," I rebut, childishly.

"Nah, not today. Your head's not on right."

His words cause me to bristle, but I relinquish the keys without arguing. Deep down, I know he's right. "So, what about Mrs. Norris?"

He shakes his head in clear disgust. "Some jackass was driving drunk and took out her fence and mailbox."

Fuck. "You okay, man?" I ask, treading carefully. Duke lost the love of his life to a drunk driver, and I know shit like this really gets to him.

"Just pissed. I'm glad no one was hurt, but why fucking chance it? Why not just Uber or…" His words fall off as he slams his mask back into place. "Yeah, I'm good. Let's check the car."

Ten minutes later, Duke cranks the ignition and radios in that we're 10-8—or in service and ready for duty.

The first half of our morning is uneventful, and Duke uses

the downtime to grill me on what has me so off my game. "Seriously, what gives? You're normally a hardass on the job."

"It's just…" I shake my head, not wanting to get into this with him.

He's not having it though. "We're partners. We don't keep shit from each other. How can I feel safe with you if I don't know where your head's at?"

He's playing dirty and he knows it. "Fine. It's Jenny."

His lips tip up. "Care to elaborate?"

I debate telling him to mind his own business. But, I don't. He's right; we're partners, and good ones don't keep secrets. "We slept together the night of Alden's wedding."

He drums his fingers on the steering wheel as he pulls off to where we like to sit and monitor traffic. There's a sharp curve here and people love to fly around it. "Figured as much when y'all both disappeared. That was over a month ago though, so what else?"

I talk him through everything that's happened between then and now. He keeps quiet for most of it until I mention being jealous over her gay cousin—then he loses it, laughing his ass off. Once he settles back down, I finish up, glossing over our bathroom rendezvous—the way she moaned my name isn't really something he needs to know—and end with how I antagonized her on and off throughout dinner just to see her blush.

"Sounds to me like you're sprung."

Now I'm the one laughing. "Who the fuck says sprung?"

"Fine, let me rephrase. You've caught feelings. You like her."

I shrug, not ready to admit it to myself, much less out loud to someone else.

The subject is dropped when a familiar white hatchback flies past us, clearly going way over the posted speed limit. We have pulled this exact car over in this exact spot twice already. He was let off with a warning the first time and ticketed the second. You'd think he would learn. Moron.

"Damn idiot," Duke mutters and I hit the lights.

For a split second, I worry that the driver isn't going to stop, but thankfully he pulls off and Duke initiates the traffic stop. I hang back while he approaches the driver's side window. I keep a close eye on them as he goes through the routine—you never know when shit's going to hit the fan, and I've seen far too many routine stops turn into shit shows.

Duke returns to our car and runs the speeder's plates and license—he comes back valid, but as a repeat offender for speeding and driving without a seat belt.

One lengthy citation later and we're 10-98—task completed—and back 10-8.

After a few more run-of-the-mill traffic stops, we pull into an empty parking lot. While Duke catches up on reports, I check emails on my phone and fight the temptation to scope out Jenny's social media accounts. I tap out pretty quickly and pull up her Instagram account. I click on her profile pic and watch her most recent story. It's a picture of the outside of Bennet's—my favorite bar to hit up after a long shift to decompress—with a caption on the screen that reads Wish me luck!

"The hell?"

"What?" Duke asks, turning his attention to me.

I show him my screen, and he grins. "If I had to guess, I'd say she's applying for the open bartender position. Mack mentioned they needed someone since Bethany decided not to come back after her maternity leave."

"But she already has a job," I say lamely.

Duke's grin ratchets up to a full-blown smile. "And no one on this earth has ever worked two jobs."

Elation and dread fill me in equal measures. The thought of seeing her regularly has me fucking floating, but the thought of watching other men hit on her has me plummeting back to earth. Chill, you don't even know for sure what's going on. Plus, even if she is interviewing, that doesn't mean she'll get the job.

By lunchtime, I'm mostly back to my normal self. "Oh, I forgot to tell you, my mom sent leftovers for you."

Duke licks his chops as he turns into the station parking lot. "Fuck yes! Definitely beats the bologna sandwich I packed."

We head in through the main door and the receptionist is quick to call me over. "Oh, Nate!"

"'Sup, Mary?"

"Something came for you." She pushes her chair back from the desk and retrieves an insulated lunchbox. "There's a note, too." She hands both items to me over the desk.

"Uh, thanks," I say, wondering what's in the cooler and who sent it.

In the break room, Duke wastes no time grabbing my lunchbox from the fridge. While his plate spins in the microwave, he turns to me and asks, "Aren't you gonna open it?"

I shrug. "I guess." Unzipping it carefully, I study the contents and pull them out one by one. An order of tacos from Zippy's, a blueberry muffin, and a snickerdoodle cookie from the bakery around the corner. "What the..."

"Read the note," Duke urges, pushing it toward me.

The microwave dings and he steps away to grab his food. I run my index finger beneath the seal and slide the card out. The first thing I'm hit with is the scent—this notecard smells just like Jenny: sweet and seductive and good enough to eat. The second thing I notice is the bouncy, feminine handwriting. She took the time to write this note...but why? She was right there when Mom made mention of sending leftovers for me to take for lunch.

Nate,

I know your mom sent you home with left-overs, but I figured you'd maybe like something to remember me by.

Your friend,
Jenny

I read the note twice, looking for some kind of clue, because Lord knows I have to be missing something.

Duke sits down across from me and digs right into his steak and potatoes. "This is so good," he says with his mouth full, making it sound more like *dis toe good*. When I ignore him in favor of reading the note a third time, he gets curious. "What's it say?"

I pass it to him, and he scans over it, a wide cheesy grin splitting his cheeks. "She's something else, brother." I stare at him blankly and he chuckles. "Went over your head, huh?"

I grit my teeth, perturbed that he got it on the first try.

"Think about it, Nate. Think." He pops another bite of steak into his mouth, chewing slowly to give me a chance to figure it out. I shake my head, still nada. "Okay, lemme break it down for you. You said you went down on her last night and that she left you high and dry, yeah? You said she tried playing it off like she was cool and calm. But looks to me like little Miss Jenny had you on her mind all night."

"What makes you say that?"

"Dude. She sent you a munchbox. Tacos...a muffin...a cookie. C'mon, put it together."

Slowly, it clicks into place. That little tease... "She wants me thinking of her... of what we did."

Duke snaps his fingers. "And he gets it! The question is, what're you gonna do about it?"

We finish up our respective lunches, with Duke eating my portion of Mom's leftovers as well and head back out. Thanks to her little stunt, thoughts of Jenny repeatedly push to the forefront of my thoughts.

Traffic stop, imagine Jenny riding me. Help a lady with a flat tire, picture Jenny bent over the hood of my car. And so on and so forth. By the end of our shift, I'm amped up and ready to exact my revenge.

Get ready, Jenny Jones, there's about to be hell to pay.

I MAY HAVE FEIGNED indifference last night toward Nate after he went down on me—or at least, I think I did—but oh Lord, my body feels anything but indifferent. Turned on, revved up, on fire, and raring to go would all be more accurate descriptors.

I spent half the night tossing and turning, resisting the urge to try and take care of myself. Not that there's anything wrong with a little self-love. Heck, I'm a big fan. I held off out of sheer stubbornness, like somehow denying myself the pleasure would loosen his hold on me.

That man's touch is out of this world, and the worst part is, he freaking knows it. It's blatantly obvious in the cocky way he holds himself. The fact that his taunting only turned me on more is even worse. I mean, who gets all hot and bothered over their crush publicly picking on them?

Me! That's who!

And after that shitshow of a hug goodbye last night, Natalie is on to me big time. Obviously, she knows Nate and I slept together, but now she knows that I'm really, truly into him in a way that extends beyond my little harmless crush.

She grilled me relentlessly when I called her, poking and prodding until I spilled the beans. So, now my best friend knows that I hooked up with her older brother in their parents' home. Good times.

Even now, her parting words echo in my head. She sounded so serious—more serious than I've ever heard—as she said, "Jenny, I want you to know that if you choose to pursue something with my brother, I'll support it. But I'd feel like a shitty friend if I didn't tell you to be careful. Nate...he's complicated, and I'm scared he'll hurt you. But, you're both grown and capable of making your own choices. So, yeah, just guard your heart, babe."

Her vagueness has my hackles up. To be honest, I've never really thought about Nate's past. He told me he wasn't the guy for me and that he didn't do relationships, and I took him at his word; I didn't wonder what made him that way. I simply accepted it. But now...now I'm curious.

About fifteen minutes after Natalie and I hung up, Jamie called. I filled him in on all things Nate, and he told me about a guy he met the other day while running one of the many nature trails by his home—they have a coffee date set for Friday.

We giggled and gossiped and schemed, tossing around theories on why Nate's so jaded until well past my bedtime.

Now, in the light of day, I still can't believe I let him talk me into sending Nate a vagina-themed lunchbox. But it struck a chord when Jamie told me I should leave him wanting, mentally and physically. Sending it is hands down one of the most immature things I've ever done, but it also made me feel clever and maybe a little powerful, like I was playing with fire, so to speak. However, I'm also a little bit on edge wondering how Nate will react. But, thanks to FoodCruise, a local food delivery app that runs 24/7, what's done is done.

I guess only time will tell, and really, I'm not sure what's worse...him flipping out or him not reacting at all.

Due to my tossing and turning, I was up with the sun this morning. I've already vacuumed as well as washed, dried, and folded a load of laundry, but I still have two and a half hours to kill before work.

Which makes this the perfect time to hit up a few of the local restaurants and watering holes to see if anyone has an opening. As much as I love working at Bayside, I could use the extra income. After all, my dreams won't finance themselves.

The first two places I hit up are fully staffed, but as I pull into the gravel lot of Bennet's—a local bar—I can't help but think that maybe the third time will be a charm.

Housed in an old natural wood barn, the exterior of the building is unassuming. If you didn't know it was here, you would one hundred percent drive right past it. There's no sign by the road, just a massive B burned into the door.

On impulse, I snap a picture of the entrance and post it to my Instagram story with the caption Wish me luck! I have a good feeling about this place, and maybe putting it out into the open will help me out. My Geema always says the universe listens, speak to it.

So, here I am universe…are you listening?

The inside pretty much matches the outside, with old, scraped-up wide plank flooring and wood-paneled walls. There's an eclectic mix of repurposed tables—a handful are made from industrial sized wooden cable spools, some are barrels of varying sizes, and there's a sprinkling of high-top tables created out of old wooden wheels and topped with glass. As cool as all of that is though, the bar is clearly the focal point. The back wall is comprised of a mixture of shattered mirrors and stained glass, and the salvaged wood bar spans the entire width of it.

The lighting is low, and peanut shells litter the floor. It's definitely not the place you'd find the trendsetters hanging out on a Saturday night, but it's cozy and authentic and welcoming in a way so many places aren't these days.

As I make my way back to the bar, I notice an old jukebox

on the far-left wall. It looks like a relic from the forties trapped in modern times. Something about its presence comforts me.

"We don't open for another thirty minutes," a craggy voice calls from behind the bar, startling me. I study the barkeep and I keep drawing closer. He's exactly the kind of man I imagined working here. Thanks to his leathered, sun-worn skin, kind milky eyes, and shock of white hair, he looks to be in his late sixties, but something tells me he's not quite there yet.

"Oh, sorry. The door was unlocked."

"Damn Mabel, never locking shit," the old man grumbles to himself. "Fact remains, we're not open yet, missy."

"I'm not here for a drink."

He assesses me coolly. "Then what're ya here for?"

"A job," I say, my voice strong and clear.

"And what's a little thing like you know about tending bar?"

He's testing me. I can sense it. "Probably not as much as you, but I bartended all throughout college."

"You don't even look old enough," he grumbles. "How old are you?"

"Twenty-five."

"Currently employed?"

"I work at Bayside Café, but it won't interfere with working here...if you hire me."

The old man nods and beckons me closer. I step up to the bar and he walks around it and hefts himself up on the stool next to where I'm standing. Expectantly, he stares at me. "Well, what're you waiting for? Make me a drink."

I quirk a brow at him but head around behind the bar all the same. What a strange turn this day is taking. "What do you want?"

"What do you think I want?"

Oh, man. His earlier questions were nothing more than a

pop-quiz. This…this is my test. I study him again, going past his outward appearance. I take in his mannerisms—the way he taps his right thumb on the bar top to the tune of Iron Man by Black Sabbath, an odd choice if there ever was one for a man dressed like John Wayne. I trace my eyes over the dips and divots in his skin; each one seems to tell a story, marking some type of occasion in his life.

Smiling, I twirl around to face the liquor stock. I study his set-up and gather the things I need and set to work. I drop one sugar cube into the bottom of my rocks glass and cover it with two dashes of Angostura bitters before adding two ounces of rye whiskey. I stir the mixture gently until the sugar dissolves completely.

Drink in hand, I turn back and set the glass down onto the bar top. The old man goes to reach for it, but I pull it back and out of his reach. I deliberate for only a second before adding one ice cube and stirring again. Satisfied with my work, I slide the drink his way.

He brings the glass to his lips, inhaling deeply before sipping it. "Well, hot damn, kiddo." It may not sound like much, but to me, it may as well be the best compliment I've ever gotten, and I beam at his praise. "You can start next week. Come back tomorrow for paperwork."

Holy. Shit. I got the job. It may have been the weirdest interview ever, but I got the freaking job! "Thank you so much…" I hesitate, realizing we haven't even exchanged names.

"Mack," he supplies, extending his hand to me.

"Jenny." I place my hand in his and give him a firm shake. "Thank you so much, Mack. I won't let you down."

"I've got a good feeling about you, kiddo. Come by any time you're free tomorrow, and Mabel will have your paperwork ready. Bring your I.D. and all of that shit."

"Will do!" I pivot and pretty much float out of the bar on cloud nine.

———

The café has been steady ever since I clocked in at ten-thirty. We weren't anywhere near as busy as we were yesterday, but the constant flow of patrons has kept me busy all day. However, now that we've hit the pre-dinner slump, I know I need to talk to Alden about Bennet's and adjusting my hours here.

After asking another server to watch my section, I head back to his office. The door is partially open, but I still knock lightly.

"Come in," he calls from inside.

Alden's tapping away at his keyboard when I enter the small room. I take a seat and wait for him to finish up. He glances from his computer screen to one of the many sheets of paper on his desk a few times before nodding. After a few more clicks of the mouse, he gives me his full attention.

"What can I do for you, Jenny?"

"I found a second job," I blurt out, ripping off the Band-Aid.

He appraises me for a few minutes. "Glad you found something. Where?"

"Bennet's."

He lets loose a knowing snicker. "Really now?"

"Why's that funny?"

"You know that Bennet's is a cop bar, right?"

"What's your point—oh…"

"Yeah. Speaking of, I heard dinner last night was…interesting."

I groan in frustration. Sometimes working for your best friend's husband rocks, and other times, like now, it sucks. "It was fine. Totally uneventful."

He nods, but I can tell he's not buying what I'm selling. "Not what I heard."

My eyes widen. I swear to God… "Whatever Nate said is a lie!"

Alden's all out laughing now. "He said you'd say that."

"I'm going to freaking murder him," I mutter to myself as anger and embarrassment races through my veins. I know Nate's a hook-up guy, but I never took him as a braggart. Especially not…about me. Him telling his buddies about a nameless, faceless girl is different than telling them about me —they know me.

When Alden notices the tears brimming my lashes, he sobers. "Oh, shit, Jenny. I'm just messing with you. He didn't say anything about you. Please don't cry."

I lift my watery gaze to meet his remorseful one. "Promise?"

"Swear it."

It may make me a fool, but I believe Alden. "Then wh-what did you mean?"

"Tatum came home talking about you and Nate hugging and when I dropped Tatum off this morning, Luke was grumbling about cold steak still. That's it."

"Okay," I whisper, feeling silly and small for letting my emotions get the best of me.

"Just, uh, let me know your schedule at Bennet's, and we'll work around it."

"Will do." I rise from my chair and exit his office, bypassing my section and heading straight for the restroom. I need to get a freaking grip.

A few deep breaths and a splash of cold water later, and I'm ready to head back out onto the floor. What I'm not ready for is the sight of Nate and Duke seated in my section. Can't a girl catch a freaking break?

JENNY'S FACE when she sees Duke and I seated in her section is comical. Her eyes are all wide and her lips—her sexy, kissable lips—form a perfect O.

"You stare any harder, you're gonna give yourself an aneurysm," Duke says, smirking. "Stare any longer, and you're at serious risk for creeper territory."

"I'll take my chances," I murmur back, distractedly. How is it that she seems to look even more beautiful now than she did yesterday?

As she approaches the table, I keep my stare locked on her. With each step closer, I'm transfixed by the sway of her hips and the bounce of her tits. She's a fucking goddess, far too good for the likes of me, placed in my path as a form of punishment for the sins of my past—that much I am sure of.

Even still, I want her. What scares me is the fact that my desire goes far beyond the carnal kind. I want her words, her thoughts, her laughter...her fucking soul. I'll never go for it though; even I'm not that much of a bastard.

"H-hello there, boys," she greets us, her voice noticeably lacking its usual pep.

Sitting up straighter in my seat, I study her. Her cheeks are pink and splotchy. The tip of her nose is red. Her eyes and smile are watery at best. My GG's upset, and I don't fucking like it. Not one bit.

"What's wrong?" I ask, skipping any and all pleasantries.

"Nothing." She shakes her head a few times. "What can I get y'all to drink?"

I'm gearing up to press her for answers when Duke speaks over me. "I'll take whatever beer you recommend."

"What about you, Nate?"

"Same."

"Great."

I glare at my partner as she turns and saunters off to get our drinks. He quickly holds his hands up in a sign of surrender. "Dude. Your girl looked about two seconds away from bawling. I get you wanna check on her and shit but now's not the time or place. You can't go starting shit at her job, brother."

"Wasn't gonna start nothing." My voice sounds sullen even to my own ears.

"Not on purpose, maybe. But shit talking and bickering is y'all's own fucked-up love language. It would've happened regardless."

"So, what do I do? I can tell she's upset about something."

"Simple…you give her a reason to smile."

The fact that my thoughts immediately divert to the gutter is not a surprise. I can think of lots of ways to make her smile…just none of them are appropriate for the setting.

"Not like that, dumbass. I meant with your words and your charm—not your dick."

"Don't need my dick to get a smile. I can use my fingers, my tongue…" A shadow falls over our table and my words dry up.

Jenny lets out an overly fake cough. "As interesting as this conversation seems to be, I'm just gonna leave these here and let y'all look over the menu."

She scampers off before either of us can stop her.

Duke cracks up. "That went well."

"Shut up."

We fall into silence as we peruse the menu. Well, Duke looks it over; I'm too busy forming a plan to not make an utter ass of myself when she returns.

Duke is the first to break the silence. "You know she brought us each a different beer?"

I glance from my bottle to his. "Huh, so she did."

"Weird, right? Since we both asked for whatever she suggested."

"Maybe she has two favorites?" I suggest.

"Asking her would be a good, safe, neutral question." He raises his brows and tips his beer toward me before taking a sip. "Damn, that's delicious."

"Glad you like it," Jenny says proudly, rejoining us. "Y'all decide whatcha want to eat?"

"Yeah, we did. But I've got a question for you."

"About the menu?"

I shake my head.

"Then what?"

"Why'd you bring us each a different beer?"

She smiles, and my heart clenches. Who am I and what are these feelings? Where did they come from? "I brought Duke an American stout because he seems contemplative and intelligent—like the kind of guy who enjoys a sipping beer."

"Okay, so then why did you bring me an IPA?"

Her smile ratchets up a notch. "Because IPAs have a bold, bitter flavor that's an acquired taste for most, and hot damn Nate Reynolds, if that isn't you to a T, then I don't know what is."

I grin back, loving this teasing side of her. "What about you, Jenny? What do you drink?"

"As much as I'd like to say something exciting, we both

know I tend to play things pretty safe. I'm an amber kind of girl."

I nod thoughtfully. "I can see that, GG. Plus, aren't ambers supposed to be a little sweet?"

"Slightly fruity with caramel flavors, usually," she elaborates.

With hooded eyes, I lick my lips and say, "Yeah, GG, that fits you real good."

Seemingly flustered, she changes the subject. "So, what'll y'all have to eat?"

I mutter the word you under my breath before speaking up. "I'll take the special."

Duke's phone buzzes on the table. "Shit, I gotta run. Nancy needs me."

My heart thuds in my chest at the mention of his almost-mother-in-law's name. "Shit. Is everything okay?"

He shakes his head. "I...I don't know. Darryl texted me saying he can't get her to come out of her room. I'll catch y'all later."

I slide out from my side of the booth and wrap him in a hug, not giving a fuck how we look or what anyone thinks. I know he loves Nancy like a mother, but also know these calls and visits really drain him. "Call me if you need me, no matter the time," I tell him as we break apart, meaning every word.

Duke nods stiffly before heading for the exit with his shoulders slumped.

Jenny nibbles her lower lip in worry. "Is...is he okay?"

I shrug. "Difficult to say. It's always hard on him when they call."

"Who are they? No, never mind. That's not any of my business. Let me go ring your order in." She scampers off, not giving me the time to stop her.

I mess around on my phone while I wait for Jenny to return. I fire off a quick text to Duke reminding him that

I'm here if he needs me; unsurprisingly, it goes unanswered.

"Look what the cat dragged in." Glancing up, I see Alden claiming the seat Duke vacated.

"'Sup?"

He suppresses a grin. "Anyone ever tell you that you have quite the way with words? A real conversationalist."

"Fuck off," I mumble before polishing off the last of the IPA Jenny brought me.

Alden nods toward it. "You like?"

"Definitely."

"It's a local brew, small batches and organic." He launches into the finer details of it—things I don't give a shit about, but I listen dutifully, because that's what friends do. After a few minutes, he laughs. "You're not hearing a thing I'm saying, are you?"

"I'm listening!"

"Listening and hearing aren't the same."

Now I'm laughing. "You're such a dad."

"Hell yeah, I am." He thumps his fist against his chest. "So, what brings you by? This isn't your usual Wednesday dinner spot."

Evade! Evade! my brain screams. "Just felt like switching it up."

"Bullshit," he coughs into his fist. "I'd put money down that you stopped by to see a certain waitress of mine."

Perceptive fucker. "Maybe."

"Tell you what, be real with me, and I'll cut her shift so she can join you."

And he knows just how to bait me...I may as well be a fish on his hook. "Yeah, I'm here to see Jenny." Alden drums his fingers against the tabletop, waiting on me to elaborate. "Because-I-might-be-into-her," I mumble the words out all together as one, but he hears me just fine just by the wide, cheesy grin splitting his cheeks.

"Ain't no might about it," he says, sounding all too pleased. "Hang tight and your dinner and dining companion will be out soon."

———

About fifteen minutes later, Jenny returns, frowning with two plates in hand. I know it's shitty of me, but I can't help but find a little bit of amusement in her obvious displeasure.

"Why the long face, GG?" I ask as she claims the seat opposite of me.

Instead of answering my question, she asks one of her own. "Why do you call me that? What does it mean?"

"What do you think it means?"

"I...honestly don't know."

"Tough luck. Let's eat." I dig into the food Jenny placed before me. "Fuck, this is good. What is it?"

"It's a play on fried chicken. Instead of a heavy batter, it's tossed in panko bread crumbs, which keep it nice and light but still crispy."

I shovel a forkful of the au gratin potatoes into my mouth, followed by a few spears of the asparagus. "It's phenomenal. What's the sauce?"

Jenny's eyes light up. "It's a sriracha butter pan sauce. Good, right?"

"Good's not the right word. I could bathe in this shit, GG."

"I'm glad you like it. I'll let Darren and Javier know."

"Something tells me you had something to do with it—the way you perked up in your seat. Spill."

Her cheeks turn that pretty shade of pink I love so much. "Not really. I just suggested a different shallot to garlic ratio." She shrugs like it's no big deal.

"Well, it's amazing. Like you."

"Don't feed me your lines, Nate Reynolds. You've already gotten into my pants. Twice."

"I hear the third time's a charm…" I smirk, and she rolls her eyes, my cocky come-on rolling right off her like water off of a duck's back.

Throughout the rest of our meal, we trade random stories between bites. Once we've both devoured every last bite, Jenny asks if I want dessert. Hello gutter, nice to see you again.

"Nate. Did you hear me?"

Nope. Too busy imagining feasting on you to listen. Try again later.

It's not until she kicks me under the table that I snap out of it. "Huh? Ow! The hell was that for?"

"I've been trying to get your attention for at least two minutes while you were off in La-La Land. Where'd you go, anyway?"

"You really wanna know, GG?"

Jenny sits up a little taller in her seat. "Wouldn't have asked if I didn't."

I debate telling her the truth for all of five seconds before deciding to go for it. Even if she shoots me down, I like watching her squirm. "I was thinking about what you asked me, and to answer, yes I would very much like dessert. Only, what I'm craving isn't on the menu."

"I'm sure I can get Darren to make—"

I lean forward, reach across the table, and press my index finger to her plump lips, silencing her.

"Only you can give me what I want." Her sharp, shuddered inhale tells me she's turned on or pissed off—please let it be the former and not the latter. "So, tell me, are you?"

Slowly, I drag my finger toward her chin, tugging her bottom lip down. Her breathing is heavy, and her pupils dilated. She's totally turned on.

"Am I gonna what?" she whispers, her tongue darting out to trace over where I slid my finger against her lips. No lie, I just about come undone.

"Are you gonna give me what I want? What I crave?"

She leans closer, the only thing separating us is this damn table. "What do you crave?"

"You," I answer simply, trying my damnedest to act cool, like I'm not ready to claim her right here on this damn tabletop for everyone to see.

Jenny shoots me a coy smile. "Then let's get out of here."

MY BOLD WORDS shock both of us. Probably me more than him, judging by the way he wastes no time leaping up from the booth. He grabs my hand and hauls me up and starts hightailing it for the door.

"Nate." He keeps on going. "Nate!"

"Huh?"

"I need to get my stuff."

"Oh, okay. Yeah."

But he doesn't release my hand from his. I tug against his hold. He offers me a chagrinned smile and lets go. "I'll wait up front."

I quickly grab my purse, knowing that if I hesitate, my common sense will return. Really, that's the thing about men like Nate Reynolds. They're so damn attractive and so unfairly charming that they rob women of their practicality—and it's not even anything they do, it's just inherently who they are.

Up front, I find Nate chatting with Alden. "Ready?" I ask, interrupting them.

"God, yes," Nate murmurs, retaking my hand and pulling me toward the door.

"You two be safe," Alden calls after us, his smile audible.

"Come home with me," Nate asks once we're outside. I nod and he steers me toward his vehicle.

The ride to his house is simultaneously the shortest and longest of my life. The entire drive is a battle of wills. He's hell-bent on teasing me, and I'm dead-set on acting unaffected.

But when his warm hand lands on my pant-covered leg and his thumb begins rubbing slow, teasing circles, it's game over. I'm so turned on, I may as well already be naked and spread out before him.

My breathing accelerates as his hand creeps higher. I come dangerously close to passing out when his thumb brushes against the apex of my thighs. On his second pass, he applies more pressure, causing a moan to slip past my lips.

I chance a glance over at him, and the smug bastard is smiling like he knows all the secrets to the universe.

By the time we pull into his driveway, he's worked me into a frenzy of want and need. I'm so out of my mind with lust for this man that I'm on him the second he shifts the car into park.

As if he anticipated my reaction, he pulls the lever, shoving his seat as far back as it'll go, and hauls me over the console into his lap. We meet in a clash of hungry lips and roaming hands.

Nate thrusts his denim-clad erection against me, and I roll my hips over his, desperate for more friction. He palms my breasts and kisses his way down my neck while I tug on his silky hair, guiding his movements.

Still wanting more, I pull away from him just long enough to tear my shirt over my head. Just as quickly, he strips me of my bra, laving his tongue over one pebbled nipple before moving to the other.

In less than five minutes, he's reduced me to a writhing, wanton ball of need.

"You feel so good, Jenny." He speaks the words against my heated skin as he kisses his way back up to my lips.

But all of the sudden, I have other ideas, and I climb off of his lap and into the back seat. Nate, being the smart man that he is, wastes no time joining me. With brave hands, I reach over and undo his button and zipper, freeing him from the confines of his jeans.

Not giving myself time to back down or him time to question me, I dive toward his lap and take his length into my mouth. My self-consciousness melts away as he moans and threads his fingers through my hair.

"Jesus, GG. Fuck." He groans out the words and they only spur me on. I want to reduce him to nothing more than goo—the way he does me. I take him as deep as I can, and he drives his hips forward, pushing himself just a bit further.

I moan at the sensation, hovering somewhere between pleasure and pain, and when he realizes I like it, he continues pistoning his hips forward until I've wrung every last drop of pleasure from him.

Until tonight, I've always imagined a blowjob would be degrading, but here and now, I feel powerful—invincible even. And the feeling only intensifies when Nate skims his fingers along my jaw. "That was…damn, Jenny."

I smile shyly.

"Let's go inside?" he asks, trailing his fingers down the line of my neck.

I nod, and he leans into the front seat, grabbing my discarded clothing as well as my bag. I tug my shirt over my head, stuffing my bra into my purse, because what's the point of adding one more layer between us if he's only going to remove it again?

Nate guides me from his car to the front door with a hand pressed to the small of my back. As much as what just went down in the car turns me on, it's these little touches that really light me up, because to me, they say he cares more than he lets on. I'm sure that's me reading too deep into things, but a girl's allowed her fantasies, right?

"You want a drink?" he asks as he locks the front door behind us.

"Sure." I follow behind him, taking stock of his place. It's definitely not the bachelor pad I've always envisioned. The flooring is a pretty oak, and the walls are a soft sort of oatmeal color, with thick, glossy white trim. There are built-in shelves in the entryway, as well as along one of the walls in the living room.

I was fully expecting week-old pizza boxes and mismatched thrift store furniture. Instead, everything's thoughtfully decorated in shades of light blue and gray. Hell, he even has throw pillows and art on the walls—I feel like I've stepped into an alternate universe. This is not the home of a late-twenties single man; it's a family home—a forever home…too bad he's made it clear that he's not my forever.

I take my time finding the kitchen, admiring the knick-knacks, books, and family pictures lining the shelves of his built-ins. When I make it into the kitchen, Nate has already made us each a glass of ice water.

I chug the icy-cold liquid down in three greedy gulps—who knew giving head would make a girl so thirsty? "Want some more?" Nate asks.

"Yes, please."

He shoots me an amused look and refills my glass. "I'd have offered you something harder, but I wanted to have a clear mind in case Duke—"

I wave off his words. "You don't need to explain it. You're a good friend—a good man—you know that, right?"

Nate's eyes take on a sort of haunted look as he nods absently. Thankfully, his phone rings, cutting through the sudden tension.

He answers the phone, skipping right over any kind of

greeting. "Is everything okay?" Covering the mouthpiece, he whispers to me, "Go make yourself comfy, I'll only be a minute."

I settle onto his ridiculously comfortable couch and set my glass down on a coaster on the coffee table. For real, what kind of single dude has coasters? I try not to listen as his voice filters in from the kitchen, but I can't help but catch bits and pieces of his conversation.

"Fuck. Is she okay? Are you okay?"

"She did what? Where are y'all?"

"All right, man, keep me posted."

Nate lingers in the kitchen for a moment or two before joining me on the couch. He doesn't come empty-handed though, passing me a beer as he settles down onto the cushion next to me.

"Everything okay?" I ask, inspecting the label wrapped around the bottle. I smile when I see it's a locally brewed brand.

He squeezes the back of his neck, massaging before dropping his hand to my thigh and his head to the back of the couch. "Same shit, a different day."

"Meaning…"

"It's a long, fucked-up story. Duke's girl, Valorie, died last year." Moisture brims my lashes as Nate continues. "She was in a car wreck—hit by a drunk driver. It's been rough as hell on Duke; they were together since high school."

A lone tear falls. "That's awful. I…I can't even imagine." Nate squeezes my thigh and scoots closer to me. I waste no time snuggling into his side.

"Valorie's mom kind of went off the deep end when it happened, and she's been wading in the water ever since. She sort of clings to Duke, and he lets her, even though all it does is drag him back down into depths with her."

"What happened tonight?" I ask, though I'm not sure I

truly want to know. It's so easy to feel all woe is me, but compared to Duke, what pain have I ever really known? I couldn't imagine losing the love of my life.

"Nancy found a photo album full of pictures from their senior prom. Downed a bottle of wine and a handful of benzos. Her husband found her sitting on the floor in the garage, sobbing and rocking, completely incoherent. Duke's the only person she'll let near her when she gets like this." Nate shakes his head, his face a mixture of sympathy and disgust. "You wanna know the most fucked-up part? Valorie has a twin, and Nancy hasn't spoken to her since Valorie died. Ain't that some shit?"

"Jesus. I don't even know what to say." Nate holds me a little closer. "I've never been in love, but I just...I don't..." Words fail me as I try to articulate how I'm feeling.

"What's that saying?" Nate asks. "You know the one...it's better to have loved and lost than to have never loved at all? Can't help but think it's a load of horseshit."

I move out of his embrace so I can look at him. "You really mean that?"

He nods vehemently. "Damn straight. Why would anyone ever willingly set themselves up for that kind of heartbreak?"

"But what if it doesn't end in heartbreak?" I press. "Think of how many people live out their lives together, happy and well. Look at your parents. Natalie and Alden."

"I guess to them the risk is worth the reward." He tries to shrug nonchalantly, but I can see the tension weighing him down. He's wearing his past hurt like a metal jacket, and I can't help but to push a little more.

"So, you'd rather go through life completely alone all because something bad might happen?"

"I'd rather not give history a chance to repeat itself. I'm not made for monogamy—I've been down that road, kind of, and I know where it leads and it's not somewhere I ever want to travel again." He takes a deep breath and shoots me a very forced looking grin.

"You really mean that? You're content to spend your days alone?"

He waggles his brows at me and runs his index finger up my thigh. "Who said anything about being alone?"

As much as his touch turns me on, I scoot closer to the arm of the couch, placing a little distance between us. "Did someone hurt you?"

Nate immediately tenses up. Suddenly the small gap between us feels like an ocean. "No." One word, that's all he gives me. I can practically see his walls coming up, his mask slamming into place.

"Then why?"

"Variety is the spice of life. Why settle for one flavor for eternity when there are so many to be sampled?"

His words pierce me like an arrow. Deep down, I know he's talking out of his ass—he's saying what he needs to hear to keep up his carefully crafted playboy persona. He forgets that I've seen behind the veil, even if only in glimpses. I've seen exactly the kind of man he is at his core—he's good and kind and one hundred percent selling himself short. But, like they say, you can lead a horse to water, but you can't make it drink. I can't force Nate to want to be with only me, just like I can't will my feelings for him to stay buried and keep things between us only physical.

"Right," I say hoarsely. "Here's the thing, Nate. I like you —a hell of a lot. But I also like myself, and I'm not willing to compromise with my heart to only be an appetizer in your buffet of women. I need monogamy and exclusivity. I need to know that I have your all."

He tries to interrupt me, but I power on.

"I'm not trying to force you into something more—I respect that you don't want to be in a relationship or to be tied down; that's your prerogative, and I'm simply telling you mine."

He rubs both of his hands over his face. "Where do we go from here?"

"Friends?" I ask, shrugging.

He mulls over my offer for a minute. "Yeah, GG. Friends."

TO SAY that tonight has taken a few unexpected turns is an understatement. I'm downright baffled as to how we went from Jenny sucking my dick to us being friends. I guess that's life, right?

"I'm gonna be real with you, GG. I've never really been just friends with a girl. There have always been benefits involved."

She laughs and the sound makes my gut clench. "Awe, poor you. I'm Nate Reynolds, and I'm so irresistible that women simply throw themselves at me, but I'm also too much of a hardass to ever settle down."

"You think you're funny?" I ask her, bringing my beer to my lips.

"Oh, I know I'm hilarious."

I swallow down the last sip and set the bottle down onto the table. "Yeah, yeah. Whatever you need to tell yourself."

She polishes off the rest of her drink. "You want another?"

"I could do one more." She rises from the couch and heads toward the kitchen like she's done it a million times before. I'd like to say that I don't watch her hips sway as she goes—since we're friends and all—but that'd be a lie.

She returns with two opened bottles and reclaims her spot

next to me. Just like the night of the wedding, our conversation flows effortlessly. Over the next few hours, I down two more beers, while Jenny moves to water. Time wastes away as we talk about the most mundane and insignificant things, and yet somehow, I'm having the most fun I've had in a while.

I check the time when Jenny lets out a long yawn. "Damn, it's after ten. I'd offer to drive you back to your car, but..." I gesture toward the collection of empties on the coffee table. I'm nowhere near drunk—not even buzzed, really—but I would never get behind the wheel after more than a drink or two. I'm unwilling to endanger my life or someone else's. It's just not worth the risk.

"S'all good," she says sleepily. "I don't mind crashing on the couch."

It's on the tip of my tongue to tell her she can sleep in my bed, but I refrain. Even though we've agreed to be friends, there's only so much temptation a man can take. "Want me to grab you something to sleep in?"

"Yes, please."

In my room, I grab her a pair of gray sweats and a navy blue Bay Ridge PD shirt. I also grab a pillow from my bed along with a blanket from the hall closet.

Unceremoniously, I toss her the clothes and drop the bedding onto the couch. "Bathroom's down the hall."

"Thanks."

As soon as she sets off down the hall, I hightail it to my room, not wanting to stick around to see how damn good she looks in my clothes.

———

Sunrise comes far too soon after a long, mostly sleepless night. I tossed and turned, dozing off, only to startle awake again and again. Dreams of the future I could have with

Jenny, if I'd only take a chance, warred with nightmares of the past I can't seem to escape.

The shit that went down with Sonia all those years ago haunts me like the Ghost of Christmas Past haunted Ebenezer, only instead of being a one-time thing, the ghost of my mistakes is recurring—primed and ready to smother me in guilt every time I even begin to think of moving on.

As much as it tears me apart—to think about her, to remember—it's for the best. Her memory is the exact reminder I need to leave Jenny the fuck alone...romantically.

At least my exhausting night ended on a high note, with a dream of Jenny beneath me, willing and ready, panting and moaning. It was so realistic that I woke thrusting against my mattress, seconds away from coming all over my sheets like a teenaged boy.

Which begs of another issue—I need to find a way to stifle my insane physical attraction to her, because that girl can get me hard just by breathing in my direction. Friends definitely don't spring wood over one another, that's for damn sure.

After a quick shower, where I take care of my—err—situation, I dress in a pair of low-hanging navy sweats and a white T-shirt. Quietly, I creep down the hall, not wanting to wake Jenny in case she's still asleep.

Imagine my surprise when I find her not only awake but in my kitchen cooking breakfast. "Morning," she greets me, sounding like she got a full night's sleep—makes fucking one of us.

"G'morning," I mumble as I make my way over to the coffee pot. I try my hardest to ignore the fact that she's still wearing my sweats and tee. But, have mercy, she looks so hot in them she may as well be in lingerie. Add in the fact that I'm currently sipping on piping hot coffee she brewed before frying up some bacon, and yeah, this shit is almost erotic.

"Your eggs weren't any good, and you don't have any fruit. So, bacon and toast it is." She spins toward the toaster—

that I've literally never used—right as the perfectly golden bread pops up. "You also don't have any jelly. When was the last time you grocery shopped?"

I take a seat at the island and accept the plate she pushes my way. My mouth waters at the scent of the buttery bread and perfectly cooked bacon. Around a massive bite, I say, "Last month sometime?" I wash it down with a gulp of coffee. "This works for me though. Thanks, GG."

She rolls her eyes and plates herself up some food, covering it with a paper towel.

"Are you not going to eat?" I ask.

"Oh, I um, I just need to take my insulin first."

"So, take it." My voice holds a hint of challenge. Not because I'm trying to be an asshole, but because she always acts ashamed of being diabetic—like it's something she chose for herself and regrets now. Which is truly bullshit. It's a fucking autoimmune disease and, if anything, she should be proud of how strong she is.

She nibbles on her lower lip, looking torn between fleeing and giving into me. "Jenny, it's fine. If you're more comfortable doing it in private, I get it. But just know you don't need to. It's nothing to be embarrassed about."

A soft smile graces her lips as she spins, giving me her back. I watch, my food momentarily forgotten as she bunches her—my—shirt around her waist and retrieves her pump from the pocket of my sweats. I can't see what she's doing, but I remember it well enough from our night together in the hotel. A few beeps later, she slips the device back into her pocket, drops the hem of her shirt, and spins to face me.

She uncovers her plate, pops a piece of bacon into her mouth, and refills both of our coffees. "Thank you, Nate."

I grin. "Ain't no thing. Thank you for this feast."

At that, she laughs. "Feast? This is sad, Nate. Tasty, but sad. You need groceries."

Shrugging, I stand and bring my plate to the sink. "I

usually eat out or order in. Unless I have leftovers from Mom or Natalie."

"You never cook?"

"Trust me, it's better for everyone this way."

She brings her plate over and rinses it. "Nope. No way. There are so many easy things that even you could handle. I remember you telling me, cocky as shit, that you worked hard for your body. Well, guess what, filling it with fast food and garbage isn't doing you any favors."

I pat my six pack. "Seems to be working well for me."

Jenny scoffs. "Muscles don't always equate strength."

"Quit playing. You know just how strong I am. Stamina for days."

"Yeah, for now. But, let's be real, you're knocking on thirty's door. It's only going to get harder to keep up with. Do yourself a favor and listen to me."

I pretend to ponder her words, but I know she's right. "Yeah, maybe. You gonna teach me?"

She does this cute little bounce and shimmies her shoulders. Like a good friend, I ignore the way her tits sway beneath the department logo. "I totally will. We can grocery shop, and I can come over one day and show you some simple recipes. I even know some you can make ahead of time and toss into the freezer until you're ready to eat them!"

"All right, grocery Yoda, you twisted my arm. Teach me your ways."

"When are you free? I'm off today, thank God, because I have to run up to Bennet's and fill out some paperwork. I'm not sure what my schedule will be like there, so really, today is the only day I can guarantee. Or Sunday."

"Shit, GG! I saw your Instagram whatever thing and meant to ask you about it. You're gonna be working there?"

She beams, proud as pie. "I am!"

"Guess we'll be seeing a lot more of each other then."

"Stop trying to change the subject. When are you free?"

I shake my head at her persistence. "I'm off today, but have plans with some of the guys. Sunday's good for me."

"Perfect. Give me your number, and we can figure everything out later today."

We exchange numbers, and I drop her off back at her car, with her still dressed in my clothes, mind you. As I head to the gym to meet Duke and Xavier, I can't help but think that maybe this friend thing won't be so bad after all.

THE REST of the week passes in a blur of working at the café, an appointment with my endocrinologist where they did some lab work, a few hours of onboarding at the bar, and a bit of spring cleaning.

My A1C—a measurement of the amount of glucose in my blood over a span of twelve weeks or so—was on target. My hours at Bennet's are a dream; I'll be working every night Wednesday through Friday, plus every third Saturday. And, my house is spotless, so really, it's been a pretty stellar week. If only I could calm my nerves about my plans with Nate today.

Sure, we've texted back and forth a few times throughout the week, but I'm still mildly anxious. I don't even know why, and it's bugging the hell out of me if I'm being honest. I mean, Jesus, we're hitting up the Piggly Wiggly, not going out on a date.

In an effort to prove to myself how un-big of a deal this whole day is, I forgo makeup, toss my hair up in a ratty bun, and dress in a pair of capri length leggings paired with a plain V-neck shirt and flip-flops.

ME

Are we still good for noon?

NATE

Shit, GG. Don't kill me...

ME

Nate Reynolds! Are you bailing on our plans?

NATE

No! Just the grocery shopping part. Bring the groceries to my place around 1 and I'll reimburse you? Please... *puppy eyes*

ME

Ugh. Fine.

I take my time meandering up and down the aisles of The Pig, filling my buggy with staples that every kitchen should have along with items specific to the recipes I printed out for Nate. It's probably a little pathetic how excited I am about teaching him to cook, but when you live alone, cooking for one isn't all that exciting. Especially when you stumble across a new recipe on Pinterest.

I'm a little shocked that neither his mother nor Natalie, has managed to give him a few lessons—though something tells me it's not from lack of trying. The fact that he agreed to let me makes me feel a little warm and fuzzy, in a strictly platonic way of course.

The clock on my dash reads 1:02 when I pull into Nate's driveway. Instead of getting out and going inside, I toot my horn like my mom always did when she returned home from the grocery store. I'm pretty sure a post-grocery-horn-honk is universal code for come help unload all of this crap!

Sure enough, not even five seconds later, Nate comes out and together we haul in the plethora of bags.

"My God, did you buy the entire store?" Nate asks on our last trip in from my car.

"Wouldn't have needed so much if you had the freaking basics."

"Yeah, yeah, smartass." He sets the four bags in his grip down onto the kitchen floor and surveys the amount of stuff we have to put away. "Seriously though, this is insane. I'm not even sure I have anywhere to put this shit!"

"So dramatic. Here's how this is gonna go: nonperishables and dry goods go in the pantry. Dairy, drinks, and most produce can go in the fridge. I'll take care of the meat. Questions?"

"What? You're gonna take care of my meat? How friendly of you." He winks, and I roll my eyes. "For real though, I think I can handle it."

We divide and conquer to make the put-away go by a little quicker, with Nate handling the pantry while I take care of the cold stuff.

I pull the notecards I printed out for him from my purse. "Okay, you ready?"

"Damn, GG, you're taking this seriously, aren't you?" I can tell he's teasing me, but I don't mind it. This is something I'm passionate about, plain and simple.

One day, I'm going to figure out what that stupid nickname means. "Sure am. I kept it simple to start you off. Enchiladas, lasagna, fajita salad, a broccoli and chicken casserole, and a one-pot chicken soup."

By the time I'm done listing it all out, Nate's eyes are bugging out of his head. "We're…going to…make all of that? Today?"

Grinning, I reach up and boop him on the nose. "You betcha!"

He groans. "Fuck my life."

"Man up, big baby. Wash your hands and tell me which one you want to start with."

"Uh. Let's do the lasagna."

"Sweet. I'll gather up everything we need while you preheat the oven to three-fifty."

In the pantry—which is shockingly large—I gather up the jarred marinara sauce, tomato sauce, and necessary seasonings. The only thing I'm missing is the packages of no-boil noodles. Where in the heck are they? I know I bought them—I triple checked that list. Finally, I spot them on the highest shelf.

I'm on my tippy-toes when Nate pokes his head in. "Get lost in there?"

"Not lost," I grumble. "Just can't reach these stupid noodles."

Nate steps into the pantry and the once-airy space now feels claustrophobic. He moves in behind me and, so help me baby Jesus, I can feel the heat of his body burning into mine. As he reaches over my head, his hips press into my bottom, pinning me between him and the freshly stocked shelves.

Friends don't get turned on by their friends. Maybe if I repeat the mantra enough, it'll be true. Because Lord knows, the feel of his rock-hard body behind me has my panties damp and my nipples hard.

Nate, however, seems completely unaffected by our nearness. I wish it was as easy for me to flip the friend-switch as it is for him. Really, it's not fair that I'm the one struggling when this whole friend thing was my idea.

"Got 'em. Is one box okay?"

Not trusting my voice to come out steady, I nod.

"Perfect." Noodles in hand, he steps out of the pantry, allowing me to take my first full breath since he stepped inside with me.

I take a few moments to collect myself before stepping out and joining Nate. From the lone bag I didn't unpack, I grab one of the disposable aluminum baking pans I bought.

"Okay, first thing you need to do is brown your meat." I

talk Nate through the basics, impressed with how quickly he picks up on things. Before I know it, our meat sauce is ready, and he's holding out a spoon for me to taste.

With one hand poised under it to catch spills, he raises it to my lips. "Mmm," I moan as the flavorful sauce hits my tongue.

"Jesus," Nate growls, sounding pained, his eyes pinched shut.

"Here, you try it." I pry the wooden spoon from his grip and dip it back into the pot for him to sample it. I bring the spoon to his lips the same way he did and basically pop a lady boner when his full lips—ones that have roved over every inch of my body—part to accept my offering.

As he moans at the taste, his growled-out curse makes a lot more sense. This may as well be foreplay, which is something else friends don't do. Time to pump the brakes. "Good, right?"

"GG, you might just be a miracle worker."

"In case you missed it, you're the one who made this. I just...instructed."

"A student's only as good as his teacher." With a soft touch, he brushes an escaped lock of hair from my face. "So, what's next?"

"Now, my favorite part, the cheese!" This time, instead of talking him through it, I show him the recipe card and have him follow the steps on his own.

While he combines the ricotta, parmesan, and parsley, I grease the two baking pans before spreading a little sauce in the bottom of each. With all of the prep work complete, we each tackle a pan, stacking layer upon layer of noodles, cheese, and sauce, topping each one with a generous amount of shredded mozzarella.

"All right, these are going to cook for forty-five minutes." He pops them into the oven while I set a timer. "Whatcha wanna make next?"

"Enchiladas," he replies, no hesitation. "Mexican food is my second favorite…right after Italian."

"Sounds good. But first, let's rinse out the sauce pot. I don't think either of us wants to deal with a sink full of dishes at the end of this."

Not wanting a repeat of the pantry incident, I send Nate to retrieve everything we need. While he rummages around, I pull the rotisserie chicken from the fridge and begin picking the meat from the bones.

When Nate steps back into the kitchen, his strong arms loaded down, he scrunches his nose. "What's that for?"

"Using this is far more convenient than cooking chicken breasts. Trust me, stick with this, and deli chicken will quickly become your savior."

"Beauty and brains, GG. I like it."

I try my hardest not to blush at his compliment, but it's a wasted effort. He could comment on something as ordinary as my nail polish color and my cheeks would probably burst into flames.

I try and laugh it off, but it comes out sounding more like a horse's neigh. Just kill me now. Thankfully, Nate doesn't call me on it.

Just like with the lasagna, Nate quickly works his way through the steps. He really is a quick learner. The only thing that trips him up is the cilantro.

"The hell is that?" he asks, tipping his head toward the green sprigs on the countertop.

"Cilantro. But you don't have to use it if you don't like it."

"Uh, I don't really know if I do or not." He leans down and sniffs it. "What's it taste like?"

"Depends on who you ask. Personally, I think it tastes like dish soap. But other people love it."

I pinch off a leaf and hold it out to him. Instead of taking it from me, he brings my fingers to his mouth. I have to summon every ounce of willpower I possess to not moan when his lips close around my index and middle fingers. I move to jerk my hand back, but he holds it in place, flicking his tongue over the tips of my digits as he samples the cilantro.

My legs are wobbly, and my knees are knocking by the time he pulls back. "I like it. Kind of citrus-y."

In a daze, I nod. At this point, he could probably tell me the sky was green, and I'd agree.

He smirks. "Thought you said you didn't like it."

"Huh? What? I don't."

"Okay, Jenny. Then we won't use any."

I try and protest, because these meals are for him, not me. But he shuts me down. "How can I invite you over for dinner one night if I make something you don't like?"

Those stupid bees give a little buzz at his thoughtfulness. "Yeah, okay. Thanks."

We resume the recipe, working in a comfortable silence, and before I know it, hours have passed, and Nate has a full freezer.

I'm loading the last pot into the dishwasher when my belly lets loose a loud rumble. "You hungry?" Nate asks.

"Yeah, all this cooking worked up an appetite."

"Let's eat then."

I look around at the now spotless kitchen. "Everything we made today is for the coming week. But if you want, I can whip something else up?"

"You sure?"

"Positive. Go relax."

Dutifully, Nate retires to the living room while I get started on a super quick salad, made up of butter lettuce, cucumbers, tomatoes, baby carrots, raw broccoli, and some of the cold rotisserie chicken. Instead of dressing, I fry up two eggs—using the warm yolk to coat the salad is one of my most favorite things. It's nothing special by any means, but I'm hoping he'll like it.

Quickly, I check my sugar and bolus, even though I know he wouldn't mind me doing it in front of him—something that blows my mind. The only people I've ever been comfortable enough to do it around is my family and sometimes Natalie—but even that took a while. After the way peers and strangers alike responded to it growing up—with either shock or disgust—it just became something I kept to myself.

After washing my hands, I bring our bowls, along with two glasses of water, out to the living room, where Nate is kicked back on the couch, looking like a king on his throne. There's just something so assertive about his presence—like he knows he's all that. The man's truly an enigma: cocky yet humble all at once.

"Looks…interesting," he murmurs, taking his bowl from me.

"Don't knock it until you try it."

I watch with bated breath as he runs his fork over the top of his egg, bursting the yolk. The yellow goodness seeps out, covering everything beneath it. He spears a healthy bite onto his fork, bringing it to his mouth. He chews thoughtfully… slowly…prolonging my torture. But he doesn't spit it out, so maybe that's a good sign.

"I gotta say, this is hella good. Definitely better than I thought it was going to be. Damn."

Something that feels like pride blossoms in my chest. I like feeding him, taking care of him. Once we've both eaten our fill, Nate grabs the remote and flicks on the TV.

Kicking his feet up onto the coffee table, he rests one arm along the back of the couch. Instinctually, I lean into him as we watch whatever sitcom rerun is playing the screen.

I'm not sure friends cuddle like this, but he makes me feel so warm and secure that I don't object.

About fifteen minutes in, Nate's phone buzzes on the table, but he makes no move to grab it. Five minutes later, it does it again. And again. "You gonna check that?" I ask him.

"I probably should. I'm just too comfy to move."

"I'll grab it." I don't mean to look at the words on the screen—I swear, I don't. But now that I've seen them, they can't be unseen.

MARY

For real. Thanks for this morning with Sarah.
You were great…

I snatch the phone up just in time for another notification to roll through.

MARY

I mean it. Why don't you swing by later and
let me thank you properly?

I toss the phone to Nate like it's a hot potato. It lands in his lap with a thud. He swipes up and reads through the messages he missed—the ones I didn't see.

"Jenny." He says my name like he's speaking to a child on the verge of a tantrum. It's probably the same voice he uses to placate Tatum. "It's not—"

I cut him off, unwilling to listen to whatever BS he comes up with. "I know we just ate, but looks like your buffet is calling." I shrug, feigning indifference. "You'd better go."

He sighs, pinching the bridge of his nose. Deep down, I'm hoping he'll correct me; that he'll tell me she's no one and that he certainly didn't blow off our plans for her. But the words never come. I guess his indifference to all of the things that had me ready to offer myself up on a platter makes sense now. Why would he want to come back for fourths from me when all of that variety he loves so much is out there waiting?

"Yeah, okay." We both stand. He takes our dishes to the sink while I collect my belongings. He walks me to the door, his eyes pleading for me to understand and really, I do. Sure, it hurts, but this is what we agreed on, and I damn sure plan to uphold my end of this friendship.

"Uh, thanks for everything today. I'll text you sometime tomorrow."

I give him a terse nod. "Sounds good. Be…safe." Friends don't get jealous, I remind myself as I walk to my car. And I repeat it several more times on the drive home.

AM I a total shit for letting Jenny misinterpret that text on Sunday? Yes, absolutely. In fact, I may even be King Shit.

I know exactly what she thought when she saw it—she assumed I ditched her for a fucking threesome. Which couldn't be further from the truth, mind you. In actuality, the department's secretary called me in a panic because her daughter Sarah—who is seventeen—was stranded on the side of the road. Her tire ran flat, and she didn't have a spare. Mary's husband would usually be the one to help out, but he was stuck in meetings all day.

Do I regret it? That's the million-dollar question I've been asking myself for the last three days. Maybe a little. But, if I'm being honest, I kind of need her to go back to thinking I'm a dog—it makes staying away from her in that way a little easier, even if the pain that flashed in her eyes made me feel about two inches tall.

We've texted daily since, and things seem to be back to normal between the two of us. We even had a brief phone call Wednesday night after her first shift at Bennet's. I hated that I couldn't be there to support her, but I was on shift. I would've gone Thursday, but Natalie asked me to watch Tatum—and in my book, family always comes first.

But now it's Friday, and I'm finally free. It's been almost a week since I've laid eyes on Jenny; strangely, I'm missing the little spitfire. I'd like to say I'm not nervous about seeing her, but that'd be a lie. I've managed to talk Duke, Xavier, and a few of the other guys into joining me, which in hindsight might have been a terrible idea. Especially since most of the guys see me as this larger-than-life player without a care in the world who jumps from bed to bed. Yeah, they see me the same way Jenny did—or does, I guess I should say.

"Yo! You ready for a night out, lady killer?" Xavier asks, completely unaware of how much that stupid-ass nickname pisses me off, as we walk toward the bar from our vehicles. I know I should just man up and ask them to stop, but that means opening the whole Sonia can of worms, and I'd really rather not.

I grind my molars together; oh, yeah, this was a terrible fucking idea.

"I know I'm ready for badge bunnies," a dumbass rookie named Jackson pipes up. Swear, the dude talks like he spits game for a living…too bad he's actually a virgin who still lives at home with his mommy and daddy. I'm ninety-nine percent positive he still has a curfew.

I shake my head at their antics, trying not to yell at them all to shut the fuck up. Duke is the only person I don't want to throttle.

"Y'all head in. I'll be right there." I catch Duke's eye over their heads.

He nods, hearing everything I'm not saying. Watch out for Jenny. Keep these jackasses away from her. Try and make them behave. Things that wouldn't have crossed my mind in the past. Hell, a few short months ago, I was the worst of them—a total womanizing asshole.

But that was then. And this is now.

I take a few moments to center myself before heading in. My eyes hone in on Jenny like there's some kind of tracking device implanted in her, sending signals straight to my corneas.

She looks completely at ease behind the bar, slinging drinks and charming patrons like she's been doing it her entire life. I move toward her, slicing through the crowd. Her black Bennet's shirt clings to her breasts, drawing the eye of every man in the place, including mine.

I sidle up to the guys and wait for her to notice me. Must be my lucky night, because it doesn't take long. "Hello, boys. What'll y'all have?" She starts on the far end of our little group, saving me for last. "How about you, Nate?"

I let my gaze slide over her. "Surprise me."

Her brilliant eyes glow like emeralds at my request, and she wastes no time filling our order. I keep my stare trained on her as she grabs a slew of cheap-ass domestic beers for most of the guys and what I know is a club soda with lime for Duke since he's our DD. She takes her time on me, though.

She keeps her back to me as she prepares my drink, and I've got to say, I'm mildly surprised when she places a scotch and soda in front of me. It's definitely not something I would ever order for myself, but if Jenny thinks it's the drink for me, then I'm damn well going to enjoy it.

Her eyes twinkle as I sip my drink. "Why this?" I ask her over the roar of the crowd.

She bites the side of her bottom lip and quirks her brows. "I read somewhere that it's what the cutest boy in the room drinks."

I can't help it; I bust out laughing. "Did you just call me cute?" She gives me a cheeky nod. "Jenny. No. Dogs are cute. Tatum is cute. Grown-ass men are not cute."

She crooks her finger at me, and I lean down over the bar. From this vantage point, I have a clear shot down her top; the swells of her lace-encased breasts distract me. Which is why I don't even see it coming when she pushes up to her tiptoes and boops me on the nose. "Guess you aren't as manly as you thought, cutie." She spins, wiggles her hips in a little victory dance, and moves on down the bar to the next group vying for her attention.

As expected, the guys have a field day over her calling me cutie. All night, it's cutie-this and cutie-that. And every time the little shit stirrer comes to check on us or refill our drinks, she makes a big show of talking to me like I'm five or whips me up some kind of ridiculous cutesy cocktail. The guys absolutely lose it when on her third pass she makes me a freaking appletini.

Joke's on her though, because while I may look like a douche drinking it, it's fucking delicious.

I'm halfway through said appletini when a gaggle of sorority-looking girls descend upon us; a stunning redhead with the biggest set of fake tits I've ever seen approaches me. Bold as fuck, she runs her cherry-red nail down the center of my chest. "There's something about a man who can order a drink like that and still look sexy, am I right?"

I hold the martini glass up in a cheers gesture before downing the rest of the sugary green liquid. "It's definitely a gift." While my words are playful, my tone isn't. I don't mind chatting up this chick, but I'm not interested in her.

"I've seen you here before," she says in what she believes is a sexy voice. To me, she sounds a little too desperate, like she'd let me hogtie her just for the hell of it. "You're a cop, right?" Ah. A badge bunny—that explains it.

"That I am."

Big Red pretty much melts into a puddle of silicone. "You're so brave. Do…do you carry a gun and everything?"

Jesus. The sad thing? Before Jenny, this is exactly the kind of woman I'd have gone home with. Now, the mere thought of sitting here, pretending to listen while she fawns all over me, pains me.

"Yes, ma'am, I do. Standard issue."

She shivers exaggeratedly and runs her right hand over my shoulder. "Mmm. And so strong."

I bring my hand up to cover hers, intent on pushing hers away, but the sweet sound of Jenny's voice distracts me.

"Y'all need anything else?" She damn near has to shout to be heard over the crowd.

A few of the guys call for a refill, business as usual. Until Jackson's dumb ass hollers out above the rest, "Yeah, baby, your number!"

I shake out of Red's hold and turn to my boys just in time to see Jackson wag his brows while making a crude gesture behind Jenny's back.

Oh. Hell. No.

In two seconds flat, I have his scrawny ass pinned to the edge of the bar. "Not fucking happening, rook."

He tries to laugh me off. "Tight little ass like hers? Why not?"

I inhale deeply through my nose, expelling the breath slowly as I run through all of the reasons I can't tear this disrespectful little shit limb from limb. I can feel the vein in my forehead throbbing. I probably look like the Incredible Hulk with the amount of unchecked fury thrumming through my veins.

"Oh, I get it. You want to keep her for yourself."

"I swear to God—"

I'm rearing back to deck his ass when I'm pulled off of him. I try and throw my weight around, ready to unleash on whoever's behind me, but they're quicker than me and pin my arms at my sides.

"Chill, brother," Duke hisses in my ear. "Kid's not worth it."

I instantly deflate and take a cleansing breath. He's right. What in God's name was I thinking?

Duke releases me from his hold, and I shove past Jackson,

stepping up to the bar, where Jenny hovers with a slightly mortified look painting her delicate features.

"I'm honestly not sure if I should be pissed off or telling you thanks," she says, passing me a bottle of water.

"Thanking me, definitely. Dude's a twit."

She snorts out a laugh. "Something I could see perfectly fine with my own eyes, Captain Obvious. I had no intention of giving him my number."

"I might have overreacted." I pinch my thumb and forefinger together, leaving barely any space between them. "Just a little."

She laughs again, and damn if it's not the best sound I've ever heard.

I'VE ALWAYS scoffed at the saying boys will be boys, but after Nate's caveman display, I can't help but to see a little truth in it. He doesn't want me, but he doesn't want anyone else playing with his toys, either. If that's not the very definition of that saying, then I'm not sure what is.

Too bad I don't much like being equated to a Hot Wheel car he doesn't want to share. Not to mention, I'm a grown-ass woman and perfectly capable of taking care of my own damn self.

Over Nate's shoulder, I catch the tail end of what looks like Duke reaming out their scrawny friend. The kid heads out with slumped shoulders, and Duke rejoins the group.

"All good?" Nate asks.

"Ordered him an Uber."

Nate holds out his hand for a fist bump. "Thanks, brother."

"As exciting as that was, I need to get back to work. Do you boys want anything to drink?"

"Nah, I'm good," Duke declines at the same time Nate says, "One more. Do your worst, GC."

A smile splits my cheeks as I catalog the girliest drinks I know. My smile doesn't last long though, because the gorgeous redhead who's held Nate's attention all night comes up behind him, standing entirely too close for my comfort.

But I will be polite and professional, even if it freaking kills me. "And what'll your friend have?"

Busty Barbie scans me from head to toe, dismissing me as a threat almost immediately. "A cosmo," she says, her voice a sultry rasp that makes mine sound childlike in comparison.

I give a tight nod to the trio. "On it."

With my heart no longer in teasing Nate, I decide to send an entirely different message with his drink—one that says I think he's kind of an asshole. I quickly whip up a specialty shot for Nate—a Mad Dog, made up of raspberry syrup, vodka, and a splash of hot sauce—along with a cosmo for his flavor of the night.

"Here y'all go. Enjoy." I shoot them a saccharine smile before moving on to help other patrons.

I greet the group of newcomers crowded in next to where Nate and his friends are, fully aware that they've been waiting on me. "Sorry for the wait, y'all."

I quickly work through their order, studiously avoiding Nate and his companion. But it's hard not to glance their way a time or two. From the looks of it, she's the one carrying the conversation. Probably because he's too busy drooling to speak.

She is contoured, highlighted, scantily dressed, and at least five inches taller than me. She's freaking gorgeous, the exact kind of woman I'd imagine Nate with.

Put plainly, she's everything I'm not. She oozes self-confidence; she's bold and assertive and not afraid to go after what she wants. Meanwhile, it took me years to work up the nerve to try to get Nate to notice me.

Envy shoots through me like poison when her throaty laugh floats my way. Apparently, I'm a glutton for punishment, because I look their way again. He's seated on a barstool with his back to me. He leans back, propping himself up on his elbows like he doesn't have a care in the world. And why would he, with a glamazon like her standing between his legs, leaning into him like he knows the secrets to everlasting youth.

I'm thankful when a group of older men signal me from the far end of the bar, stealing my attention away from them. I know he has a healthy sexual appetite—hello, he ditched me for a freaking three-way—but seeing him work his magic in person hurts way more than reading about his exploits in a text message.

"Take a break, kiddo," Mack says as I finish up with my latest order.

I glance around the crowded space. We are crazy busy. I'm talking bodies jammed wall-to-wall, I hope the fire marshal doesn't pop in for a drink because he'll definitely shut us down, packed. "You sure?"

Mack shoots me a mean glare that I know he doesn't mean. "Don't wanna see you for at least half an hour. Got it?"

I smile at his surliness. "Got it."

Even though my feet are aching, I freaking love it here. I love the fast pace, the commotion, the hoots and hollers—all of it.

My stupid, traitorous eyes seek Nate out as I untie my apron and stash it under the bar. Only, instead of finding him with his tongue shoved down Red's throat, he's kicked back chatting with Duke and another guy—no beautiful, man-stealing women in sight.

Not your man, Jenny.

My plan to slip out to my car unseen is foiled before I can even come around from behind the bar. "Where're you off to, GG?"

I pause in front of Nate's barstool. "Taking my thirty."

He nods. "Want some company?"

It was my intention to politely and cordially decline his

invitation. So, imagine my shock when what I say instead is, "You sure your latest flavor won't mind?"

His boys—save for Duke—all ooh and ahh. The one I briefly met at the wedding—Xavier, I think—helpfully adds, "He struck out. He talks like he has all this game, but our lady killer couldn't seal the deal tonight."

Nate's jaw clenches tight, and I feel like I'm missing something.

"He didn't strike out," Duke corrects. "He sent her packing because he wasn't interested."

Xavier's eyes bug out. "Should've sent her my way, man." I've got to say, I'm as perplexed as he is—the girl was a knockout and a sure thing. Why on earth wouldn't he go for it?

"C'mon, GG, let's go." I nod and duck under the bar. Those damn bees flutter to life again when he grips my hand and tugs me behind him toward the exit.

"What does that freaking mean?"

Nate ignores my question entirely as we step outside.

The humid night air hangs heavy around us as we walk to my car, causing a fine sheen of sweat to coat my skin. I slide into my driver's seat and Nate drops into the passenger side. He's a big guy in an open space, but here, in my little sedan, he may as well be a giant.

A laugh slips past my lips when he shoves the seat back as far as it will go and still looks cramped. "Small-ass shoebox of a car," he grumbles as he reclines the seat as well.

"It's a perfectly normal-sized car."

"Maybe for a midget."

I scoff. "I am five-five, perfectly average, thank you very much."

Nate mumbles something under his breath that sounds very much like ain't nothing average about you. I chalk it up to my mind playing tricks on me and my ears hearing what they want to.

Reaching into the back seat, I grab my lunchbox as well as what I refer to as my kit—it contains my meter, backup insulin, and all of that jazz. With my lunchbox balanced on my lap, I open my kit and grab everything I need to check my sugar. According to my CGM, I'm in a good range, but it isn't always accurate, so double checking never hurts.

Reaching down the front of my shirt, I unclip my pump from my bra, leaving it to rest awkwardly on top of my breast. A quick finger prick later, the reading is sent to my pump and I calibrate my sensor to help it achieve better accuracy—though it really wasn't far off. I bolus for the dinner I packed, reclip my pump, sanitize my hands, toss my kit back into the back seat, and unzip my lunchbox.

My mouth waters at the sight of my dinner, even though it isn't much—a turkey sandwich on sugar-free bread, a golden delicious apple with peanut butter, a piece of cheese, and a bottle of water to wash it all down with. I'm so hungry that it may as well be a gourmet feast.

As I dip an apple slice into my peanut butter, I decide to finally address the elephant in the room—er, car. "Wanna tell me why you're here with me and not getting lucky with Red?"

Nate doesn't reply immediately. Knowing him, he's probably thinking of some smartass reply.

"You...you did..." He trails off, waving his left hand in my general direction. "...Your sugar stuff in front of me."

Instantly, my cheeks flame with embarrassment. When did I become so comfortable in his presence? "Oh. Uh. I'm sor—"

"I know you're not about to apologize," he barks, cutting me off.

My eyes drop to my lap.

"GG, we've been over this. You have nothing to say sorry for, and fuck anyone who's ever made you feel otherwise."

"Right, okay." I let out an awkward laugh. "Enough about me. Seriously though, why are you out here with me? I bet that ginger would have been down for some men's room action."

Nate makes a tsk-ing sound. "You really shouldn't slut shame."

Again, I scoff. "So, you admit you're a slut?"

"Touché, GG." He grins boyishly, and my freaking thighs clench at the sight. "And no, I am not a slut; I just like—"

I speak over him, "Variety, I know. And for the record, I wasn't implying she—or any woman who enjoys casual sex, even in public—is a slut. I would never judge someone for embracing their sexuality."

"So, public sex isn't off the table?" he asks, his voice all husk and smoke. This man is dangerous—lethal even. He could probably charm the panties right off of a nun.

"That's your takeaway?"

He has the good sense to look sheepish. "I'm a guy. A hot girl mentions sex, and my snake brain takes over. Truly, it can't be helped."

Our conversation tapers off into a comfortable silence as I munch on my sandwich. That is, until Nate asks, "Really though, like how public? Are you secretly into voyeurism? Are we talking somewhere private but you could get caught, like a fitting room…or perhaps a car in a bar parking lot?"

"You're too much, you know that?"

"I've been told a time or two." I go to uncap my water, but Nate snatches it out of my grasp. "Stop ignoring me. I won't be able to sleep tonight without this information!"

"Oh, well, I can't have that kind of guilt on my shoulders, now can I?"

He grumbles under his breath, and I decide to throw him a bone.

"I don't know. It's not something I've ever done, but I've definitely thought about it. There's no specific place in my mind—it could be a break room, an elevator, an alley, in the ocean—just somewhere anyone could stumble across."

Reaching down to rearrange himself, Nate groans. "Now I'm definitely not gonna get any sleep."

I laugh at his misery. "Pretty sure friends don't get hard talking about sex with each other." I pat his thigh to torture him a little more. "Now, give me back my water."

"Pretty sure most guys don't have friends that look like you, GG."

"You ever gonna tell me what that means?" I ask, recapping my bottle.

"Already told you, you gotta guess."

Feeling emboldened, I ask, "Does it mean gorgeous girl?"

Nate leans toward me, running his knuckles over my cheek. "Nope, that's not it. But you definitely are gorgeous."

Slack-jawed, I stare at him. Does he really think I'm gorgeous? Cute, sure. Pretty, I can see that. But...gorgeous? That's next level, and I'm just...me. It's on the tip of my tongue to press him further, but ultimately, I decide it doesn't matter one way or another. We'll never be anything more than intimately acquainted friends and I'm okay with that —mostly.

"Okay, playboy. My break's over. You gonna head out?"

"Nah, I'll stick around until the end of your shift." It doesn't escape my notice that he never answered me about Red, but I figure it, too, doesn't really matter.

"You sure?"

"There's nowhere I'd rather be." I can hear the truth in his words, and it warms me and makes me green with envy in equal parts. This man is going to make some woman very, very happy one day. I only wish it was me.

OVER THE PAST FEW WEEKS, Jenny and I have fallen into an easy pattern of sorts. Whichever one of us wakes up first texts the other one. We've also taken to sending each other riddles to solve. She's better at them than I am, which kind of turns me on—weird, right?

Any time we're both off is spent together. To date, we've hung out with my sister and Alden, been bowling, played mini golf, seen a few movies, and today we're hitting up the go-kart track.

We also talk on the phone almost every night—sometimes until one of us falls asleep. Honestly, some days I find myself wondering when I grew a vagina.

I haven't been laid in almost three months, what with little Miss Jenny occupying all of my free time. Hell, the last time I got off with another person was when she went down on me.

Needless to say, my sexual frustration is at an all-time high. There's only so much my right hand can do to satiate my needs, but that doesn't stop me from trying. The nights we talk for hours are the worst. My good girl sounds so sultry and tempting over the phone—I could probably get off listening to her read me her shopping list. Yeah, I'm that hard up.

Even worse…she doesn't seem to be affected at all. I mean, here I am, lusting over my best friend, while she's carrying on business as usual.

Go fucking figure.

———

We're supposed to meet at the track a little after eleven, yet here I am at barely ten pulling up to Jenny's house—if you can call it that, really. It's more of a…really well-made shack.

I'm out of my car and knocking on her front door within a span of seconds, not wanting to leave enough time to doubt randomly showing up or question my intentions.

My breath lodges in my throat when her door cracks open just enough for her to see out. "Nate?"

"Surprise!"

"Uh, yeah. Hi." Her eyes flit down toward her feet then back up to me. "You're here."

I nod slowly. "I am. You gonna let me in?" Jenny is acting kind of weird; maybe showing up unannounced wasn't the best idea after all?

"Yeah, um, yes." She pulls the door the rest of the way open, keeping her body behind it. "Come on in."

When she closes it behind us, her odd behavior instantly makes sense. My girl is clad in nothing more than a small, white towel. The offending piece of terrycloth barely makes it to mid-thigh, and I'm pretty sure a miracle is the only thing holding it up.

It's not very friend-like, but internally, I'm praying for the towel to drop so her delectable body will be bared to me. Another non-platonic thing—the hard wood I'm rocking beneath my khaki cargo shorts. If she notices the tent I'm pitching, she doesn't mention it; thank God.

"So, I'm, uh…just gonna run upstairs and get dressed."

My eyes rove over her body, recalling in great detail exactly how she looks and feels under me. "Uh-huh."

"Nate!" She stomps her foot, causing her perky tits to jiggle beneath the material and the knot to loosen. My breath catches in my throat. "Are you even listening?"

Now I'm the one struggling for words. "Uh, yeah, you said—"

Jenny ekes out a laugh. "You're such a guy. I said I'm going to get dressed."

She turns without another word and heads up the stairs. Like the perv I am, I track her every move, enthralled with the tantalizing amount of skin she reveals with every step. Girl's sex on a stick without even trying.

While she fiddles around doing whatever it is girls do when they get ready, I chill out on her couch, calling to mind every unsexy thing I can think of to will my hard-on away. It mostly works, until she descends the stairs looking like something straight out of a country music video, minus the boots.

She's dressed in a white tank top that hugs her chest and cutoff denim shorts so tiny they could pass for panties, with a plaid shirt tied around her waist and red Keds on her feet. I'm honestly not sure which is worse—this or the towel.

"You ready?"

"Mmhmm," I hum, trying my best not to drool at the sight of her sexy, toned, tan legs. For a girl on the shorter side, they look a mile long. Memories of how they feel wrapped around my waist and shoulders fight their way to the front of my mind.

When I make no move to stand, she pops a brow at me. "'Kay…you gonna stand up?"

"Yeah, just give me a minute, GG." Speeding tickets, DUIs, perp walks, home invasions, vandalism, drunk and disorderlies. Finally, I feel steady enough to stand. "Let's go."

She studies me, her head tilted to the side. For a split second, I worry she's going to call me on my shit. I release a heavy exhale when instead she says, "Ready to have your ass handed to you on the track?"

Damn, I love her sassy mouth. "You do realize defensive driving is literally part of my job description, right?"

She brushes off my words and sashays out the door like she has not a worry in the world. I follow behind her, more than excited to gloat when I leave her cute little ass in my dust on the first lap.

———

"I can't believe you fucking beat me," I complain for at least the fiftieth time since our race. "Seriously, how? Did you slip the kid some money to give me a slower go-kart?"

Jenny giggles, and damn if it isn't the sweetest sound I've ever heard. "Nate Reynolds, a sore loser. Who would've guessed it?"

"I'm not a sore loser. You're a cheater." I wrap an arm around her shoulder, pulling her into my side as we follow the path from the kart return to the on-site ice cream shop.

She laughs harder. "And how, pray tell, did I cheat?"

"Hell if I know. Probably some kind of witchcraft."

"So now I'm a witch?" she cries in mock outrage, shoving away from me.

But I don't let her get far, lacing our fingers together holding her hand in mine. Do friends hold hands? Maybe so, because she doesn't pull away. "Hell if I know, Jenny Jones, but you've sure as shit cast a spell over me."

A brilliant smile lights up her face as she looks at me. "C'mon, I'll treat you to ice cream to make up for my witchy ways."

I knock my shoulder into hers. "Sounds fair," I concede even though I have no intention of letting her pay.

Turns out getting ice cream was the worst idea ever. I

thought I was safe when she ordered a cup of lemon sorbetto, but watching her lick and suck the spoon is pure torture. I have to suppress a groan with every bite she takes.

"Oh, wow, that was so good," she moans as she polishes off the last of her frozen treat. "What are your plans for the rest of the day?"

"You work tonight, right?"

"Yup. Four to close."

"Then I guess I'll be chilling at Bennet's."

She rolls her lips inward. "You don't have to—"

I don't give her a chance to protest. "I want to." She nods, letting the subject drop. "C'mon, I'll drive you home."

The drive to Jenny's passes in the blink of an eye. Even though I know I'm going to see her tonight, I'm not ready for our time together today to end. At the bar, I'll have to share her with a room full of people, so I want to soak up as much one-on-one time with her as possible.

As if she's reading my thoughts, she asks, "You wanna come in and watch a movie?"

I make a big show of checking the time, not wanting to look too eager. "Yeah, that sounds good."

Inside, I throw myself down onto her couch, pulling her down with me. I land on my back, with her body partially draping over mine. The weight of her on top of me feels like the best kind of agony. She tries to move off of me, but I roll, turning us so that I'm on my side. She's facing me, her head resting on my arm.

"Stay. I'm comfy."

"Can I at least roll so I can reach the remote and you know…see the TV?"

I let out a long, overly dramatic sigh. "I guess. Needy."

Jenny grins and rearranges herself so that her back is to my front, making sure to keep a little space between our bodies. She leans forward slightly and grabs the remote from the coffee table and hits the power button. Not bothering to check what's playing, she tosses the clicker back down and relaxes into me. Within minutes, we're both out cold.

JENNY

Waking up next to Nate Reynolds is something I'll remember for the rest of my life. Obviously, I don't have much to compare it to, but something tells me the feelings rushing through me aren't the norm. The way his strong arms hold me close, combined with how his leg is wedged between mine, has me walking the line between feeling safe in his embrace and turned on enough to rub up against him like a cat in heat.

I attempt to move out of his arms, but he yanks me back into him, nuzzling his face into my neck. "Five more minutes, GG," he murmurs, his warm breath skating over my skin.

I glance up to the clock on the wall—it's three. I really need to get ready for my shift at the bar, but the comfort I feel in Nate's arms has me agreeing all too easily.

"If you could be any animal, what would you be?" Nate asks, his voice still gravelly and thick with sleep. Leave it to him to make tired sound erotic.

"Random. But I'll humor you. I'd be…" I pause, really wracking my brain. "This is going to sound so lame, but I'd be a cat."

He stretches out his body, yawning. The action presses us

closer together and I have to suppress a shiver. "Like a jungle cat?"

Twisting, I turn my upper body so I can see him. "No, like a house cat."

He smirks. "You're a weird girl, Jenny."

"Yeah, well, you're one of my best friends, so what does that say about you? I believe the saying is it takes one to know one."

He flexes his hips forward, retreating just as quickly. Still, it was more than enough time for me to feel his post-nap erection dig into my bottom. "I might be weird, but I'm definitely not a girl."

I try and play it off, like the feel of him doesn't make me want to jump his bones. "You loser." I shake out of his hold. "I gotta get ready for work. I'll see you tonight?"

"Why don't I just stick around, and we can head over together?"

I blink at him a few times. "You do realize if we do that you won't be able to leave...if you...meet someone." Ugh. The very thought of watching him walk out of those doors with a woman—the thought of him taking her home and worshiping her body the way he did mine—makes me feel ill, but I know it's bound to happen.

"Aw, GG, are you worried about my sex life?"

Even with the playful delivery, his question stings. Because while I'm basically a nun, he still has an active and healthy sex life. Get a grip, girl, this is what you wanted.

"Ha!" I laugh him off. "You wish."

He licks across his bottom lip, searing me with his dark brown eyes. "Go get changed. I'm driving you, and that's final."

His authoritative tone has heat unfurling low in my belly. "Yes, sir."

He winks. "Good girl."

Ever since the night Nate drove me to work, he's made it his mission to be at the bar for every shift of mine that he's not working. Some nights, he lets me test drink recipes on him, other nights he sips on water and basically loiters until I'm off the clock. Occasionally he brings me dinner.

From time to time, one or two of his buddies will join him—those nights are my favorite, because as much as I love our one-on-one time, I really love seeing him joke around with his boys. Not to mention, they're always more than willing to help me pick on him.

Plenty of women approach him. Some of them are so over-the-top stunning that my heart lodges in my throat, because it's only a matter of time before one of them sways him off of his stool and into bed. But strangely, he never flirts back with any of them.

On the same token, he doesn't let any guys flirt with me. It's like he's decided since he can't have me, no one can. Not that I'd go home with any of them—I mean, my Lord, I've been with all of two people in my entire life—I'm not exactly chomping at the bit to add another notch to my bedpost. If anything, sleeping with Nate and trying to keep things casual only reinforced that I'm a relationship kind of girl. For me, sex and emotions go hand-in-hand. So, no bar hookups for me.

Guard dog tendencies and repressed feelings aside, having Nate as a friend definitely has its perks. Like today, for example, he's invited me to tag along to the police department's annual Memorial Day picnic.

He's due to pick me up in thirty minutes, but knowing him, he'll be early. Meaning, I need to get my ass in gear and get dressed. It feels like I've tried on every stitch of clothing I own—twice. For a picnic. A freaking picnic. The man's seen me naked, he's seen me dressed to the nines, and everything in between; yet here I am, obsessing over what to wear. As sad as it is, I want to look good for him.

Finally, I admit defeat. It's time to call in reinforcements. Grabbing my phone, I video call the one person I know won't lead me astray—my cousin Jamie.

He answers almost instantly, his handsome, chiseled face filling my screen. "Jenny-cake, to what do I owe the pleasure?"

I shrug defeatedly. "I need help."

"With what? I'm not a mind reader."

"I need outfit advice. Nate invited me to a picnic and—"

Jamie squeals in the most unmanly fashion. "Are y'all finally together?"

"Nope. Just friends."

"Oh. Well, then obviously you need to make that man's tongue wag."

"Jamie, he's seen me butt naked—I doubt there's some miracle outfit—"

"Hush and let me work my magic, woman. Throw on a pair of Nike shorts, a strappy sports bra, and a loose-fitting tank that shows off said bra. Tie your hair up in a high pony-tail and put a little blush on your cheeks and some gloss on your lips."

"Really?" I ask, my skepticism clearly written on my face.

"Really, really. Low-key sexy is in, girl."

"You're a lifesaver, Jamie-pop."

He flips his imaginary hair. "Tell me something I don't know."

We end our call, and I immediately follow his instructions. A quick glance in the mirror tells me my cousin dearest definitely knows what he's talking about. I look casual and attractive all at once—the walking embodiment of I woke up like this. Hopefully Nate likes what he sees as well.

Judging by the sound of my front door opening—yes,

we're past the point of knocking—I'm about to find out. "GG, you ready?" Nate hollers from my living room.

"Well, I would be if you weren't" —I check the time on my phone— "fifteen minutes early!"

His heavy footsteps sound as he climbs the stairs. "Couldn't wait to see—" His words drop off like a cliff. He rakes his teeth over his bottom lip as he stares at me. "Damn, Jenny."

Playing it clueless, I twist a strand from my long ponytail around my finger. "What? The mess?" I nod my head toward my clothes-covered bed.

Nate steps closer to me. "What mess? All I can see is you."

His words light a fire in me, and I can't help but to push a little more. Spinning, I give him my back, revealing the way my shirt is cut to expose most of it, along with the criss-crossing straps to my bralette. "You're not so bad yourself, cutie."

He groans, and I do a mental fist pump. "You're trying to kill me, aren't you?"

"I have no idea what you mean. It's just shorts and a tank top." He grumbles something under his breath that sounds a lot like bullshit. "I'm just gonna slather on some sunscreen and then we can go."

Nate clears a spot on my bed and plops down onto the mattress while I grab my SPF 50. I make quick work of rubbing the lotion into my arms and shoulders but decide to mess with him a little when I do my legs.

With my back still facing him, I bend at the waist, making sure to pop my ass out just a smidge. Slowly, I work the sunblock into the skin of my right leg. A quick glance toward the bed shows me that Nate's not only watching, he's enthralled. I move to my left leg, giving it the same treatment, prolonging my little show. Finally, he's had enough.

"Stand up, Jenny." His tone is harsh, and I snap to attention. "Face me," he commands, and like a good little girl, I do.

"Give me the bottle." The dark tenor of his voice has me reacting on autopilot—he sounds so lethal and sexy, as if he's completely in control and barely restrained all at once.

Sitting at the edge of my bed, he spreads his legs apart. "Come closer." I step into the space between his knees. He squirts a dollop of lotion into the palm of his right hand and tosses the bottle onto the floor behind me, causing anticipation to snake up my spine.

With his free hand, he grabs the hem of my shirt and tugs me closer still so that the end of my bed is flush against my legs. He snakes his left hand beneath my shirt, moving it far enough away from my body for his right hand to join. His arms encircle my waist and his hands meet my skin—the cold sunscreen a shock against my heated flesh.

I release a breathy gasp at the sensation, followed by a whimper as he begins massaging the cream into the skin of my back. His fingers sensuously knead and caress, reducing me to a trembling pile of need.

As his hands move higher, skimming over the dips in my waist, I swear I almost say fuck it and climb onto his lap. But, we're only friends, so I suppress the urge and count down from one hundred in my head. Things are going great until he skims his fingers just beneath my breasts right when I hit 69.

Sweet mercy, take me now. Nate has me so turned on that I can hardly breathe. Right as I'm about to give in to my urges —because, really, why do I need Nate as a friend when I can ride him like a stallion instead?—he withdraws his hands from my body.

"There." He stands, forcing me to take a step back. "Wouldn't want your back to burn, would we? Let's roll, time's a wasting." He moves around me and trots down the stairs like he didn't just almost get me off from his touch alone.

Nate: 1, Jenny: 0.

NATE

This entire day is going to be a test of my patience. From the minute I woke up from a dirty dream involving me doing unspeakable things to Jenny in my gym's locker room—weird as hell because she's never even been there—I just knew. And then I show up at her house to find her dressed in damn near the outfit I ripped off of her in the gym shower during my slumber…shit has to be some kind of omen.

And then she started teasing me, wiggling her pert little ass right in my face and running her hands all over her gorgeous legs. It was all I could do to stop myself from throwing her down onto her messy bed and reminding her just how good we are together. However, with Herculean strength, I was able to not only resist but to turn the tables as well. Who knew sunscreen could be so sexy?

"You ready for some fun?" I ask, guiding my car into the designated parking area.

"What kind of fun are we talking?"

"Aside from good food, there are games."

Jenny scrunches up her cute little nose. "What kind of games?"

"Water balloon toss, tug-o'-war, sack races—field day stuff."

Jenny rubs her hands together. "Oh, this will be fun!"

I throw the car into park and turn to her. "Are you competitive, GG?"

"You don't even know."

———

After watching Jenny kick ass in ring toss and the obstacle course the chief set up, I can safely say she is ridiculously competitive—she can also talk shit with the best of them. Girl can also put away some barbecue like nobody's business. Honestly, I don't know where she puts it all.

Currently, we're seated side by side on a blanket, relaxing while watching some of the guys play tug-o'-war. Well, I'm relaxing. Jenny is screaming like a banshee, cheering on Duke's team.

"Pull! Harder!" She leans forward, bracing her elbows on her knees. "C'mon! Don't tell me all those muscles are just for show!"

Spurred on by her cheerleading, the guys on Duke's team all give one final hard tug, pulling the middle of the rope over the marker, declaring them the victors. Jenny springs to her feet as a chorus of hell yeahs ring out, her voice being one of the loudest.

Here, in this moment—this completely insignificant moment—I'm struck with the desire to make her mine. And I don't just mean between the sheets. Jenny Jones is damn near perfect, and my desire for her is slowly beginning to override my fear of destroying her.

I mean, we've managed being friends…so why couldn't we be more? My family already loves her, she gels with my boys like she's known them her whole life, and she accepts me. My brain whispers that I'm no good for her, that I'll only hurt her, that she can't accept my scars because she doesn't even know what they are, but my heart is fucking shouting to me that if I don't at least try, I'll regret it forever. And I'm not sure I'm willing to live with anymore regrets.

In fact, I'm not even willing to wait.

Bringing my thumb and index finger to my lips, I let out a sharp whistle, grabbing the celebrating group's attention as a whole, but it's only hers I want. "Jenny!" I beckon her my way. "Need to talk to you."

She worries her lip between her teeth as she steps toward me. "Is…is everything okay?"

I shake my head and lace my fingers with hers. "Not even remotely."

"Wh-what's wrong?" she asks. "You're scaring me. Are you okay?"

"I'm about to be," I murmur before wrapping her long ponytail around my fist and crashing my lips to hers. She freezes against me for a split second before melting into my touch. She pushes herself up onto her tiptoes, bringing us closer, as her arms encircle my neck.

My teeth tug at her bottom lip, and she opens for me, allowing our tongues to tangle together. I slide my free hand around her waist, arching her back and drawing her closer. At the sound of one of the guys yelling for us to get a room, we reluctantly break apart.

Dazedly, Jenny brings her fingers to her lips. "What was that?" she whispers lowly.

"That was me doing what I should have done a while ago."

"I…I don't understand. We're friends, Nate—"

"I don't wanna be your friend, GG."

Her eyes widen at my bold declaration.

"I want more, so much more. I'm so greedy for you, I'll take any little morsel you give me, but I crave all of you. I want your words, your thoughts, your laughter, I want to hold your hand and kiss you for the whole world to see. I want to give us a chance to really explore this thing between us." I suck in a ragged breath and hoarsely add, "Please tell me you want that, too?"

When tears fill her pretty green eyes, I fear I've misread everything and completely fucked up. That is, until she launches herself into me, her arms around my neck and her legs around my waist. "Yes. Really? Oh, God, yes!"

She peppers my face with little kisses, and I bask in it, feeling like king of the world. There's still a smidgen of doubt niggling at the back of my mind, telling me I'm making an irreparable mistake, but right now, I'm too happy to care.

"Let me take you to dinner tonight," I murmur into her ear. "On a date. A real date."

I set her down, and she nods, a bright beaming smile gracing not only her lips but her entire face.

Once again, I clasp her hand in mine. "You ready to get out of here?"

"Uh, yeah. In case you haven't heard, I've got myself a hot date to get ready for."

I can't help but grin. "Hell yeah, you do."

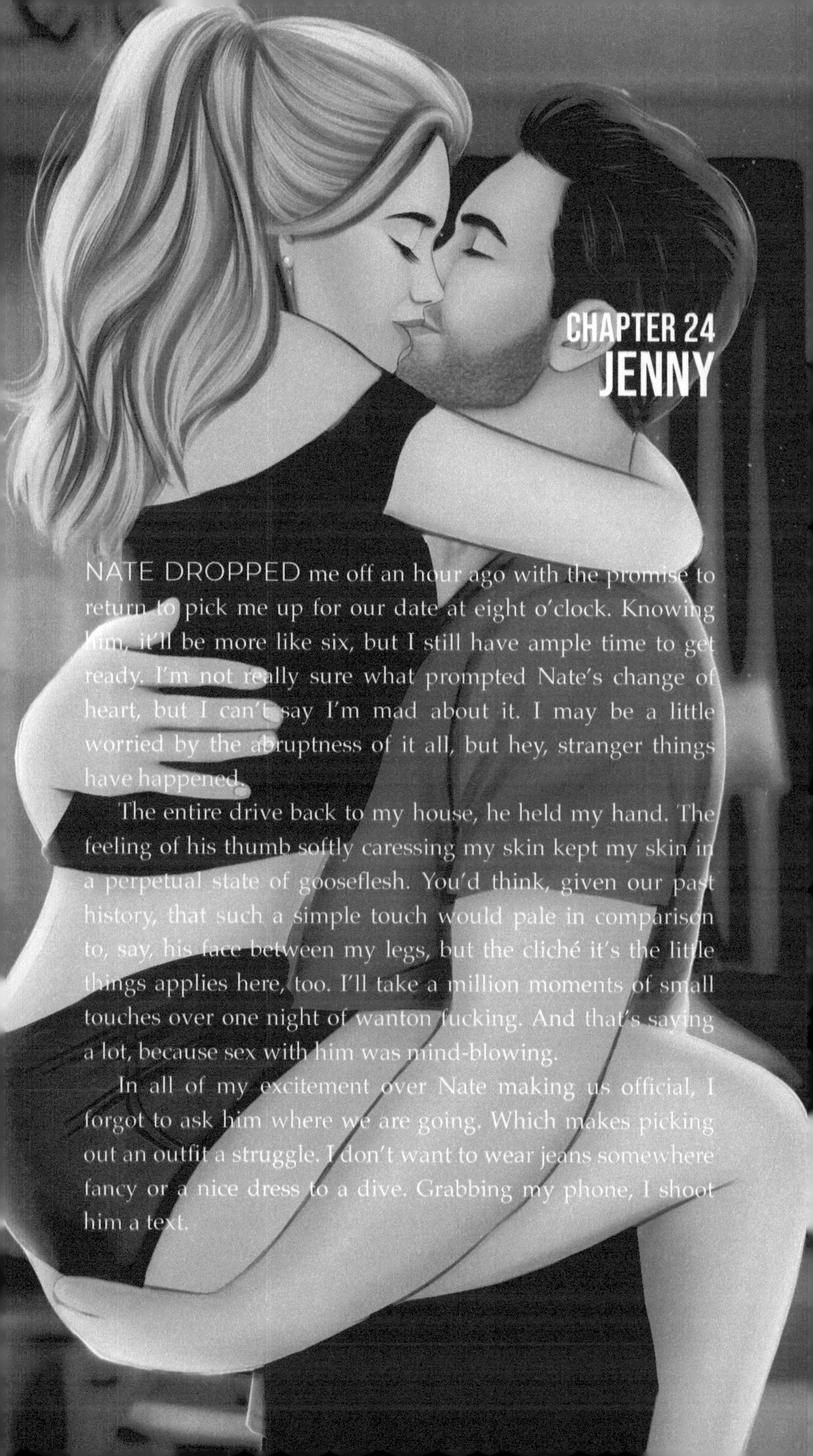

NATE DROPPED me off an hour ago with the promise to return to pick me up for our date at eight o'clock. Knowing him, it'll be more like six, but I still have ample time to get ready. I'm not really sure what prompted Nate's change of heart, but I can't say I'm mad about it. I may be a little worried by the abruptness of it all, but hey, stranger things have happened.

The entire drive back to my house, he held my hand. The feeling of his thumb softly caressing my skin kept my skin in a perpetual state of gooseflesh. You'd think, given our past history, that such a simple touch would pale in comparison to, say, his face between my legs, but the cliché it's the little things applies here, too. I'll take a million moments of small touches over one night of wanton fucking. And that's saying a lot, because sex with him was mind-blowing.

In all of my excitement over Nate making us official, I forgot to ask him where we are going. Which makes picking out an outfit a struggle. I don't want to wear jeans somewhere fancy or a nice dress to a dive. Grabbing my phone, I shoot him a text.

NATE

Hmm. Not really.

ME

Wanna tell me where we're going tonight?

ME

Okay, let me try again. *Will* you tell me?

NATE

Ask nicely. ;)

ME

Oh, Nathaniel, will you kindly divulge to me the location of tonight's dinner? I'd be ever so grateful.

NATE

Smartass. You're lucky I like you so much.

NATE

I was thinking the Black Sheep. That cool?

ME

OMG. Yes!

The fact that Nate's taking me to the Black Sheep has me slightly giddy. Their chef is a farm-to-table culinary genius. Alden tried poaching him when we took over Bayside, but Chef Macon Wright is as loyal as he is talented—which is to say very.

I've eaten there a time or two, but usually solo; sharing it with Nate has me ridiculously excited. The fact that he chose it tells me he pays attention to me and my passion for good food. It says he knows me.

Even though the food is five-star, the ambiance is low-key, which means I can dress up or down. Normally, I'd ask Jamie or Natalie for help, but tonight is special, and I want to pick my own outfit, as silly as that may be.

Flipping through the hangers on the rod in my makeshift closet, I grab a few things that I think will work. Option one: a pair of high-waisted, white shorts with black pinstripes and a black tank top. I try it on, but it's not right.

Option two: a pair of medium washed skinny jeans with an off-the-shoulder white top with fluttery sleeves. Still not what I'm going for.

Option three: a denim mini-skirt with the white top from option two tucked into it. Oh, yes, this is definitely it. I strip back out of the outfit and rehang the rejects before hopping into the shower.

Twenty minutes later, I'm lathered, conditioned, shaved, and moisturized. My hair and makeup, however, will have to wait until the mirror unfogs. Back in my bedroom, I select my shoes and accessories—brown leather wedges along with a pair of big gold hoop earrings and a few dainty bangle-style bracelets.

After another twenty minutes, give or take, and I'm dressed, my hair is styled in soft, tousled waves, and my makeup is soft and natural looking. The only thing I'm missing is a swipe of gloss across my full lips.

As predicted, Nate lets himself into my cottage a little after six o'clock. "GG, I'm hoooome!" he hollers, channeling his inner Ricky Ricardo. I know he's only being silly, but the thought of one day sharing a space with him and calling it home has those pesky bees flapping their wings.

"Whatever happened to eight?" I holler back from the kitchen.

The sound of his footsteps approaching has me turning to look his way. "Oh, wow," I murmur, taking in his appearance. It never ceases to amaze me how good looking he is, especially dressed in a pair of form-fitting khakis and a red and white plaid button-down that looks like it was tailor-made for him. "You look…"

"Thanks. You do, too." He steps closer to me, his right hand moving to grip my waist. "And I'm early tonight for the same reason I always am—because I couldn't wait another minute to see you."

I press my lips to his cheek, inhaling the spicy scent of his cologne. "Such a sweet talker."

"Only for you. Now, let's go."

The car ride is filled with mindless chatter, the kind where even though we aren't talking about anything important, it almost means more because we're learning the silly, small things about each other. For example, I am absolutely shaken when Nate divulges to me that he eats Kit-Kats as a whole instead of breaking it apart into bars. I mean, who does that? Barbarians, that's who. I think he was equally distraught when I confessed to eating my string cheese in bites instead of peeling off slivers. Look at us, a match made in weird food habits heaven.

In what feels like the blink of an eye, we're pulling into the parking lot for the Black Sheep. "You wanna check your sugar before we go in?" he asks, a soft smile on his face.

I return his smile. "Yeah, thanks."

He reaches into the back seat and grabs my purse. I retrieve my kit and quickly run through the steps of checking my sugar—it's a little high, but after the picnic this afternoon, I'm not surprised. I wasn't quite as careful as I should have been.

Once I'm finished, Nate exits the car, coming around to open my door. We're parked at the far end of the lot, which isn't shocking, given that it's a Saturday. They're jam-packed. "You think the wait's gonna be long?" I ask, looking at all of the cars between us and the building.

With a hand to the small of my back, he steers me toward the entrance. "Probably, but I made us reservations."

I stop dead in my tracks, staring up at him. "How did you make a reservation when you told me you wouldn't even be picking me up until eight?"

He shrugs. "I knew I'd be early."

Grumbling good naturedly, I say, "You better be glad I knew you'd be early, too."

Inside, Nate gives our name to the hostess, and she guides us to our table, letting us know that our server would be by shortly to take our drink orders and to tell us the specials— not that I need to know them. I know exactly what I'm getting —the pork tenderloin served with a butternut squash puree, brussel sprouts, and an apple chutney. It's what I get every time I eat here, though this time I'll probably hold the chutney due to my blood sugar being elevated.

Within seconds, our server is tableside, menus in hand, rattling off the specials. After we thank him, he takes our drink orders and promises to return with bread in hand— another thing I'll be skipping tonight, sadly.

When I make no move to pick up my menu, Nate smirks. "You already know what you're getting, don't you?"

"Yup," I say, popping the P.

"Okay. Well, wanna order for me, too?"

His request blows me away. "Really?"

"Yeah, GG. Show me what you've got."

Our server returns, and I order my meal, along with the chateaubriand—a cut of steak taken from the thickest part of the filet—served medium rare alongside asparagus and mashed potatoes with au jus.

Nate eyes me as he butters a slice of bread. "I don't know what you just ordered me, but you sounded sexy as hell doing it."

Laughing, I tell him, "It's a steak, cutie." He scowls at the use of the nickname, which only makes me laugh harder.

While we wait on our meals, the conversation flows effort- lessly. There's no awkward first-date jitters between us, which

I guess is one perk of dating someone you already know. An upside specific to Nate is him knowing about my diabetes— something I never thought I'd say. But because he's aware my sugar is elevated, there are no uncomfortable questions about why I'm only drinking water or why I'm not eating the bread. Most guys would assume it was me doing that thing girls do when they only order a salad and pick at it like a bird, but with Nate…he gets it. He gets me.

When our food arrives, we waste no time digging in, our table blanketed in silence save for the sound of our utensils scraping our plates. Nate finishes his meal first, seemingly content to watch me eat mine. If he were anyone else, I'd feel self-conscious. But judging from the way his eyes darken every time I slide the tines of the fork out from between my lips, he's got other things on his mind.

Things I have no qualms about playing into.

On my next bite, I make sure to lick at the morsel of pork before lightly placing it on my tongue, moaning exaggeratedly at the flavor. Nate's hands form fists on the tabletop as I slowly withdraw the fork from my mouth. "Oh, God, that's so good, Nate. So good." My voice comes out soft and breathy, causing his fists to clench.

"Don't push me, Jenny."

I bat my eyes at him, transforming myself into the picture of innocence. "Maybe I like pushing you."

Nate groans and my center pulses with need.

When our waiter comes to check on us, Nate whips his debit card out to pay without even seeing the check. "I mean it. I want you something fierce, and I haven't…been with anyone since you."

I stare at him, a mixture of shock and disbelief swirling through me. "Wait, what?"

"I haven't so much as touched another woman since we were together."

"You mean since I went down on you, right?" I ask, careful to keep my tone even.

Nate shakes his head back and forth. "No, I mean, since the wedding. Hell, I haven't so much as gotten myself off to thoughts of anything other than you."

My riot bees buzz to life, hope fluttering along with their wings. "But…what about…Mary and Sarah?"

"She's the receptionist for the department and old enough to be my mother. Her daughter, Sarah, had a flat tire, and her husband was caught up at work."

My eyes gloss over with moisture. "Oh, Nate. I-I assumed the worst. I'm so sorry."

"You don't need to apologize, GG. I let you believe it because it made pushing you away easier. I figured if you thought the worst of me…" He trails off brokenly.

I give him a sweet smile. "You should know by now, there's nothing you could do to make me want you less. Hell, you straight-up ignored me for almost two months, and I still wanted you."

A dark shadow crosses over his face before he wipes it away with a smile. "Lucky me."

Our server discreetly deposits the credit card slip, and Nate signs it, tucking his card back into his wallet. "Ready to go?" He pushes his chair back from the table.

"Yeah, Nate, I'm ready," I tell him, meaning it in more ways than one. I'm ready to head home. I'm ready to invite him inside and for him to hopefully stay the night. I'm ready for his touch. I'm ready to see what our future holds. I'm ready for him—to show him that he is the guy for me.

THE DRIVE back to Jenny's is delicious torture. The way she keeps glancing at me, sighing and rubbing her thighs together, has the ten-minute trip feeling like an eternity.

Unable to resist, I bring my right hand down onto her leg, just above her knee, my fingers kneading the soft skin of her thigh as I slide my hand higher. She gasps when I move beneath the hem of her skirt, teasingly running my fingers along the line of her panties, wondering if she's already wet for me.

"Jesus, Nate," she whimpers, squirming against the leather seat.

"You like that?" I ask, turning down her long driveway. "You want more?"

"Yes. God, yes." Those three words alone have me rock hard and ready.

I throw the car into park and withdraw my hand, even though it kills me. "Then invite me in."

I watch with rapt attention as she unbuckles her seat belt. My hope dwindles when she exits the car without a word and reignites when she braces her arms on the roof and leans down, her eyes boring into mine, fiercely...daringly. "Well, what're you waiting for?"

I'm unbuckled, out of the car, and sweeping her up into my arms in five seconds flat. Add another two seconds to get us up the steps and to her front door, and I've been waiting seven seconds too long.

Jenny quickly unlocks the door, and we slip inside. I waste no time spinning us, pinning her against the door as I devour her lips, tasting every inch of her mouth. She mewls, and I swallow down the noise, anxious to coax every single moan from her, desperate for the whisper of her skin on mine. I work both hands under her skirt, palming her ass and lifting her. Like the good girl she is, she wraps her legs around me, locking her ankles at the small of my back. The feel of her core pressed tightly against where I need her the most has me dizzy with want.

I kiss my way down her neck and across her shoulders— seriously love this fucking shirt she's wearing, but I'd love it more on the floor. She whimpers when I remove my lips from her skin, her hips shifting against mine, seeking friction, her desperation driving mine higher. Using the door as leverage, I lean back and strip her of her shirt and bra. The sight of her dusky pink nipples and perky breasts. They're gorgeous and, as of tonight, all mine. Unable to help myself, I reach between us and palm myself, trying to gain a modicum of control as I dip down for a taste.

I draw one tight bud into my mouth, sucking hard. "Fucking delicious." I speak the words roughly against her skin, and she bucks her hips, demanding more.

I continue my ministrations, drunk on the breathy sounds spilling from her lips...the same lips she's guiding me back up to with her fingers in my hair.

"Take me to bed, Nate. Make me feel good." Her words are a soft pleading noise that I'm helpless to resist.

I carry Jenny up the stairs to her loft, kissing my way up her neck, licking at the sweet spot behind her ear, sampling the warmth of her skin with my lips; she tastes like sweetness and sunshine and mine. When I reach the edge of her bed, I release my hold on her, allowing her to slowly slide down my body until we're standing toe-to-toe. With my forefinger, I skim her jawline before tilting her face up to mine. "Are you sure?"

"So very sure." With nimble fingers, she begins unbuttoning my shirt, causing my heart to hammer in my chest—damn, I want her. When she reaches the last one, I shrug out of it, letting it fall to the floor.

I swipe my thumb over her plump bottom lip as I take her in. Her green eyes are glazed over with lust—and some other emotion that I can't quite put a name to, but whatever it is, I like it...a lot.

Popping the button on her skirt, I tug the zipper down as I drop to my knees before her. I shimmy the skirt over her hips, revealing a pair of navy blue satin panties with a little bow at the front. As I work the denim down past her knees, allowing it to fall and pool at her feet, I notice an ivory-colored lace band snug around her left thigh.

Reverently, I skim my hands up her legs, starting at her ankles. My lips join the action at her knees, and I kiss my way up to her thighs, alternating from leg to leg. When the soft lace of her garter meets my lips, I groan. Fuuuuuck...is it weird that the piece of fabric housing her insulin pump makes me that much harder?

When my mouth reaches the apex of her thighs, I hook my fingers into her panties. "These have to go, GG."

"Yes." She hisses out the word, her head thrown back as she wiggles her hips restlessly.

I grin and slide them down her legs, where they join the growing pile of clothes on her floor. "You're so fucking sexy," I whisper as I place my lips all over her body—except where she wants them the most.

Impatient with my teasing, she urges me to stand. The second I'm upright, she attacks my lips with a fervent kiss that drives me to the brink of insanity. After what feels like an eternity, we break apart. "Get on the bed, Jenny."

It pleases me to no end when she does exactly as I say. Jenny looks so damn good, naked and ready for me, that I have to stop and stare. She's this perfect mix of innocence and seduction as she shivers under my stare. How did an undeserving jackass like me get so lucky?

"Aren't you going to join me?" she asks, trailing her hand between her breasts and down her belly, essentially snapping the final thread of my already fraying patience.

I shed my remaining clothes and crawl onto the bed between her legs—she doesn't have to ask me twice. Finally, we're skin to skin, and I groan low in my throat as she threads her fingers through my hair. I seal my lips against hers, and I can feel how ready she is for me as I thrust against her.

"Please, Nate. Please."

I roll us so she's on top, careful to not displace her pump. "Ride me," I command, expecting her to blush and go shy on me. Instead, she braces her hands on my chest and sinks down onto me. "You feel so good. So, so, good, GG."

She circles her hips in slow, controlled movements, seemingly hell-bent on driving me crazy. And, oh, God, is it working. A small moan leaves her lips, and she picks up her pace. Finally, when I can't take it a second longer, I palm her hips and guide her movements, meeting her thrust for thrust until we're both on the edge of bliss.

"Kiss me," she begs, leaning down toward me. The moment our lips meet, she clenches around me, calling out my name as she topples over the edge, with me right behind her.

Minutes later, Jenny is still slumped in a heap on my chest with my arms wrapped around her, holding her close. "I... that was...thank you, Jenny."

She stirs against me before rolling off me. I follow after her so that we're facing one another. Her once-soft curls are now a mess from my fingers, her eye makeup is smudged, and her skin glistens with a fine sheen of sweat; she's never looked more stunning than she does right now.

"Did you just thank me for fucking you?"

I pin her with a glare. "That was so much more than fucking, GG. That was...hell, I don't know, the creation of new planets or something."

Jenny laughs at my ineloquent declaration. "Yeah, cutie, you're right. That was something special." She blinks at me, words clearly forming on the tip of her tongue.

"What's on your mind?" I probe, brushing her hair from her face.

"We didn't use protection. I...I'm on the pill though, so you don't have to worry or anything."

I cringe at my thoughtlessness. "I'm so sorr—"

She cuts me off. "Don't apologize. I wanted it just as badly as you did. As long as you're clean, no worries."

"Then we're good." I drop a kiss to the tip of her nose. "Let's get cleaned up and go to bed."

Jenny pinches her eyes closed, hesitating briefly. I already know she's recalling the last time we slept together and waking up without me.

"I swear I'll be here in the morning. There's nowhere else I'd rather be."

She nods, seemingly soothed by my words. But words are only words, and I plan on proving how I feel about her through my actions.

THE FIRST THING I notice as I lazily blink myself awake is Nate's warm body ensconcing mine. I sigh happily as I commit this moment to my memory in vivid detail. And while this isn't my first time waking up with him, it's different now that we're together. Being tucked in my sheets, with sunlight filtering in through the skylight while wrapped safely in Nate's arms, is easily one of my top-five favorite things—it's up there with cute puppies, coffee, and the smell of a new book. As I lie here, my body still deliciously sore from last night, I can't help but wonder what made him change his mind about me—about us.

Yesterday, he said he wanted all of me, and I believe him; but for how long and in what capacity? Are we…together… exclusively? Is he in this for the long haul or am I a fleeting fancy?

"Jenny," he grumbles, his morning voice grating me like sex and sandpaper. "I can feel you worrying from here."

"I'm not worrying," I lie. "I'm thinking."

"About what? Talk to me."

"It's nothing."

"Don't do that—don't minimize your feelings because

you're worried about how I'll react. That's no way to start off a relationship."

"Is that…are we in a relationship?"

Nate snuggles closer to me, tucking his head into the crook of my neck. "Damn straight we are. I'm yours, and you're mine." He tilts his face toward mine and brushes his lips against my temple before sitting up. "I'm not good at this shit, Jenny, but you make me want to try. There's stuff in my past that I'm fully ready to talk about, but you make me see past all of my hurt. I'm sure I'll mess up, but don't give up on me, okay?"

The honesty of his words wraps around my heart, cocooning it with a warmth I've never felt before. "I'll always fight for you—for us. And I won't push you to talk until you're ready; plus, it's not like you killed someone." I giggle at my stupid joke, hoping to lighten the mood and let him know that I'll be patient with him.

Nate tenses beside me before forcing a laugh. "I'm gonna grab a quick shower and then we can do breakfast." He grazes my cheek tenderly with his knuckles before hopping up from the bed, naked as the day he was born.

I breathe in deeply and release it as he pads from the bed to the bathroom. My knee-jerk reaction is to worry, to assume he's hiding something, but that's exactly what I said I wouldn't do. He deserves the benefit of the doubt, and I have to trust him if we're going to grow this newly blossomed relationship into something more.

While he showers, I slip into a pair of sleep shorts and his police department shirt I never returned. Popping into the bathroom, I quickly check my sugar, wash my face, and brush my teeth. "There's a spare toothbrush under the sink. I'm gonna start breakfast."

"Sounds good," comes his gruff reply. The temptation to say screw breakfast and join him under the cascading hot water is strong, but I resist. I need to eat.

In the kitchen, I set to work on whipping up my famous avocado egg cups. With the oven preheating, I halve two avocados, removing the pits before carefully scooping a bit more out of the centers. I salt and pepper my yummy green friends before cracking an egg into the divot I created in each of them.

After I add a pinch more salt to each egg and top them with finely diced tomato, a bit of basil, and a generous sprinkle of feta cheese, into the oven they go. I set the stove timer for eighteen minutes and start a pot of coffee.

With five minutes left on the timer, Nate steps into the kitchen, dressed in only his boxers with his hair still damp. "Damn, that smells good."

I find myself a little tongue-tied at how delectable he looks. "Uh-huh."

He laughs and moves closer to where I'm seated on my lone barstool. "Cat got your tongue?"

"Something like that," I murmur as he leans down to kiss me. What started as a peck quickly ramps up to a full-on make-out, complete with over the clothes groping and a little bit of grinding.

I break away from him as the beeping timer fills the small space. "The food is ready, and there's coffee in the pot," I say lamely, my voice sounding foreign to my own ears—all soft and thick with desire.

"Good, I'm starved." His words hold a dirty promise that has me shivering with anticipation.

After we eat our breakfast, Nate makes good on his unspoken promise by eating me. Swear to all that's holy, a girl could get used to this. We spend the rest of the day lazing around, talking and touching. All in all, it's the best Sunday I've had in a very long time.

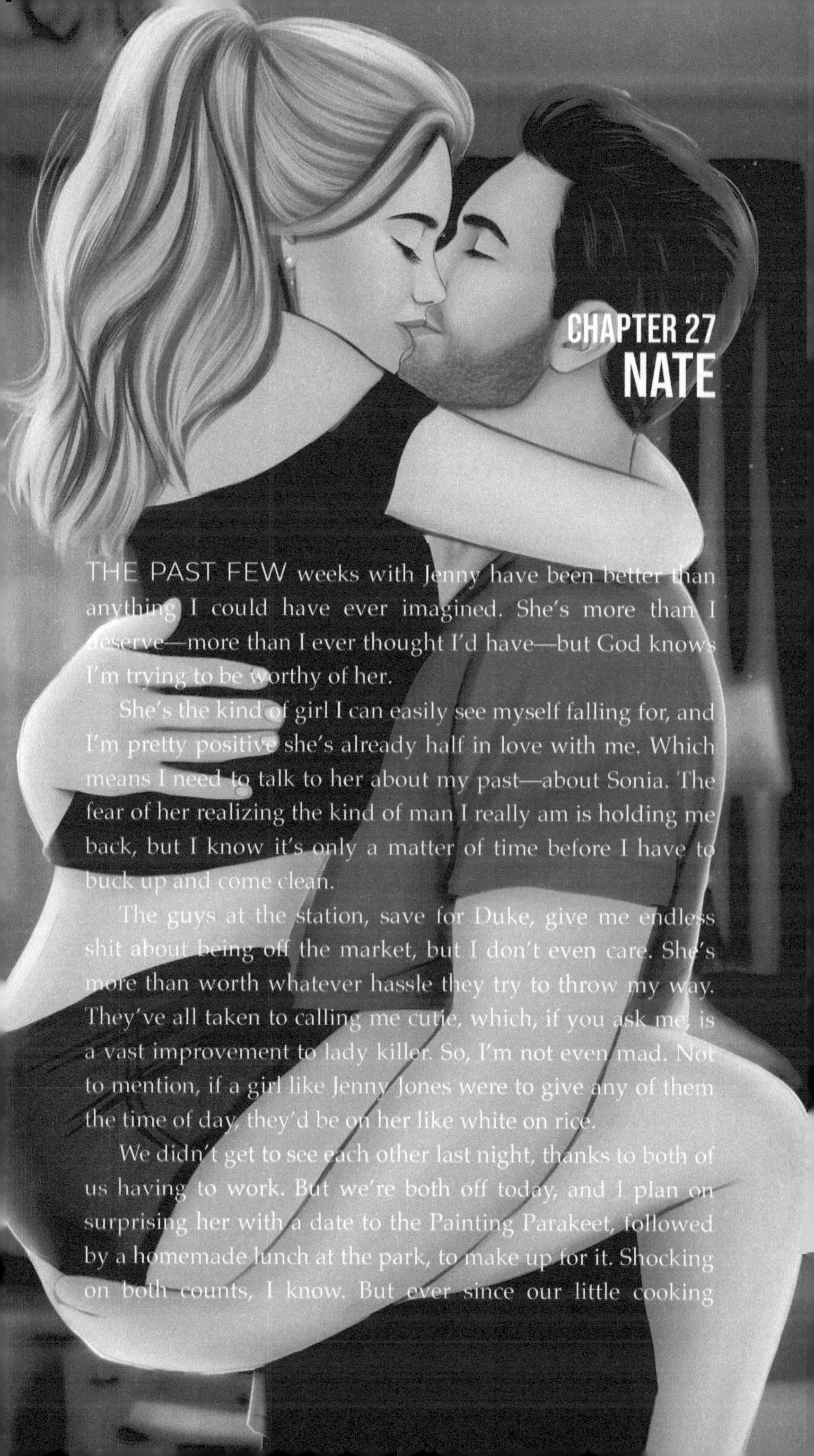

THE PAST FEW weeks with Jenny have been better than anything I could have ever imagined. She's more than I deserve—more than I ever thought I'd have—but God knows I'm trying to be worthy of her.

She's the kind of girl I can easily see myself falling for, and I'm pretty positive she's already half in love with me. Which means I need to talk to her about my past—about Sonia. The fear of her realizing the kind of man I really am is holding me back, but I know it's only a matter of time before I have to buck up and come clean.

The guys at the station, save for Duke, give me endless shit about being off the market, but I don't even care. She's more than worth whatever hassle they try to throw my way. They've all taken to calling me cutie, which, if you ask me, is a vast improvement to lady killer. So, I'm not even mad. Not to mention, if a girl like Jenny Jones were to give any of them the time of day, they'd be on her like white on rice.

We didn't get to see each other last night, thanks to both of us having to work. But we're both off today, and I plan on surprising her with a date to the Painting Parakeet, followed by a homemade lunch at the park, to make up for it. Shocking on both counts, I know. But ever since our little cooking lesson, I've stuck with it. Hell, I even bring Duke lunch twice a week now. And as for the painting crap…well, she's mentioned wanting to go a time or two, and if decorating matching coffee mugs will make her smile, then I'm down. I'll do just about anything to see her smile.

I dial her number as I sip my morning coffee. She answers on the third ring, her sleepy voice echoing through the line brings a smile to my face. "G'morning."

"Rise and shine, GG. We've got plans today."

She yawns, and I wish I was there, in bed with her, to see the sweet stretch that I know accompanies it. "We do?"

"Mmhmm. So, get ready. I'll be by to scoop you up in two hours. And before you ask, dress casual."

"What are we doing?" she asks, sounding far more alert than she did a moment ago.

"Nope. It's a surprise. See you soon." I disconnect the call before she can attempt to wrestle any details out of me.

I gulp down another mug of coffee while gathering ingredients for our lunch. Everything is diabetic friendly: I have buffalo chicken roll-ups made with low-carb tortillas, a quick broccoli slaw, and mini cheesecakes in a jar. I was on the fence over the dessert, but after some Googling—and maybe a Pinterest search or two, though I'd never admit it—I found a recipe that would fit in with Jenny's carbohydrate allowance.

Just like Jenny taught me, I use the meat from a rotisserie chicken for my roll-ups, folding it in with my cream cheese, ranch seasoning, and buffalo sauce mixture. I add a handful of shredded cheddar, skipping over the blue cheese that the recipe calls for, because I know my girl doesn't care for it.

I divide and spread the mixture over six tortillas—another Jenny lesson, leftovers are a godsend during a busy week— before rolling each one tightly and wrapping it with plastic wrap. Technically, I'm supposed to refrigerate them for twenty-four hours before slicing…here's to hoping that an hour and a half is sufficient.

While the wraps chill, I whip up the slaw and start on the cheesecake jars. Everything's coming together nicely when my phone buzzes to life on the counter with Natalie's ringtone. "Little sister. To what do I owe the pleasure?"

Her panicked voice bleats out, "Please tell me you can watch Tatum? I honestly don't know who else to call. I tried Jenny, but she didn't answer."

"Nat, take a breath. Slow down and tell me what's wrong."

She releases a shuddery exhale. "Alden's setting up at Taste of the Bay, and I need to go down and help him, but Mom and Dad both have the flu!"

"What is Taste of the Bay?"

"It's like a culinary who's who. It's being taped and everything. They're gonna air it tomorrow morning on the local news. I can't bring Tatum. Please tell me you can watch her. Please?"

My excitement over today dwindles. As much as I'd like to tell my sister I'm busy, I'd never leave her in a lurch where my niece is concerned. "Yeah, Nat. Give me twenty minutes, and I'll be there."

"Oh my God. Thank you!" The relief in her voice eases my disappointment. Besides, spending time with Tatum always brings a smile to my face.

Downside: now I have to break the news to Jenny. Phone still in hand, I redial her number. This time, she answers on the first ring. "Oh my God. Nate Reynolds, if you're calling to tell me you're already here, I'm gonna freak!"

I sigh. "I'm not. I'm actually calling to cancel."

"Oh," comes her dejected reply. "Is everything okay?"

"Yeah, Natalie called me just now—she's in a pinch and needs someone to watch Tatum." An idea pops into my head. "Hey, why don't you come with me?"

"To babysit?"

"Mmhmm. You've watched Tatum before, and she loves

you. Not to mention, I'll still get to see you. Really, it's a win-win."

She mulls over my offer for a minute. "Yeah, that sounds good."

"Toss your swimsuit into your bag; I'm on my way."

After I rinse my mug in the sink, I trek back to my room and dress in my swimming trunks and a T-shirt with the sleeves cut off. On my way back to the kitchen, I grab my ice chest from the back of the hall closet so I can pack up the lunch I made—no need for it to go to waste just because our plans have changed.

———

Thirty minutes later, Jenny and I are strolling up to my sister's front door. I ring the bell, and the door flies open, revealing a very flustered Natalie. "Oh, thank God you're—" Her words evaporate when she sees Jenny at my side, her fingers interlaced with mine.

"Uh, I'm gonna need someone to explain this right quick." She doesn't sound mad. Hell, if the smile stretching across her face is anything to go off of, she's thrilled. Confused, but thrilled.

"Not too much to explain, little sister. I dig her, she digs me. We decided to give this thing a go."

It's at that moment Tatum comes flying up to the door. "Uncle Nate! Miss Jenny! Are y'all talking 'bout digging? Because I'm real good at making holes. Big ones! One time, I even found creepy, crawly worms!"

Jenny ducks her head behind my shoulder to hide her smile while I let out a loud laugh. "Oh, Tater Tot. Not that kind of digging."

Tatum pouts for all of five seconds before honing on Jenny's hand in mine. "Is Miss Jenny your girlfriend? Do you love her? Are you gonna marry her? Y'all should make a baby. I keep asking Mama and Daddy to, but they just smile and change the subject. But babies are awesome. Will y'all make one? I'll even babysit!" Now it's Jenny and Natalie laughing while I practically choke on my own spit.

"Slow down, kid, we just started dating."

Tatum's big brown eyes widen. "She is your girlfriend! Mama was Daddy's girlfriend before they got married. So that means y'all's gonna get married, too!"

A few months ago, the very same thought would have had me running for the hills, but now…now it doesn't seem so farfetched. Truth be told, I could easily see myself putting a ring on Jenny's finger—you know, way on down the line.

"Hey, Tatum," Jenny cuts in, finally finding her voice. "You wanna run and throw on your swimsuit, and we can swim?"

"Yes!" Tatum screeches, taking off toward the stairs like a bat out of hell—or a toddler out of a candy store.

"Thanks, GG," I murmur in her ear before addressing Natalie. "Go on, we've got this. I even packed lunch."

My sister's brows lift. "You made lunch?"

I nod proudly. "Yep. This one taught me a thing or two about cooking, and now it's a regular occurrence at Casa de Reynolds."

Natalie looks impressed. "Well, I never thought I'd see the day." From somewhere in the house, the sound of her cell phone trilling steals her attention. "Gah! I've got to go. You both know the drill and how to reach me. Y'all have fun!"

She darts back inside to gather her stuff, pausing only long enough to hug and kiss Tatum goodbye before she's out the door and on her way.

"So, we're really gonna play in the pool?" Tatum asks Jenny. "Do you know how to swim with your head under the water? Daddy's trying to teach me, but I'm scared."

Jenny smiles at Tatum's over-the-top enthusiasm. "We

sure are, just as soon as I change, and yes, ma'am, I can—I can even do a handstand under the water."

Tatum stares up at Jenny with something akin to hero worship in her eyes. "Hurry, Miss Jenny! Hurry!"

Jenny smiles and ruffles Tatum's hair before setting off down the hall to the half bath to get changed. "C'mon, Tater Tot. Think you can grab us some towels while I stick our lunch in the fridge?"

Without another word, Tatum darts off down the hall.

The three of us reconvene on the back deck, me with three bottles of water, Tatum with three towels, and Jenny with a bottle of sunblock—oh, shit. My mind flashes back to the Memorial Day picnic, but I will the thoughts away. I will not get hard in front of my niece.

Tatum and I wade into the shallow end while Jenny hangs back. She hesitates briefly before unknotting the sash of her cover-up, revealing her beautiful body clad in only an olive green bikini. She slides her pump from the pocket of her cover-up and fiddles with it for a second before disconnecting the tube from where it inserts into her abdomen.

"What's that thing on your tummy?" Tatum asks with all the finesse of a child—which isn't much—as Jenny descends the pool steps to join us.

I tense up, worried about how Jenny will react. But my girl responds with ease and grace, taking the time to explain her disease to Tatum in a way that she'll understand. She patiently answers all of her questions and as I watch how absolutely amazing she is with my niece, I swear I fall a little bit in love with her.

Time seems to pass in a blur as we splash and play in the water. Jenny demonstrates her handstand for Tatum no less than fifty times, but I'm not complaining, because with every dive down, I get a great view of her legs.

After a while, Jenny's pump lets out a series of beeps. "Everything good?" I ask as she swims toward the steps.

"Yep. Just time for me to reconnect. It alerts me when I've had my delivery suspended after twenty minutes." She dries off and reconnects her pump. "Why don't y'all keep swimming, and I'll grab the food you brought?"

Tatum squeals her approval over Jenny's plan as she doggy-paddles in circles around me.

A few minutes later, Jenny returns with the food I made, plus a PB&J for Tatum, which is smart thinking on her part; the kid may have a sophisticated palate, but the roll-ups pack some serious burn. After lunch, the three of us head inside and cuddle up on the couch to watch a movie, which is exactly how Alden and Natalie find us an hour or so later.

I'M NOT REALLY sure why Nate was so gung-ho on him not being the guy for me, because these last few weeks have been some of the best of my life. Not only is Nate an insatiable beast in bed, he's also caring and kind and attentive in the day-to-day stuff.

For example, last Thursday he knew I was running late for work at Bayside thanks to a late night at Bennet's—and an even later night with him—and damn if he and Duke didn't roll up to the café in their cruiser just to bring me a coffee.

Sweetness aside, we still haven't really delved into either one of our pasts...especially his. If this thing between us is going to work, we need total transparency. You can't build a stable foundation off of secrets and half-truths, and I know he's keeping something from me.

He has these moments where he seems to get lost in his shadows, and that's fine, but how can I help guide him back into the light if I don't know what I'm up against? Which is why I plan on sitting down and flat-out asking him tonight.

We're both off today, and I figure maybe we can go down to the pier and walk along the shore, and then I can cook for him at his place...ply him with some good food and hope like hell he opens up to me.

With a plan in place, I pick up my phone and call him.

"GG," he rumbles into the phone after the second ring. The sound of his deep voice—mmm—I wonder if it will always make my core ache and my nipples pebble?

"Hey, cutie. Whatcha up to today?"

"Honestly? I feel like there's something I'm supposed to do today, but I can't remember what for the life of me. What about you?"

I quickly fill him in on my hopeful plans for us, and he readily agrees. We aren't meeting until two, so that gives me some time to do a little light cleaning and to grab some groceries—for the week and dinner tonight.

Around one-thirty, I toss the ingredients for tonight into an insulated bag and head down toward the bay. A quick scan of the parking lot tells me that Nate's already here, and as luck would have it, there's an open parking spot next to him.

Nate sees me immediately and hops out of his car, coming to open my door for me. He greets me with a scorching, not-appropriate-for-public kiss and a swat to my ass before we head down toward the shore.

We leave our shoes under a shady oak tree and walk hand-in-hand at the coastline, letting the wake of the lapping waves tickle our toes. Everything about this moment is so perfect. My heart feels bubbly and full, and my soul feels light and content.

Here's to hoping these good feelings remain after tonight.

———

NATE

Today with Jenny, like every day with her at my side, has been amazing. She not only makes me laugh, she challenges me and makes me strive to be the man she deserves. But what it really comes down to is—do I deserve her? While my heart says yes, my brain screams no.

To make matters worse, I've had this niggling feeling all day in the back of my mind that I'm forgetting something important. I just don't know what. I've been so wrapped up in the goddess slaving away over dinner in my kitchen that everything else in my life—save for family and work—almost seems inconsequential.

I offered to help her cook, but she shooed me to the living room, saying she wanted to surprise me. Being the shit that I am, I keep hoping maybe she'll surprise me by offering herself up as the main course.

The thought alone is enough to have my cargo shorts fitting a little too snug in the crotch. I flick on the television, intent on distracting myself while I wait. I channel surf before finally landing on some sci-fi show that looks mildly promising.

By the second commercial break, I'm hooked, and plotting ways to get Jenny to binge the series with me from the start.

Two things happen as the credits roll—Jenny calls out to tell me dinner is ready, and my phone buzzes with an incoming text. A quick glance at my home screen tells me it's Duke. But with a hot plate of food and an even hotter woman waiting for me in the next room, I slide my phone into my pocket with his text unanswered; I can see what he needs later.

On my kitchen table is a spread fit for a king—seared chicken breasts topped with what I now know is a balsamic glaze, served with roasted red potatoes and asparagus, plus a salad. "Damn, GG, this smells amazing."

She gives a humble shrug. "Thanks. Let's eat while it's hot."

Her stilted response gives me pause. My girl's acting weird. "Everything good?" I ask, spearing a bite of salad into my mouth.

She worries her bottom lip between her teeth before slowly nodding. "Yup. Totally fine."

Red flags wave and sirens blare at her use of the dreaded F-word. Everyone knows that when a woman says fine, she's anything but.

Calmly, I set down my utensils, focusing all of my attention on her. "Talk to me. What's wrong?"

"It's nothing. Not really. I…just…"

"You just what?" I try and stave off the worry that threatens to settle in my gut like lead.

"I was hoping we could talk about…" She trails off again, glancing around the room as if she's expecting some kind of divine intervention. "About why you were so adamant about not being the guy for me. Don't get me wrong—I'm so-so-so glad you changed your mind, I just want to know why and what made you hold back at first. I just want to know you, Nate. All of you."

My phone buzzes again in my pocket, and I'm more tempted than ever to ignore her in favor of it. But she deserves the truth, even if it kills what we have—pun intended.

"Shit, Jenny," I sigh.

"If…if you want, I'll tell you about my baggage and stuff first?"

I snort. What baggage could this girl possibly have? As soon as I think it, I regret it. I'm not that guy—comparing hurts gets you nowhere.

Judging from the pained look on Jenny's pretty face, she read my shitty thoughts loud and clear. Fuck. This day is spiraling from good to bad quick, fast, and in a hurry.

"It's…it's fine. Never mind." She pushes her chair back from the table, snatches up her half-eaten plate, and scrapes the food into the trashcan.

My phone buzzes again.

"I think I'm gonna clean up and head out. We can talk tomorrow."

I feel helpless. I know I need to get my ass up and go to her—to talk to her, to explain—but I remain frozen in my seat.

With robotic movements, she packages up the leftovers. As she loads the dishwasher, my phone vibrates again. "Might wanna get that," she mumbles.

Resigned, I pull it from my pocket. Duke has texted me four times now.

DUKE

Hey, man. Call me…

DUKE

Please.

DUKE

I miss her. Fuck, I miss her.

DUKE

I need you.

Hastily, I toggle out of my texts and over to my calendar app to check the date. Oh, shit. No. Suddenly the weight of what today is crashes around me like a tidal wave. I've been so caught up in Jenny that I completely forgot.

"I…I've gotta go. We'll talk soon—tomorrow—something. Lock up." I damn near sprint to my car, leaving a very confused Jenny behind in my kitchen. It's a shitty thing to do, but I'm caught between a rock and a hard place here, and I know Duke needs me more.

———

I drive like a bat out of hell on my way to Duke's, repeatedly calling him, only to get his voicemail every time. It feels like I hit every single red light as worst-case scenarios flash through my brain.

When I pull up to his place, I don't bother parking neatly at the curb—nah, I pull haphazardly into the grass and fly out of my car without even pulling the keys from the ignition.

I pound on his front door hard enough to shake the frame, but he doesn't answer. Fuck, fuck, fuck. Testing the knob, I find it's unlocked. "Duke?" I yell his name, but he doesn't answer.

Panic grips me as I venture farther into his house. "Duke, goddamn it!" The house is dark and eerily quiet—where in the hell is he? I move through the house methodically, clearing each room as if I'm searching for a perp.

As I near the master bedroom, the sound of broken sobs has me on high alert. I shoulder open the partially closed door and step into the dark space. Light spills through from under the bathroom door and I rap my knuckles over the frame before stepping into the space.

The sight of Duke—my partner, one of my best friends—lying in a crumpled heap on the bathroom floor, a half-empty liter of Jack by his side and a pill bottle in his hands, has the small amount of dinner I ate threatening to come back up.

"N-Nate," he slurs. "Y-you came."

I drop to my knees and shift him so that his head is in my lap and pry the bottle from his hands. "Fuck. Are you—how many did you take?"

Duke shakes his head back and forth, mumbling incoherently as his tears soak my shorts. It fucking kills me to see this man—this stoic, behemoth of a man—so broken.

"I need to know. C'mon, man. Talk to me." My tone toes the line between panic and calm.

After a few gut-wrenching moments, his sobs ebb, and he clumsily moves to a semi-upright position. "N-none. F-fucking none."

Relief rushes through me. Thank. Fuck. "Good."

He shakes his head. "N-nothing's good without V-Val. She left and t-took my light with her."

"You being here is good. I know every day without her hurts, brother, but you're still here, and we both know she wouldn't want this for you."

"I miss her," he whispers brokenly as a fresh round of tears start. "I'm al-always so goddamn s-strong for everyone else. Always p-putting them first. I just want her back."

I stand and start the shower for him. "C'mon, D. Let's get you sober." Using the ledge of the tub, he pulls himself to standing. He staggers to me, and I guide him under the spray fully dressed. "I'm gonna start a pot of coffee. Holler if you need me."

He braces himself against the tiled shower wall and nods. I turn to leave, but he calls out to me. "Dump the Jack."

I nod and head out to the kitchen, swiping the bottle as I exit.

As I start the coffee pot, I can't help but imagine all of the different ways tonight could have played out; while I'm glad he's okay, it doesn't ease the guilt over not being there for him when he needed me.

Fifteen minutes later, Duke drags himself into the kitchen, immediately slumping down onto a barstool. I pour him a mug of coffee and slide it over to him. "I'm sorry I wasn't here, man. I—"

He waves me off. "My shit's not your shit."

I slam a fist down onto the island. "That's where you're wrong. You're more than my partner. You're my brother. Your shit will always be my shit. You're a tank for everyone in your life—let me carry some of your weight when it gets to be too much."

Duke sips his coffee, letting my words soak in. "When will it stop hurting? Some days I feel like my old self, and other days, I keep expecting her to walk through the damn door."

I shrug. "Wish I knew."

WHAT IN GOD'S name just happened? is all I can think as I finish picking up the kitchen. And how lame am I? Nate all but runs out on me, and here I am worried about leaving behind a mess.

No, you know what? Fuck him. He can clean his own damn kitchen. Did I push him too hard, too soon? Maybe. But that doesn't give him the right to just up and leave like that.

But I guess that's the Nate Reynolds's way—when the going gets tough, run like hell.

Angry tears wet my cheeks as I debate my next move. I don't want to be alone right now, but I don't know where to go, so I drive aimlessly, trying to figure out how everything went so wrong.

Before I know it, I find myself turning down Natalie's street. Guess my driving isn't so aimless after all. Can I really talk to her about this, though? Laying this burden on her would be like trapping her between a rock and a hard place—how selfish would I be to expect her to rally behind me when her brother is involved?

Then again, maybe that's exactly what I need—someone to help me see his side.

Mind made up, I turn into the driveway and dial her number.

The phone rings twice before her voice floats through the line. "Hey, girl, what's up?"

"Hey," I whisper, hating how broken I sound. Somewhere between Nate's and here, my anger morphed to sadness.

Natalie immediately goes on high alert. "Jenny, are you okay?"

"No. I'm in your driveway. Can I come in?"

A few seconds later the porch light turns on, flooding the yard with its bright glow. "Of course. Alden just unlocked the door, let yourself in."

I end the call and check my phone, hoping to find a missed call or text from Nate, but of course, there's nothing.

I enter the house quietly, not wanting to wake Tatum in case she's sleeping. Following the sound of low talking, I find my best friend and her husband in the kitchen. They both look up when I enter the room, and Natalie immediately rushes over to me, wrapping me in a tight hug, which only makes me cry harder.

"Oh, babe, what happened?"

Alden excuses himself to the living room, and I recount the events that led me here. Like the good friend she is, Natalie listens without interrupting, even though I can clearly see she has something to say. When I finally finish spilling my guts, she pulls me into her arms again, offering her comfort.

"I don't know how to fix this, Nat. Did I push him too hard? Was I too needy?"

Natalie pours us both a glass of wine. "I wish I could say. Nate…he's complicated. He has layers, like an onion."

Even though I feel miserable, I laugh. "Did you just Shrek me?"

She shrugs, her lips tipped up in a small grin. "Maybe. But it fits."

"Why is he so closed off? What…what happened to make him that way?"

Natalie sips her wine before replying. "It's not really my story to tell."

"I know. Believe me, I know. And under normal circumstances, I'd never ask you to betray his confidence, but, Nat…" My voice breaks as a fresh round of tears start. "He's the best thing to ever happen to me, and he's slipping away. I-I don't want to lose him."

My best friend massages her temples. "Lord, don't let this blow up in my face," she mutters under her breath but still loud enough for me to hear her.

"In college, Nate had this on-again, off-again girlfriend. Their relationship, according to him, wasn't much to write home about. She thought she was in love with him and was way more serious about their relationship and future together than he was. Nate thought they were on the same page—that she knew he didn't want to settle down until after school. Now, I'm not sure if he led her on, or if it was all in her head; turns out she suffered from bipolar disorder.

"But things got really bad, and she tried to take her own life when he ended things between them. Honestly, he kind of shut down when it happened, and I know he harbors a lot of guilt over the way things went down."

"How awful," I murmur. Suddenly his staunch anti-relationship stance makes sense. "I can't even imagine."

"It was rough, and Alden wasn't here at the time—he'd already moved off to Europe—so he was all alone to wade through the aftermath. Only, instead of rising to the surface and moving on, he found himself caught in his grief like quicksand."

My heart aches for him, but I also can't help but wonder what this means for us. "What do I do, Natalie?"

"Do you love him?" she asks, bluntly, and I nod; there's no point in denying it. "I thought so. Unfortunately, all I can suggest is to be patient. I know that's probably not what you wanted to hear, but it's all I've got. Nate's like a wild cat—you back him into a corner and he's bound to attack."

I don't reply, because really, what is there to say? Instead, I pull out my phone and text Nate.

Me: I'm sorry about tonight. Please let me know you're okay.

I stare at my screen, willing him to reply, but nothing comes through.

"You wanna crash here?" Natalie asks.

I nod, not trusting my voice.

"There are fresh sheets on the guest bed. I'll see you in the morning, okay?"

With one last parting hug, she goes off in search of her husband, and I head upstairs. I fall asleep with my cell phone clutched to my chest.

Nate never texts me back.

AFTER ANOTHER NIGHT of tossing and turning, I'm dragging ass as I get ready for work. It's been two days since everything between Jenny and me imploded. And as much as I want to rage and lash out, I know I have no one to blame but myself.

She's texted me a few times, but I can't bring myself to reply. I mean, what's the point...what the fuck would I even say?

I zone out for most of roll call and do the minimum in inspecting our patrol car. I'm a fucking mess today; I'm caught in this downward spiral, and I don't know how to escape it.

After Duke radios us in as 10-8, he wastes no time laying into me. "What's your deal? You've been a mess ever since the other night."

"Don't know what you're talking about," I grunt back.

"Bullshit, brother. Start talking."

I scrub a hand over my face. "Some shit went down with Jenny, and we haven't really talked in two days. I don't know what to do or how to fix it."

Duke chuckles. "That depends. What'd you do?"

"I was so caught up in her, I completely forgot about the

anniversary of…" I let him fill in the blank. "We were having dinner, and you were texting me, and I fucking ignored you. You needed me, and I straight-up ignored you. All these what-ifs keep swirling through my head and fuck."

"I don't blame you. Trust me, if Val was here and I was with her, and you texted me, I'd probably ignore your ass, too. It's easy for the love of a good woman to blind you a bit. Doesn't make you a bad friend—it makes you human, Nate."

"That's not all. She was pressing me to talk about our pasts, saying she wanted to know me better. I froze up and then ditched her to come to you."

"Oh, shit. Yeah, you're in the doghouse now, huh?"

I let out a longsuffering sigh. "Nah, more like the pound. I haven't talked to her since that night."

Without warning, Duke pulls the car off onto the shoulder. "I'm gonna be real straight with you. Girls like Val and Jenny, they only come around once in a lifetime. If you love her, or even think you could love her, you need to buck up, talk to her, and make things right. Because, brother, you never know when someone's gonna be taken away permanently."

———

Duke's words about losing Jenny for good have been ringing in my ears all day. I desperately want to reach out—to text or call her—but I don't know what to say. So, like a dumbass, I say nothing and continue stewing in my guilt and regret.

I'm on my sixth beer when I finally give in and text her.

ME

I miss you.

ME

I fucked up.

ME

But you already know that.

I watch my phone like a hawk, but she never answers. Not that I even deserve a response.

Somewhere between beer seven or eight, there's a knock on my door. Who the fuck? I sink further into the couch and raise the bottle to my lips—whoever it is can wait.

Then Jenny's sweet voice reaches my ears. "Nate, open the door. Please. I know you're home."

I do a quick recount of the empty bottles on the coffee table—I haven't drunk nearly enough to be hearing things. So…that must mean…Jenny's really here.

She knocks again, and I stumble to the door, flinging it open. "Jenny." Her name passes my lips like a prayer.

"Can I come in?"

I open the door wider, and she steps in, her sweet scent scrambling my already-cloudy senses as she passes me.

I follow behind her, wondering why on earth she's here. She claims the chair, leaving me alone on the couch.

"Are you…sober enough to talk?"

Involuntarily, I scoff. "Sure am."

She looks wary. "'Kay. I got your texts, but my phone died. Nate, what…where do we stand?"

I shake my head, searching for the right words. "I-I dunno."

She sucks in a deep breath. "I need to tell you something."

Immediately, I'm tense, assuming the worst. "What?"

"The other night, I…talked to Natalie. She told me about you and—"

I cut her off. "She told you about what?"

"About your college girlfriend," she whispers, her voice small.

"So, instead of waiting for me to open up, you ran to my sister to get the dirty details? Is that it?" My voice is hard, angry—though I'm not entirely sure why.

"I didn't mean to go behind your back or break your trust."

"Oh, so you accidentally asked Natalie, is that it? Did she accidentally tell you that I was such a selfish, careless prick that I drove Sonia to try and take her own life?"

Jenny whimpers. "N-Nate, that…it wasn't your fault."

I laugh bitterly, sure Sonia's parents said she suffered from mental illness, but I know I'm the bastard who drove her to it. "You really fucking believe that? Are you that naive?"

"I may be inexperienced, but I'm not naive. You're so determined to be the bad guy, so intent on keeping me out—"

"Because I'm fucking trying to protect you!" I roar. "Because I don't want to ruin you like I did her!"

Tears run down Jenny's cheeks. "Don't you get it? You can't ruin me, Nate. The only thing you're ruining is us. You're shutting me out and not even giving us a chance."

"We never had a chance."

She springs up from the chair. "That's a load of shit, and you know it! It's funny, when Natalie and I talked the other night, she compared you to a wild cat—but you're more like the cowardly lion."

"Oh, so not wanting to hurt you makes me a coward?"

Jenny shakes her head at me, like she's thoroughly disappointed in me—yeah, well, welcome to the club. "You're already hurting me." She moves closer to me, dropping to her knees at my feet, bracing her hands on my knees. "I love you, Nate, do you hear me? I. Love. You. And I think you love me, too, but we'll never be anything if you don't find a way to get some closure."

I shake out of her hold, and she stumbles back, catching herself on the coffee table. The hurt in her pretty green eyes is almost too much to bear, but I press on. She's better off without me. "You don't love me—you hardly know me."

My venom-filled words seem to do the trick.

"What? You don't know how I feel. Please don't do this. Let me help you, Nate."

I pin her with a cold glare. "Go home, Jenny."

She stands, staring me down like a soldier going off to war. "If I walk out that door, I'm done, Nate. I truly do love you, but I love me more."

As much as it kills me, I nod and say, "Just go."

Without another word, she turns and leaves, the door slamming in her wake.

"Such a clusterfuck," I mutter to myself as I grab another beer. Regret over sending her away claws at me from the inside, but she deserves more than I'll ever be able to give her.

———

Jenny's words about closure echo through my mind. Fueled by regret and way too much alcohol, I find myself doing the one thing I swore to myself I never would. I look up Sonia's Facebook page.

My phone trembles in my grip as I try and type her name in the search bar. It takes me a few tries to get her name right, but nothing comes up. After a few more tries, I remember that I blocked her way back when everything went down, at the request of her parents. I feel kind of shitty unblocking her, but…I have to know—I need to know how she's doing now.

I chug down the remainder of my umpteenth beer as her profile loads. The room spins and my gut churns as I attempt to prepare myself for what I might find. What's that fucking saying…prepare for the worst, hope for the best? But what I find shocks me more than anything I ever could've imagined —and I've imagined plenty over the years.

Sonia—the girl I thought I broke—is not only doing well,

she's fucking thriving. Married, with a kid, and another on the way, from the looks of it.

Jesus. My phone clatters to the floor.

All these years, I've spent drowning in my guilt, and she's fine—healthy and happy. Don't get me wrong, I'm fucking thrilled to know she's doing well…to know I didn't ruin her life.

Nah, the only thing I ruined was my future with Jenny.

Jenny. My Jenny. Not your Jenny, my brain shouts. Not anymore.

I click around on Sonia's profile a little more when I notice her chat icon is green, meaning she's online. Before I can over-think it, I message her.

ME

Long time no talk. I won't bother you, but I wanted to…fuck, I don't know what I wanted. I guess to make sure you're okay. That your life is good. That you're…happy.

I don't expect a reply, so imagine my surprise when those three little bubbles bounce across the screen.

SONIA

Whoa! No kidding it's been a while. I'm doing really well, Nate. I actually tried looking you up a year or two ago. But I couldn't find you. I owe you an apology. As you know, I was diagnosed with bipolar disorder in high school. What you don't know is when I got a taste of freedom in college, I quit taking my meds. I thought I could manage without them…clearly, I was wrong. I hope you don't blame yourself for anything that happened, though judging by your late-night message, I'm guessing that's not the case. We were practically kids, Nate. Stupid, reckless kids. I think about you often. I hope you're living your life to the fullest. I know I am. I've been married to Kent for three amazing years, and we're expecting our second son any day now. Anyway, I'm rambling. I hope you're well. 🖤

I read her message three times before replying.

ME

Thank you.

Jenny was right; I needed closure. Only, I'm pretty sure it's come a little too late. Backing out of Sonia's profile, I bring up my contacts and call Jenny. It goes directly to voicemail, so I leave a message after the beep.

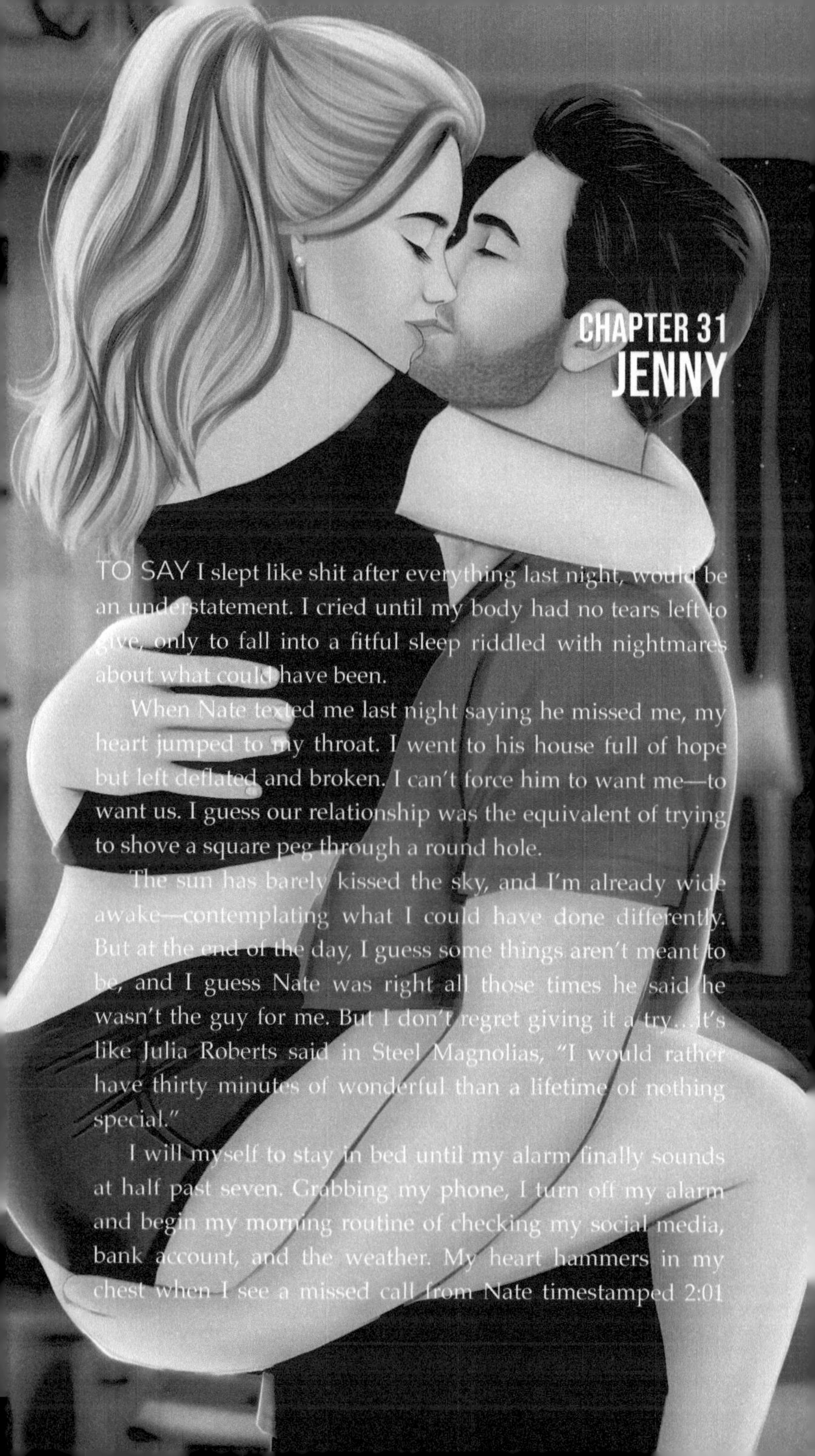

TO SAY I slept like shit after everything last night, would be an understatement. I cried until my body had no tears left to give, only to fall into a fitful sleep riddled with nightmares about what could have been.

When Nate texted me last night saying he missed me, my heart jumped to my throat. I went to his house full of hope but left deflated and broken. I can't force him to want me—to want us. I guess our relationship was the equivalent of trying to shove a square peg through a round hole.

The sun has barely kissed the sky, and I'm already wide awake—contemplating what I could have done differently. But at the end of the day, I guess some things aren't meant to be, and I guess Nate was right all those times he said he wasn't the guy for me. But I don't regret giving it a try...It's like Julia Roberts said in Steel Magnolias, "I would rather have thirty minutes of wonderful than a lifetime of nothing special."

I will myself to stay in bed until my alarm finally sounds at half past seven. Grabbing my phone, I turn off my alarm and begin my morning routine of checking my social media, bank account, and the weather. My heart hammers in my chest when I see a missed call from Nate timestamped 2:01

a.m.—that definitely wasn't there when I placed my phone on Do Not Disturb last night.

When I see he also left a voicemail, my body fills with a mixture of hope and dread. What could he possibly have to say after last night? Did he call to apologize or to dig the knife deeper?

Only one way to find out…

I take a deep breath and press play. "Jenny. I fucked up. You…you were right. D-don't give up on me."

I listen to the stupid message twice, trying to read between the lines for some hidden and undecipherable message, but I come up empty every time. What does he mean don't give up on him? He's the one who gave up on us. He's the one who decided that clinging to past hurts was better than working toward any future we could have had.

He's the one who gave up. Not me. But even still, hope flutters softly in my gut.

———

NATE

I wake groggy and hungover and sore as fuck—that's what passing out on the living room floor gets you when you're pushing thirty, I guess. But I also feel a little bit lighter than I did the day before. That is, until I remember I no longer have Jenny. I need to find a way to convince her to give me another chance—just one more chance. Not that I deserve one.

But before I can formulate any kind of plan to win my girl back, I desperately need to shower.

As the scalding water pelts down on me, I rack my brain for ways to get back into Jenny's good graces. Too bad I keep coming up blank. Maybe coffee will help.

Spoiler alert…coffee doesn't help either. I'm completely drawing a blank still; probably the universe's way of telling me to leave her alone, that I've hurt her enough. But if I've learned anything in the past twenty-four hours, it's better to try than to live with regrets over the unknown.

I also realize that if I'm going to formulate any kind of plan, I need reinforcements. Natalie was willing to help Jenny; here's to hoping she's willing to help me as well.

Fifteen minutes later, I'm knocking on my sister's door, donuts in hand—it's the least I can do, showing up here unannounced before eight o'clock in the morning.

After a few minutes, I knock again a little harder and the door swings open to reveal my scowling sister, wrapped in her robe, with a cup of coffee in hand.

I brush past her and head straight for the kitchen. "Please, come in," she mutters sarcastically in my wake.

"Who was at the—oh, hey, man," Alden says when he sees me. "Coffee?"

I nod and help myself to a mug.

Natalie joins us and gets right to the point. "What brings you by so early?"

"Can't a guy just want to spend time with his baby sister and his best friend?"

Hands on her hips, she gives me the same glare our mom gave us growing up when she knew we were lying to her.

"Fine. It's…about Jenny." Her eyes soften, and a guilty look blankets her features. "I already know you told her about Sonia. I'm not mad—well, I am mad, but not at you."

"I'm guessing things didn't go well?"

I laugh dryly. "Understatement of the century. I was a few beers deep when she came by last night, and when she brought up Sonia, I got defensive and spewed a bunch of bullshit her way. She…she told me she loved me, and I pretty much told her she was wrong and to leave."

With tears in her eyes, my sister wraps me in a hug. "Oh, Nate. You big freaking idiot."

Tears sting my eyes, but I don't let them fall. "What do I do? How do I fix this? Can I?"

It's at that moment Tatum bounds into the room. "Uncle Nate! Did you bring Miss Jenny again?"

I pinch my eyes shut and shake my head. "No, Tater Tot. Not today."

"Why?" she asks, earnestly, and like the assholes they are, Alden and Natalie leave me to answer her.

"Because…" I trail off, searching for the right words.

"Because she's mad at you. I wasn't tryin' to listen because I know I'm not supposed to easy drop when grownups talk, but I heard you anyway. By accident."

All three of us have to hide our grins behind our coffee cups.

"Can I give you some advice, Uncle Nate?"

What can it hurt, right? "I'd love some, Tatum."

She climbs up onto the barstool next to me and takes my big hand in her little one. "Falling in love is like learning to tie your shoes, Uncle Nate. It's hard and it takes time—like a lot of time. But once you get it, you know how to tie them forever. You don't just forget."

I smile at her sweet, albeit confusing analogy. "I'm not sure I'm following."

She sighs dramatically. "Uncle Nate! What I'm saying is, y'all's are still tied together. Sure, maybe the double-knot came loose, but the love is still there! You just gotta tighten your laces!"

I still don't have a freaking clue what she's trying to tell me, but I smile and give her a big bear hug all the same. "Thank you, Tater Tot. You want a donut?"

"Yes!" Natalie plates one up for her and sends her to the table to eat.

"You wanna know what you really need to do?" Alden asks, finally speaking up.

I nod. If anyone knows about relationships and making shit work, it's him.

"You need a grand gesture. Go big or go home. You gotta show her you love her."

"You do love her, right?" Natalie asks.

"With every beat of my heart."

They both grin. "Then go get her, brother."

IT'S BEEN crazy at the café today, and with my emotions still all topsy-turvy from everything, I'm dreading working at the bar tonight. Thankfully, Thursdays aren't too bad; now I just have to hope none of Nate's buddies pop in for a drink. I may be strong, but I'm not that strong.

I end up working past my scheduled shift, leaving me with less than an hour between jobs. Even though I'm mentally and emotionally drained, I don't complain, because the extra hours keeps my mind busy and off of a certain heart breaking cop.

When I finally pull up to my house, I have just enough time to change and freshen up before heading to the bar. As I climb the porch steps, I notice what appears to be a bouquet of flowers by my front door. How strange. Upon closer inspection, I see they're not just any flowers—they're pink peonies and white roses with baby's breath, the same flowers that were in my bouquet for Natalie and Alden's wedding.

Inside, I open the attached card.

Jenny,

I'll never forget the first time I really and

truly saw you. We were at Natalie and Alden's for a cookout, and I remember thinking damn, this girl is gorgeous. And you were so cute and tongue-tied around me.

And then when shit hit the fan over there that day, the way you swooped in and helped with Tatum blew me away. I wanted you, even then. Hell, I planned on making a move, but something you said that day stopped me in my tracks.

I remember it as clear as day. My sister asked how Alden looked at her, and you said, "With fire and forever in his eyes." Well, guess what, GG? That's how I look at you, too.

You're the best thing that's ever happened to me, and I'm going to fight for you...for a second chance.

Always yours (even when I was too damn dumb to admit it),

Nate

Big, fat tears roll down my cheeks as I read and re-read his letter. It's basically everything I could've asked for from him...but isn't it too late? Hasn't our ship sailed? Suddenly, I'm more confused than ever.

Unfortunately, I don't have time to process this confusing development—not if I want to make it to Bennet's on time.

Between the happy hour crowd and the thirsty Thursday-ers, the bar is packed. So packed that I don't notice a certain tatted-up cop slip onto a stool until it's too late.

"What can I get—oh, Duke…hey. Wh-what can I get you?"

He gives me a soft smile that's a complete juxtaposition to his hard features. "Nah, nothing. I'm just here to give you this." He slides a sloppily wrapped gift across the bar toward me. "Give him another chance, Jenny," he murmurs before leaving just as quietly as he entered.

"Jenny!" Mack yells, startling me. "Take your break!"

I cock my head to the side. "My break? Mack, we're slammed, and I haven't even been here—"

"Save it, kiddo. I'm the boss, and I said to take your break. No lip."

Shrugging, I duck out from under the bar and head to my car, gift box in hand.

With shaking fingers, I unwrap the box Duke delivered. I remove the card and place the box on my center console. I slide the card from the envelope. The front simply has a frowny face on it.

Nervously, I flip it open and read it.

Jenny, did you know my dad keeps an apology notepad for whenever he messes up with my mom? It's like this little prescription pad for saying sorry. Clever, right? Only my transgressions are too big for its little checkboxes. So, here's my own version just for you.

To: The best thing that's ever happened to me
From: The idiot who desperately wants you back
Date: To-damn-day

Infraction: Stupidity, stubbornness, lack of communication, and then some.

Reason(s) for my behavior: There's not a reason on earth that can justify how I acted. All I can say is, I'm a sorry-ass man whose head was so far up his own ass that I couldn't see the good thing right in front of me. I can also say, if you give me another chance, I'll do everything in my power to make it up to you, and I'll show you every day just how much I love you.

I really do love you, Jenny, and if there's any way in hell you can find it in your heart to forgive me, meet me down at the pier on Saturday at 9:00 a.m.

Still yours, whether you want me or not,
Nate

For the second time today, I'm a crying mess. And these tears, they're the worst kind—they're hopeful. After laying the card on my passenger seat, I finish opening the package.

Carefully, I remove the lid and stare at the contents housed inside of it. Each item has a sticky note stuck to it. One by one, I examine the contents.

A package of my most favorite, splurge-worthy coffee— Jenny, I know this is your favorite, just like I also know you save it for special occasions, but every day with you is special.

Next is a bundle of hair ties—I know you like to wear the same one until the elastic is completely stretched out, but I also know you only have two left in your drawer.

Beneath that is a three-pack of my favorite lip balm—after the first time we kissed, I made it my mission to discover what made your lips so soft and sweet. Hopefully I get to kiss you again.

The last item is a poorly painted heart-shaped ceramic dish with a stack of sticky notes attached to it—you're probably scratching your head over this one, huh? The day we watched Tatum, I planned on taking you to the Painting Parakeet. Even though we didn't get to go together, I coerced Duke into coming with me so I could make you this. I know it's ugly as sin, but I'm hoping you can look past that. This is me giving you my heart, Jenny—it's yours for the taking. Hell, it's yours whether you want it or not. But I really hope you want it.

I'm a full-blown blubbering mess by the time I finish reading the little stack of Post-it notes. Jesus. This man. Turns out Natalie was mostly right with her Shrek-ology. Only Nate's not an onion, he's a coconut—with his hard and gruff exterior that's protecting his sweet, sweet center.

NATE

It's five minutes until Jenny's supposed to meet me, and I'm a hot mess. Can guys be hot messes? Hell if I know, but if they can, that's what I am—what I've been all week. I was hoping to hear from Jenny on Thursday, but it's been two excruciating days of radio silence.

Natalie said she hasn't spoken to her either, but I'm not so sure I believe that.

Either way, I'm nervously twiddling my thumbs under the oak tree that separates the parking lot from the sand, anxiously waiting to see if the woman I love is willing to give me another shot.

My eyes flit back and forth between my watch and the road, simultaneously counting down and looking for her. Please God, let her show.

When nine o'clock comes and goes, my heart sinks. But, hey, maybe she's running late, right? At five minutes after, the sound of a car pulling up has me on alert. Frantically, I scan the parking lot—oh, shit, yes, she's here. She's. Here.

It takes all of my willpower to stay put, to let her come to me. Oh, fuck it, who am I kidding? We meet in the middle, and she practically tackle-hugs me to the ground.

"You came." I cradle her face in my hands. "You're really here."

Jenny nods, a single tear rolling down her cheek. "I'm here. D-did you mean all of those things you said…in your notes?"

"One thousand percent, GG—with all of my heart."

She inhales a shaky breath and presses her lips to mine. My heart soars in my chest, and I put my everything into our kiss. I move one hand to the back of her head and the other to her waist, holding her to me.

Her grip on my shirt is like a lifeline tethering her to me. We stay locked together until we have to separate in order to breathe. But I don't let her get far. Pressing my forehead to hers, I murmur, "I fucking love you, Jenny Jones. You're every good thing in this world, and even though I know I don't deserve you, much less another chance, I'm begging for both."

"It's yours. I'm yours. You're worth every chance and then some. I love you, cutie, so much."

I press a chaste kiss to her lips. "Say it again."

"I love you."

If anyone would've ever told me that hearing those three little words would get me hard enough to pound nails, I would've laughed until I was blue in the face. Yet, hearing Jenny say them has that exact effect and judging from the way she's softly shifting her hips against me, she knows it.

"Let's get out of here?" I ask, hoping like hell she says yes.

And she doesn't let me down. "God, yes."

The rest of the day—hell, the rest of the weekend—is spent with me lost in her body, making love, only breaking long enough to eat or sleep. And let me tell you, being inside her tight body, with her clenching around me as she chants, "I love you-I love you-I love you," like a prayer…yeah, there's nothing on this earth that's comparable.

JENNY

Tonight's our first dinner at Nate's parents' house as a couple. As much as I'd like to say I'm totally chill about the whole she-bang, I'd be lying. I'm a freaking mess. While I know that Melanie and Luke like me just fine as Natalie's best friend or as an occasional babysitter for Tatum, that in no way means they'll like me as their only son's girlfriend.

"Are you sure it's not too soon to introduce me as your girlfriend?" I ask Nate for the millionth time since we've left his house to head over to theirs.

"We've been over this." Nate holds up his index finger. "First: They already know you, so you can't really call this an introduction."

He adds another finger. "Second: We've been together—officially, not counting those days apart—for a month and you already know I plan on keeping you for the long haul, so why wait?"

He's now holding up three fingers. "Third: Like I've told you countless times, my mom totally ships us—her words, not mine—and she's gonna be over the moon to hear it's official. I legit wouldn't be surprised if she asks about a wedding date or when we plan on giving her grandkids."

I take a deep breath and smooth my hands over my skirt. "Okay…if you say so."

Nate reaches over the center console and grabs my hand. "I know so."

His touch soothes me, and I relax into the seat. Until we turn onto their street and their house comes into view, that is. At the sight of the picturesque red brick, my riot bees begin buzzing in full force, fluttering nerves from my belly all the way up into my throat.

"Maybe we should just cancel?" I ask, panic creeping in as we turn into their driveway. "Or you can go, and I'll just wait here."

Nate turns to me, his eyes squinted. "You do realize you're acting a little bit insane, right?"

As much as I want to balk at his words, I can't, because he's right; I am acting insane. But this is my first time ever meeting a boyfriend's parents. It's a big deal, a big step. Their approval of me—in this capacity—means a lot to me. Straight up, I'm more nervous now than I was when Nate told me he loved me for the first time.

"GG, take a breath. They already love you. Not to mention, my mom has already tried setting us up once."

I shake my head. "No…no, she has not."

He nods, smirking. "Yes, ma'am. When you came to dinner with Natalie the week after Tatum's party—that was all Mom's doing. She saw the way I was looking at you and was smart enough to put two and two together long before I ever did."

"For real?"

"Swear on it. So, c'mon."

Feeling slightly more settled, I reach across the center console and take his hand. "One last thing…are you ever gonna tell me what GG means?"

Like the cocky little shit he is, he just winks.

I do my best to calm my frazzled nerves as we walk from the car to the front door, but it's no use. My brain is muddled with every possible worst-case scenario. Logically, I know Nate's right and that I'm being insane, but my logic has seemingly abandoned the hive.

Sensing that I'm approximately zero-point-five seconds from a meltdown, Nate grabs my hand, giving it a squeeze before softly rubbing his thumb over my knuckles in a soothing gesture. And damn if the bees don't simmer down—it's kind of mind-blowing the way such a simple touch from him can put me at ease.

My quasi-calm shatters the second he flings open the door and hollers, "Mom, Dad! We're here!"

I tighten my grip on his hand. "We?" his mom calls back, her voice moving closer. "Who's we—oh, hello, Jenny dear."

"H-hi, Melanie."

Her eyes flit between the two of us briefly and then down to our clasped hands. A small smile plays on her lips and I can't help but wonder if maybe Nate was right...maybe she is okay with us. The jury's still out on her actually shipping us though.

"Oh, Nathaniel. Is she...are y'all..." Melanie's words fall away.

"Together?" Nate supplies. "Yeah, Mom, we are."

The next thing I know, Nate's mom is swooping in like some kind of bird of prey—only instead of pecking out our innards, she's wrapping both of us in the tightest, most motherly hug on earth.

When she finally releases us from her hold, we're both nearly gasping for air; Melanie pays us no mind though. "Oh, Nate. You finally pulled your head out of your ass. I'm so happy." Nate scowls at his mother as she focuses her attention on me. "Welcome to the family, sweet girl. If he doesn't treat you right, you let me know."

"Uh, okay—I mean, yes, ma'am?" My reply comes out sounding more like a question, causing us all to laugh.

"Alright, Mom, that's enough. Let's go eat."

"Not until your sister gets here. You know the rules."

The three of us head into the family room, joining Luke, while Nate grumbles all the while about how hungry he is and how it's just like Natalie to keep everyone waiting. Luckily, she strolls through the door with Alden and Tatum not even five minutes later.

Dinner is delicious and the conversation flows easily. I'm pleasantly surprised when no one makes a fuss about Nate's changed relationship status—at least, until Tatum catches on to the fact that we're together.

"Uncle Nate, why are you holding Miss Jenny's hand? Is she your girlfriend again? Did you fix stuff?"

Grinning, Nate confirms to his niece that we are indeed together again.

"So, now will y'all get married and have babies? In all of my movies, when the prince wins the princess back, he hurries up and marries her so that way when he messes up again, she has to stay." It takes my all to contain my laughter when she turns her wide eyes on me. "And Uncle Nate will mess up again, Miss Jenny. It's just what boys do. Mama says they can't help it—something about it being in-brained in their NBA. So, marry him and stay, okay?"

"It's a little soon for all that, but don't worry, I'm not going anywhere, okay?"

Tatum sighs dramatically. "But the longer you wait to get married the longer until you have babies!"

I can't help but smile—this kid really wants a sibling something fierce.

"Tater Tot," Natalie interjects. "You do know that not all married couples have children, right? Families come in all shapes and sizes."

"I know, Mama. But, since you and Daddy won't give me a baby, maybe Uncle Nate will!"

I turn to Nate, expecting him to look horrified at the mere mention of wedding bells and babies, but that's not at all what I find. Nope. In fact, he has a downright dreamy look about him.

My eyes are glued to Nate as he speaks up, his voice sounding soft and far away. "You know what, Tater Tot, maybe I'll do just that."

"What?" I choke out on a gasp.

Nate smiles warmly at me. "You're telling me you've never thought about the two of us settling down and starting a family? Because I gotta say, GG, it sounds damn good to me." My eyes fill with tears—as do Natalie's and Melanie's.

Melanie lets out a small sob at her son's declaration, but Luke is quick to speak over everyone, ending the emotionally charged moment before it ever really starts. "Got plans for the Fourth?" he asks gruffly, aiming his question at no one in particular. I guess the senior Mr. Reynolds is not one for all the lovey-dovey talk.

Everyone launches into their plans for the following weekend—it looks like we'll all be together enjoying the annual Bay Ridge fireworks display on the bluff. Which is just fine by me, seeing as the café is catering the event and all of my favorite people will be there—minus my family of course. But that just means we'll have to make a trip up to Tennessee sometime soon.

———

The fireworks start in an hour, yet instead of being down at the bluff, I'm trapped in my loft with my best friend while she goes through every article of clothing I own. I'm not even exaggerating either. I know I tend to overthink my outfit choices, but this girl's taking it to a whole other level—like cuckoo-crazy, she hit her head level.

"Natalie, babe, what gives? It's a cookout."

She rolls her eyes and tosses another dress down onto my bed.

"I'm not kidding, Nat. Why does it matter so much? Not to mention, shouldn't you be there helping your husband?"

"I was down there from the crack of dawn until like two hours ago. He's fine," she says dismissively. "Oh, try this on!"

I barely catch the dress she tosses my way, but I slip it over my head knowing that arguing with her won't help—she's apparently on a mission and honestly, at this point, I don't really care. The faster I comply, the faster I get to see Nate, who has been blowing up my phone asking me where I'm at. Once I told him his sister was holding me hostage, the ass sent back a winky face emoji and told me he loved me.

I turn and appraise my reflection in the mirror. The dress Natalie picked is pretty cute—a breezy little white spaghetti strapped number with a sweet V-shaped neckline and a thigh-skimming hemline trimmed in eyelet lace.

"Do you like it?" my best friend asks.

I shrug. "Sure. It's cute and comfy." She finishes off my outfit with a pair of red espadrilles and a gold and navy tasseled necklace. According to her, I'm festive and cute. According to me, I'm overdressed and ready to see my man.

Natalie insists I ride with her and I don't put up a fight— hell, I'd probably agree to riding horseback if I got us out of my cottage and on our damn way.

By the time we make it to the bluff, the sun is almost kissing the waterline. People are everywhere; it's a veritable minefield of lawn chairs, beach blankets, and frolicking chil- dren. I let Natalie lead the way as we weave through the crowd.

"There they are." She points off in the distance, and sure

enough, the entire Reynolds clan is set up beneath the shade of one of the many ancient live oaks.

The minute Nate spots us, he starts our way and we meet in the middle where he sweeps me into his arms as if it's been an eternity since he last saw me.

"Missed you, GG," he husks into my ear, sending a wave of shivers down my spine.

"I missed you, too, even though I saw you last night."

"Still been too long."

I shake my head at him and press a quick kiss to his lips. "You ready to tell me what GG stands for? I think I'm all guessed out."

Like the infuriating man he is, he simply shrugs and links his pinky with mine. "Let's grab some food before they run out."

I let the subject drop, because while I've tasted the individual components of these Italian hoagies, I've yet to enjoy the finished product. Here's to hoping I don't drop a glob of sauce on my white dress.

We both make quick work of our hoagies, finishing them just as the first of the fireworks start. We stand together, chest-to-chest wrapped in each other's arms as the night sky bursts with colors.

"Love you," Nate murmurs against my temple and I tilt my face up toward his, intent on stealing a kiss. But he beats me to it, capturing my lips with his. He tugs at my bottom lip and I open for him. He licks into my mouth, our tongues tangling as he owns me with his kiss.

His hands slide to my hips and mine tangle in the collar of his shirt, clutching him to me as he deepens our kiss just a little bit more. We spend what feels like hours, though it's probably only minutes, so completely lost in one another that the fireworks that once held me captivated have nothing on the ones Nate has lighting up my body.

When he finally pulls away, I start to mumble out a breathless love you, too, but my words evaporate when he drops down to one knee before me. Holy. Shit.

"Nate…wh-what are you…"

He takes my hands in his. "Jenny, you're the best thing that's ever happened to me. I spent years thinking I wasn't enough, that I didn't deserve the love of a good woman. Hell, I figured being alone was my penance, but you've shown me just how wrong I was. You've shown me that I'm not defined by my past and that I'm more than my mistakes. You've shown me that I am worthy of love and then you went a step further and gave me the greatest gift of all—your love."

Tears fill my eyes as he releases my hands and fishes a ring box from his pocket. He flips open the lid, revealing an incredibly stunning cushion cut sapphire surrounded by two halos of diamonds.

"Is this real—"

"Shh, be a good girl and let me finish?"

I give him a sniffly nod.

"I know this probably seems rushed, but, GG, I can't go another day without putting my ring on your finger. Please tell me you want this, too, that you'll marry me—that you'll be my wife?"

Before his words truly have time to soak in, I tackle-hug him to the ground, peppering kisses all over his face while murmuring my agreement again and again.

The sound of clapping and congratulatory hoots fills the air, almost muffling the sound of the fireworks finale, and Nate and I break apart. Alden and Natalie rush over to help us both up; I should be embarrassed that I literally just mauled my…fiancé…to the ground in public, but I'm too elated to care. I mean, holy shit, the man of my dreams just asked me to marry him!

Once we're both upright, Nate slides the ring onto my finger and presses a kiss to my forehead.

"Move and let me hug my sister," Natalie demands, wriggling between the two of us. She wraps me in her arms, and I'm suddenly hit with a realization.

"You knew!"

She steps back and winks. "I did and I'm so freaking excited!" She moves on to hug her brother.

Alden is next in line to hug me, with Tatum in tow. He murmurs his congratulations in my ear before Tatum flings herself into my arms. "Does this mean I gets to call you Aunt Jenny? Will you live with Uncle Nate? You should! Then we can have spend-the-nights and you can help when I give him makeovers and all kinds of fun!"

Her excitement is downright adorable, and I hug her close promising we can do all of those things in the future.

When Alden eventually swoops her out of my arms and over toward Nate, Melanie and Luke approach. She folds me into a tight, motherly hug that makes me wish my family was here.

"Oh, pumpkin." I hear my mom's voice say and I snap my gaze up, searching, wondering if I'm losing my mind. In all of the excitement, I completely missed the fact that Luke has his tablet in hand with the screen facing outward.

Sure enough, my parents, grandparents, and Jamie are all crowded together watching through video chat. It's not the same as having them here in person, but holy crap, the fact that Nate thought to include them means the world to me.

Luke gives me a quick side hug before passing his tablet to me. I slink off to the outskirts of the bluff. "How?" I ask, not knowing what else to say.

"That handsome man of yours got in touch with Jamie somehow and while I wasn't too keen on him when he first called, he won me over."

I laugh, because damn if that doesn't sound exactly like Nate. "He is charming, that's for sure."

My family and I chat a little longer before we end the call

with promises of Nate and I coming up to see them in person soon.

———

Later that night, we're in his bed wrapped in nothing but each other and the sheets after our little private celebration. He's holding me close, trailing his calloused fingers over the notches in my spine, while his proposal replays in my head. I'm in the middle of dissecting every moment, every word, every syllable when something hits me. "Oh my God! Nate Reynolds!" I screech, bolting upright. "Good girl! Does GG stand for good girl?"

Nate nods and grabs my wrist, tugging so my chest crushes into his. "It does. I've always thought of you as too good for me and that morphed in you being a typical good girl and then to you being my good girl."

I can't help the cheesy grin that splits my cheeks. "You're something else, cutie."

Nate pretends to grumble, and my grin transforms into a full-blown smile. Nate beams right back, pulling me closer. "Love you so much."

"You made tonight the best night of my life. I love you, too —more than you'll ever know."

He kisses my temple. "Wanna know what would make it better?"

My brows dip...what could possibly make this night any better? Maybe another round of celebratory sex? "What's that?"

"You moving in. Just think, we could do this every night. And have lazy Sundays. And—"

I silence him with a kiss, moaning when I feel him harden against my belly. "You don't have to convince me. Where you are is where I want to be."

He captures my lips again and before I know it, round two

is in session as he grips my hips and helps seat me on his length. We set a slow, sensuous pace. We're not in a hurry as we seek our pleasure—after all, this is only the beginning of a lifetime together.

The End.

EPILOGUE

NATE

IF SOMEONE WOULD HAVE ASKED me a year and a half ago how I saw my future playing out, I would have given them some bullshit, half-assed answer—something shallow and meaningless, because that's exactly what my life was before Jenny.

My good girl changed everything for me. Jenny showed me just how fucking amazing life could be; she showed me, through her love, that there's more to living than simply going through motions.

While there's not a single day with her that I take for granted, today is especially sweet—because in exactly forty-three minutes, she'll become my wife.

"You ready?" Alden asks, echoing my question to him on the day he married my little sister.

"So ready it's not even funny. I feel like I'm about to come out of my skin watching the clock."

"Then don't watch it," Duke adds helpfully. *Smartass.*

"Can't help it, brother. With every rotation of the second hand, I'm a minute closer to kissing my bride." I grin, all too eager to see Jenny—to claim her in front of God and man, to officially and truly make her mine.

"Eager much?" Jamie asks, smirking like the little punk-ass shit he is.

"Like you couldn't believe."

Jamie nods, pleased with my reply. For as rocky as mine and his relationship started off, he's been one of the biggest supporters of our relationship—dude would do just about anything to see his cousin happy and that makes him all right by me.

I check the clock again: forty minutes. Swear to God, time has never moved so slowly.

Unlike Alden and Natalie's wedding, Jenny and I opted to keep things low-key. We're exchanging vows under the same tree where I begged for her forgiveness, right at the edge of where the sand meets the grass.

Our ceremony is small and intimate—immediate family and close friends only. Neither of us wanted some big to-do; we just wanted to say *I do*.

Funnily enough, Jenny would have been cool with a Justice-of-the-Peace-courthouse-drive-by, but I convinced her —via multiple orgasms—to have an actual wedding. As sappy as it sounds, I want to be able to tell our future kids about the day their Mama took my name; I want to have pictures of her decked out in white for me; I want to eat freezer burnt cake on our first anniversary.

The guys and I continue to shoot the shit until finally, after what feels like two eternities, it's time to head to the ceremony site. We pile into Alden's car and make the quick drive down to the pier.

We didn't do much in the way of decorating the space; between the soaring pine trees, moss covered oaks, vibrant green grass that gives way to sugary sand, and the bay water lapping at the shore it's safe to say Mother Nature got it right all on her own.

We meet the officiant beneath the shade of our tree and take our positions. Since our wedding parties are uneven,

Jenny thought it made the most sense for the girls to walk alone.

Guests trickle in and music starts to play through the Bluetooth speakers Alden set up this morning, but I hardly notice any of it. I'm too busy watching the parking lot for my girl.

Finally, an SUV pulls up, idling at the edge of the grass. My mom and Tatum are the first out and my best friend beams as his daughter walks toward us. Straight up, I'm beaming too, because as I watch my niece, I can't help but imagining a sweet little girl with my dark hair and Jenny's striking green eyes.

Natalie's next, and objectively, she looks beautiful, but I barely spare my sister a glance. I'm too busy anxiously awaiting the appearance of my bride.

And merciful Jesus, when she steps out of that car, with her parents right behind her everything else on the planet fades away. As she walks toward me, her cream-colored dress hugging her curves and swishing around her ankles, she looks like an angel—a fucking goddess—meant only for me.

Once my good girl makes it to me, the music cuts off and the officiant begins. I probably should be paying attention as he works his way through the opening and expression of intent, but I'm too damn infatuated with my bride. Her face is fresh and dewy and her eyes are overflowing with love— truly, she's never looked more beautiful.

"Today, the bride and groom have prepared their own vows, which they will exchange now."

Jenny and I both go to speak, our voices overlapping, but I urge her to continue. "Ladies first, GG."

She smiles widely, reaching for my hands. "Nate, I'd write my love for you in the sand, but the tide would wash it away, and my love for you is unending. There's not a day that passes where I don't find myself falling for you a little bit more. I know things between us won't always be easy, but nothing worth having ever is. I know things between us won't be perfect, but nothing real is and cutie, we're as real as it gets."

Unable to help myself, I yank her forward and press a chaste kiss to her lips. "Jenny, you're the best thing that's ever happened to me. You're everything good in this world and somehow, I'm lucky enough to call you mine—and I'm even luckier because you call me yours. There's no way to know what the future holds, but I swear right here and now, that I will be by your side through every up and down life can throw at us." I pause for a moment, so fucking taken with Jenny. This woman, she was made for me. "I love you GG, damn I love you."

"And now," the officiant resumes his part, "do you Jenny take Nate to be your lawfully wedded husband? Do you promise to love, honor, cherish, and protect him forevermore?"

My girl nods, her eyes shining with unshed tears. "Yeah. Yes...I mean, I do."

"And Nate, do you take Jenny to be your lawfully wedded wife? Do you promise to love, honor, cherish, and protect her forevermore?"

Without even a lick of hesitation, I practically shout, "Hell yes, I do!"

We exchange rings and the officiant spouts off some more words about happiness and forgiveness and love, but all I can think about is kissing my bride.

"Now by the power vested in me by God, man, and the great state of Alabama, I now declare you married; you may now seal this declaration with a kiss."

I hook an arm around Jenny's narrow waist and pull her body flush against mine before sealing my lips to hers. My intention was to keep our kiss G-rated, but something comes over me, knowing that she's officially my wife and I can't help but to nip at her bottom lip and lick into her mouth.

Pouring my love into our kiss, I show Jenny— and everyone else here— exactly how I feel about her.

Day turns to night in a blur of champagne and dancing, but all I can think is how glad I am that my girl was stubborn enough to fight for us— for me—when I was too blinded by my past to do it myself. Even though I tried my hardest to stay away from her, to fight the magnetic pull between us, she showed me that while I had the best of intentions, we're just so much better together.

The End.

KEEP READING FOR A SNEAK PEEK OF DUKE & MALLORY'S BOOK, BEST OF ME

SNEAK PEEK

PROLOGUE

DUKE

The first time I ever laid eyes on Valorie Parsons, I could've sworn I was looking at an angel. I remember it as if it were yesterday…

It was the first day of tenth grade, and I was posted up at my usual table in the cafeteria with some guys from the team, shooting the shit and talking about our first game later that week. And then she walked in. Swear to God, the air crackled with her presence. She was only a freshman, but she waltzed into the room like she owned that school. Her long blonde hair was done up in those messy waves that immediately makes guys think of sex, her skin sun-kissed like she'd spent the entire summer lounging at the beach, and her lips…her glossy, perfectly kissable lips had my heart—and my shorts—feeling more than a little tight.

As crazy as it sounds, I knew right then and there that she was it for me. Right hand to my heart, I leaned over, nudged my buddy's arm and said, "I'm gonna marry that girl." Laughing, he replied, "You don't even know her." I shot him a grin and hopped up from my seat. "Not yet, but I'm about to."

The rest, as they say, was history. From that day on, Valorie Parsons was my girl. The two of us were damn near inseparable, spending all of our free time wrapped up in each other. And now, eleven years later, I'm hoping like hell that when I drop down to one knee and offer her my all, that she agrees.

"Rook, are you even hearing me?" my partner, Cal, asks as he hangs a sharp right onto the four-lane highway.

I jolt in the passenger seat. "Huh? What? I've been riding shotgun with you for the better part of four years, asshole; I ain't no rookie."

Cal laughs, a deep gruff sound. "You're damn sure acting like one, sitting over there looking like a possum on the side of a busy street. You got something on your mind?"

I shrug, not quite sure how to verbalize exactly what I'm feeling; hell, I'm not even sure I'd want to, even if I could.

"Listen up, Kincaid. We may not be blood, but we're family. We talk. We break bread. We work through our shit so we can stand in the sun together, you feel me? We don't keep secrets. So, I'm gonna ask you again, what's got you so out of it?"

I glance over toward my partner, the man who's had my back for the last four years, who eyes me warily. He's fucking right. If there's anyone I can tell my deepest fears to, it's Cal. "I got plans to ask my girl to marry me tonight."

"That's good, man, real good." He quirks a brow. "Y'all are still pretty young though, huh?"

I heave out a deep sigh. He's not saying anything I haven't heard before. But I've been thinking about asking Val to marry me since she agreed to that first date all those years ago. What she and I have is special—it's that once in a life-time, knock-you-on-your-ass kind of love.

I wanted to marry her the day she graduated high school. Hell, I even went as far as dropping down to one knee outside of our favorite summertime ice cream spot with nothing but a waffle cone of rocky road to accompany my proposal. But she always said she didn't want us to be two dumb kids who stumbled down the aisle in a fit of lust and bad decisions. She wanted to finish college first so we could have a solid foundation to build our future on, and who was I to argue with that logic?

But now, I'd say we're well on our way.

Last month, Valorie donned her cap and gown and collected her diploma. I was proud as punch when my girl told me she wanted to study law. In my mind, we'd be like superheroes, working to keep our small town safe. I could just see the headline in the local paper: *Local cop and his prosecutor wife working together to fight crime by day and make babies by night.*

Then she dropped the bomb that she wanted to be a defense attorney, and my dream shattered. Us being on opposing sides of the law was a fissure in the armor of our relationship, but I knew our love was enough to mend the crack.

Last week, she accepted a position with a hotshot law firm over the bridge in the city. Some Ivy League asshole with a reputation for fucking his female employees and representing the worst of the worst runs it, and even though it burns my gut, I know Val getting hired there before she's even passed her bar exam is a big deal.

"Yeah, Cal, we're young. But...I think we've got what it takes to make it for the long haul."

My partner eyes me knowingly. "You sure you're not just rushing to put a ring on her finger before she starts working for that greasy little shit?"

My heart clenches in my chest. I've asked myself that same question. And, yeah, maybe I want him to know she's one hundred percent off limits to the likes of him, but I also trust her all the way down to my soul. Eleven years we've been together—I know she's faithfully mine, just as I'm hers. I have loved the girl as long as I've known her, and I'm more than ready for us to take this step. The thought of seeing her walking down the aisle toward me in a white gown...her belly swollen with our first child...our first Christmas as a family...those are things I dream about at night.

We've worked hard to build up our foundation, and now I'm ready to frame up some fucking walls—I'm ready for her to wear my ring and to take my name and for us to officially start the rest of our forever together.

So even though there's a sliver of doubt niggling around in the back of my mind, I decisively nod my head and snap, "That's not it. I'm just ready for her to be my wife. She's... she's everything to me, plain and simple as that."

Cal holds one hand up in surrender. "Okay, Kincaid. No need to get your panties in a wad; I was just askin'."

"You ready to head in?" I ask, nodding toward the clock. Our patrol shift only has twenty minutes left, and by the time we drive our loop and make it back, it'll be time to punch the clock.

"Yeah, man. Let's roll."

The closer we get to the station, the more my anxiety gives way to pure, unadulterated excitement. By the end of the night, I'll be the luckiest man on the damn planet, and I have big plans to celebrate, starting with reminding my girl just how good we are together.

With only ten minutes left on our shift, the radio crackles with a call from dispatch. "Report of a motor vehicle accident, injuries unknown, just past mile marker fifteen on ninety-eight. Available units, please respond."

We're less than two miles away. "Shit, let's go," I say, a sick feeling settling in my stomach.

As much as I love being a cop, car wrecks are the worst for me. My parents were in a horrible accident when I was in middle school; my dad got behind the wheel drunk and wrapped his car around a telephone pole. Of course, that jackass walked away with barely a scratch, but my mom wasn't so lucky. It was the passenger side of the vehicle that had wrapped around the telephone pole, leaving her with a shattered pelvis, a punctured lung, and a bleed in her brain. In the end, her injuries were too great for her to recover, and she died a day later.

"10-4," Cal calls back, and with a flip of a switch, the sirens are screaming and we're on our way.

The accident scene comes into view, and I see a mid-size, blue vehicle in the tree line with parts and pieces scattered about. As we draw closer, the details come into focus with startling clarity. Time stops and that sick feeling from earlier turns to pure fucking panic. Policy and procedure be damned —I'm out of the car and hauling ass toward the scene before Cal even has the squad car in park.

"No, no, no! It's not her. It *can't* be." My throat constricts and my chest heaves as I draw closer. "Jettas are common— It could be anyone..." I try and reassure myself, but it's in vain.

I stop in my tracks when I see her hot pink monogram decal on the trunk, my heart dropping to my feet. "Fuck. *Fuck!* Val, baby? Valorie?" I yell her name, taking off at a sprint. Cal lands a hand on my bicep, trying to stop me, but I shake him off. There's nothing on this earth that will stop me from getting to my girl. Not even the pleading, frantic shouts of my partner.

I draw up short when the front end of the car comes fully into view. It's mangled to the point of being unrecognizable, but even still, I'm holding on to hope that Val's fine. I'm desperately clinging to the notion that she's going to walk away with nothing more than a few bumps and bruises—no worse for wear. But it's utterly destroyed, and there, in the grass, is the woman I planned to make my wife.

She's covered in glass and blood, broken and bent in the most unnatural angle, completely still. I squeeze my eyes shut, sucking in ragged breaths, praying like hell that when I lift my eyelids, this will all have been a nightmare—that Val will be sitting up, awake and fine.

However, when my eyes open, the scene is wholly unchanged, except now the tinny smell of blood—*her blood*—fills my nostrils, along with various fluids leaking from the engine.

A guttural scream tears past my lips as I drop to my knees and pull her into my arms. My brain switches to autopilot, and I check for a pulse, "Please, baby, please." My voice grows hoarse as I beg her to open her eyes…flinch…*anything* to let me know she's still with me.

Shards of glass from the shattered windshield dig into my knees, but I don't feel anything but a staggering sense of loss and despair. I know I shouldn't be touching her, moving her, and there will be consequences to my actions, but none of that matters as I cling to her, sobbing, blood seeping through the fabric of my once- pristine white shirt.

"Kincaid!" Cal shouts, his hand coming down hard on my shoulder. "The ambulance is here. You…you gotta let the medics get her." His voice cracks on his last words. He knows what we've just rolled up on. We've all known a fellow brother in blue that's responded to a scene where he knew the victim. But this time it's different.

This time, it's me.

It's my accident scene.

It's my loved one.

It's my life—my fucking future—that's vanishing before my very eyes.

He drops to his knees beside me, wrapping an arm around my shoulders in support. "Please, you gotta let the guys take her. We'll follow them to the hospital."

I glance over my shoulder at my partner, seeing my own grief reflected back at me, before looking back down at the woman I'd been planning to spend the rest of my life with. Shaking my head, I pray to God for him to bring her back; I plead with Him to take me instead. But it's useless…He's not fucking listening.

With her head cradled in my blood-streaked hands, I lean down and press my lips to her skin one last time. Even in death, she's still the single most beautiful person to ever walk this earth. The first time I ever laid eyes on Valorie Parsons, I could've sworn I was looking at an angel.

And now…she is one.

READ BEST OF ME FREE WITH KU

ALSO BY LK FARLOW

All of LK's titles can be read as standalones & most are available with Kindle Unlimited.

An * beside a title denotes it is also available in audio.

A 🖤 denotes it is available with KU.

His to Save (a stepbrother/heroine on the run romance suspense) 🖤

His to Keep (an enemies to lover/forced proximity romantic suspense)

Sweet Little Nothing * (an enemies-to-lovers/bully romance)

Dirty Little Secret * (an older brother's best friend/second chance romance)

Pretty Little Thing * (a single mom/forced proximity/mistaken identity romance)

Best Laid Plans * (an older brother's best friend/secret baby romance) 🖤

Best of Intentions * (a friends-to-lovers/little sister's best friend romance) 🖤

Best of Me * (a second chance at love/forbidden twin romance) 🖤

Rebel Heart (an enemies-to-lovers jock/tutor rom-com) 🖤

Rebel Soul (an arranged baby/friends-to-lovers rom-com) 🖤

Rebel Desire (an unrequited soulmates/surprise single dad rom-com) 🖤

Coming Up Roses * (a small-town/single mom romance) 🖤

An Uphill Battle * (a frenemies-to-lovers romance) 🖤

Weather the Storm (a second chance at love romantic suspense) 🖤

Come What May (an age gap/single dad romance) 

ABOUT THE AUTHOR

Known by Kate to most, LK Farlow is an Amazon Top 40 bestselling author of more than a dozen romances, ranging from sweet, to sexy, to rip your heart out, and everything in-between.

She has a heart built for happily-ever-afters, which is lucky since she found hers at the young age of nineteen. Now, at thirty-something, she is the wife to one hunky man and the mother to four semi-feral humans, three lizards, a chameleon, a tortoise, and a handful of stray cats.

Kate often jokes that her life is all out chaos on most days, but she wouldn't trade it for the world.

www.authorlkfarlow.com